G000060033

The Leah Chronicles

An After it Happened Story

Andorra

Devon C Ford

PRESS

Copyright © Devon C Ford 2018

All rights reserved. No part of this publication may be reproduced, stored in or introduced into a retrieval system or transmitted in any form or by any means, electronic, mechanical, photocopying, recording or otherwise without prior written permission from the publisher.

This novel is entirely a work of fiction. Names, characters, places and incidents are either the product of the author's imagination or are used fictitiously, and any resemblance to any person or persons, living or dead, is entirely coincidental. No affiliation is implied or intended to any organisation or recognisable body mentioned within.

Published by Vulpine Press in the United Kingdom in 2018

Cover by Claire Wood

ISBN: 978-1-912701-24-7

www.vulpine-press.com

Dedicated to single malt whisky; without you, I wouldn't have come up with half of this stuff…

Author's Note

If you're reading this, then you probably made a strange noise when you first heard I was revisiting the *After It Happened* series. One person even admitted to being so excited that he punched a co-worker in the head, so I apologise to that poor, unintentional victim.

I have no regrets about the epilogue of *Rebellion*, at all, but I did leave two generations of time between where the exploits of **[INSERT FAVOURITE CHARACTER(S)]** left off and the epilogue ended.

It's a terrible thing for an author to do, to complain about nagging fans, but as I was working on the other projects I always have on the go I found my attention slipping out of the 1980s zombie world my mind was inhabiting and thinking more and more about what Dan and Leah had been up to since I abandoned them to their future after the wild fan theories tugged at my insomnia. I relented one Sunday afternoon and started to jot down some ideas about how Leah *et al.* would progress their lives, and before I came up for air I had written a few thousand words.

When I first ended the series I promised myself that I couldn't put them through any more, as I had punished them enough in their plight for survival and freedom and prosperity.

Well, it's been long enough.

When I first gave the draft of this story, of which there will be more, to a trusted team of beta readers they commented that they felt themselves returning to the comfort of old friends and were immediately able to dive headlong back into their universe as though they had never left. Be it another terrible Dad joke from Neil, a classic Ash moment, the tense anticipation of knowing that Dan's blood is up or the kick-ass Leah action, I hope you enjoy a dip of the toe back into the *After* world and grow to love the new characters emerging as you did the original members of Dan's unhappy campers.

DCF

Epilogue From *Rebellion*

Stretching her aching back, the old woman rose from her chair and picked up the battered carbine she had carried for years. It was so worn in places that the dappled camouflage pattern she knew every inch of was rubbed down to the smooth metal. Her weapon possessed the last of the working parts for that model, and was as close to its end as she was. She hadn't fired it in nearly ten years, and even then it was to drive away a curious predator, but couldn't quite give up on it. She said she would be buried with it and didn't want it far from her reach; like a Viking warrior wanting to go to Valhalla with her hand gripping a sword's hilt.

Walking slowly, she took the stone steps one at a time until she stepped out onto the exposed walkways and turned to face the bay as her stiff-limbed and tired companion flanked her without instruction. The loyal mongrel hadn't left her side in over a decade; a proud warrior heritage of its great ancestry still present despite the dog's advanced age.

The sinking sun had dropped behind the far cliff and silhouetted the watch tower beautifully, bathing Sanctuary in a rich, golden, fiery glow.

She never got used to how powerful a sunset was. How it stirred feelings in her which reminded her very soul that she was alive.

She had grown sentimental in her old age; prone to reliving stories to an audience who had heard them before but listened out of reverence, respect and entertainment. *The good old days,* she called them, even though there was little that happened during those days which was good. She was permanently wearing her rose-tinted glasses, as was her right having survived for so long through everything the world had thrown at her.

Age did nothing to dull her senses, however, and soft footsteps betrayed the approach of two people. She knew who they were before they got to her, and she was also certain that they were hoping to startle her with their sudden appearance.

Her two nephews, born two years apart and startlingly different in their looks; one tall and broad with a mess of thick, dark hair whilst the other was a head shorter, blonde and smaller in stature with big eyes which seemed to stare straight into a person's soul. Both had the undeniable looks of their grandparents but took more of their personalities from their adoptive aunt.

Between them they held the stewardship of the town now, as she had taken a step back many summers before after twenty years of training them as best she could. Both were effective soldiers, but more than that they were leaders; just like their grandparents. Their joint reign was a return to the times when they at Sanctuary were a warrior clan; a force to be reckoned with.

Before she acknowledged them, something in her subconscious made her turn to the distant watch tower where her parents were buried side by side. She often joked they were buried so close to each other that they could carry on their loving bickering into eternity.

She still missed them, and the pain of their passing lessened only a little each day. She knew they were still watching over their home, buried close to their son who had fallen ill and died not long after they had passed.

She liked to believe that they were still keeping everyone down where she was safe as they had always done, at whatever cost.

"You'll have to be better than that to get the drop on me, boys," she croaked with a smile to herself.

"Still got it, Auntie Leah," said the taller one, leaning in to give her a rough kiss on her cheek which still bore the scar from the battle for Sanctuary.

"I've forgotten more than you know, sunshine," she said with a grin, goading them both into a good-natured argument for her amusement.

"Always," said the shorter one, deftly and diplomatically avoiding the bickering she tried to antagonise as he bent to scratch under the chin of the German shepherd cross who looked up at him expectantly. Producing a scrap of dried meat, he rewarded Ash's descendant as she knew he would.

"All quiet," said Jack before the woman cut him off.

"You don't need to tell me," she said. "I'm retired."

Her nephews exchanged a look, which she somehow detected even though she still gazed out over the ramparts.

"And don't roll your eyes at me," she said before turning to face them. She knew they didn't want to report anything to her; they wanted advice on something whist they could still call on her experience.

"What can an old woman do for you?" she enquired with sweet sarcasm.

"Nothing," said Peter, the shadow of the old compound bow

jutting out above his shoulder, "we just wanted to see how you were."

"I'm fine," she said, "in fact I was just about to go and visit my granddaughter."

Jack smiled back at her before saying, "We'll walk with you, Auntie Leah."

A little over a week later, over a hundred men and women of all ages made the long and arduous journey on foot to the top of the cliff overlooking their beautiful home.

They lowered her shrouded body into the rectangular hole as her daughter knelt in the dirt to reverently lay the battered and ancient gun on her chest. Her body was almost covered by the time everyone had filed past and sprinkled a handful of dirt over her, leaving her nephews little work to do in replacing the remainder of the excavated soil. Her granddaughter was the last to stand over her with her uncles; fourteen years old and strong, with a fierce sense of pride in her heritage, she was the very image of the woman they laid to rest. In reverent flattery of her grandmother, she carried with her an old rifle everywhere she went. The short barrel with its angular foregrip. The dual sight on the top rail. It had belonged, originally, to a man now immortalised in the legend of her home. A man she had never met but felt like she knew nonetheless.

Carefully arranging the stone slab to align with the others, they gently patted down the earth to tuck her in tight, next to Dan.

She was in fine company on that ridge. The vanguard of warriors who fought their whole lives to protect the group, never once giving up or putting their own needs ahead of others. Those responsible for the safety they now enjoyed.

She lay beside her Uncle Neil. Mitch beside him.

The best friend of her childhood, Ash.

She lay beside her younger brother, taken too soon.

She lay behind the woman who had become her mother, and a mother to so many others.

Andorra

PROLOGUE

"Sit down, boys," said the woman as she groaned, lowering herself to the high-backed chair in the corner of the room, "do you want to hear a story of your grandfather?"

The two young boys, one larger and dark-haired who was eerily quiet and the other, younger and fair-haired with a permanent buoyancy to his attitude, sat on the rug beside the ancient black and grey dog. It raised its large head, the fur about its muzzle long turned white, surveyed the arrival of the boys and flopped back down to ignore their presence; he was damned if he was giving up a prime spot on the rug in front of the fire.

"So what do you want to hear?" she asked, brushing her greying hair out of her face and revealing a scarred cheek from an injury earned long before her nephews were born. "The defence of Sanctuary? The tale of how I got *this*?" she asked, pointing at the faded stripe across her cheek.

The boys exchanged a look; the fair one pulling a face and the dark one glowering at him before shaking his head at the woman.

"Or how about the story of how we crossed the ocean, riding on *Hope*?"

"Uh-uh," said the younger one petulantly, giggling as his brother swiped at him because he had predicted it and dodged clear.

"Maybe the terrifying time that your auntie fought a pack of wild dogs and barely escaped with her life?" she said in a theatrically menacing tone, making the younger one chuckle and recoil in mock terror.

"How about the time we rescued the slaves from the evil giant?" she tried.

"You told us that one last week," the older boy, Jack, said quietly. Although only six years old, he had a depth and authority to his voice which lent him an oddly brooding air.

"Did I?" she asked, her face registering annoyance and feigned shock. "My old memory isn't what it used to be..."

"You're not old," the younger one, Peter, said with a wide smile and a laugh.

"I am!" she snapped back indignantly. "I'm forty years old. *Forty! Me!*"

Peter laughed with her, and even the seemingly sullen Jack cracked a smile which she had to admit that she hadn't seen much of since their father passed away less than half a year before. Their mother, stricken with the grief and stress of her partner's painful illness, had quietly taken her own life along with him, and both were now buried high on the cliffs to overlook the walled town below. Beside them were their parents, *her* parents, and a dozen more besides, but she didn't like to consider that too much in company, especially company so young, and preferred to pay her respects in private with a glass of the fierce liquor they brewed there as she stared up at the watchtower from her ramparts.

And they were *her* ramparts, as she had been leading the town and its inhabitants in the years since her father's passing. That day still stung her memory, threatening a tear which never seemed to run dry when thinking of the grumpy man she owed her entire life to, but her lapse into recall was burst by the door opening.

A slim, young woman poked her head around the door and smiled at the scene. The dog, the first descendant of the best friend a young girl could ever have wished for, disturbed once more by the arrival of the troublesome humans interfering with his warm nap, looked up again and grumbled loudly.

"Pipe down, Ares," the woman in the chair said, although not unkindly, earning an exaggerated sigh from the dog as its chest rose and fell.

"It's time for their bath, *Maman*," she said in English with a subtle French accent, prompting a complaining noise from Peter and a sullen glance from Jack.

"I was just telling them a story, won't be too long, *chérie*," she replied, seeing her daughter smile and duck back out of the room to leave them to their history lessons. The woman in the chair let her own smile linger a moment on the closing door, her love for her daughter radiating warmth.

"What about the one about the highwaymen?" Jack asked her hopefully.

"Which ones?" she replied with a smirk. "There have been so many over the years I can't really remember them all…"

Responding to the goad like a fish taking a lure, Jack sat up on his knees and spoke faster than usual.

"The one where you and grandpapa had to fight in the dark through the long tunnel. When Ash and Nemesis hunted the bad men and you saved the people from the thing…" He trailed off, his excitement having flowed uncharacteristically before he composed himself once more.

"Oh, *those* highwaymen," she replied, "you don't want to hear that old tale, do you?"

"*Oui*, please, Auntie Leah," Peter blurted out, as he often did mixing the two common languages of their town.

"Okay, okay," she said, "settle down and I'll tell you. It started at the end of the summer when I was nearly eighteen…"

LIFE IN PEACETIME

"Keep up, old man," I said, trying to keep the breathlessness from my voice. A huff of a grunt from behind me, closer than I expected, told me that Dan wasn't as old and unfit as I thought. I dug deep, pushing myself harder to try and extend a lead over him as we raced up and down the intricate stone stairways of the central keep. We'd abandoned our usual practice of exercising wearing our heavy equipment because the summer had been long and very hot. That heat alone sapped the oxygen from the air and made exercise harder, but we had both felt the spread of comfort in the almost four years since we had last been forced to fight for our survival.

Ash and my own dog, cursed to wear a thick fur coat all year round, had been left out of our daily exercise regime which especially annoyed Ash at first, but as the sun grew hot shortly after sunrise he had been content to lounge about in the shade being annoyed by the other dogs in the town as though he was some kind of lazy monarch or esteemed village elder. Some of those other dogs were his own descendants, and I had adopted the short-coated bitch which shared his temperament and ability but her mother's looks. I had called her Nemesis, or *Nem* for short, as Dan insisted that a working dog should always have a single-syllable name to shout at them when time was of the essence.

Even Nem, with her thinner, lighter coat and far superior

youth, was banned from our run due to the oppressive heat.

Bursting out of the confines of the stairwell and turning a hard right onto the partly covered walkways leading towards the main gate, I felt more than heard Dan catching up with me. His longer legs and superior strength were serving him better in the open, when my smaller size made the stairwells easier. Forced to slow to take the ninety-degree left to reach the gate, my brain snapshotted the repaired parapet and gates showing different coloured stones and the marks where the explosion had scorched a huge patch of the ancient construction. We accelerated off as one, but he had somehow managed to out-brake me and get the inside line like a racing car driver.

"No fair!" I gasped, dropping my body low and accelerating like a sprinter off the line to try and beat him on the last fifty paces. I didn't look at him, but I knew he would have his head down and be willing his tired, old legs to drive him forward.

Both slowing and standing upright as we crossed our imaginary finish line neck and neck, our breath came in ragged, panting gasps against the heat and the exertion.

"Draw," I said, bending down with both hands on my knees.

"Bollocks," Dan growled through a pained smile, "I had you at the end!"

"Did you... really?" I said, breathing in hard and forcing my outward breath to be slower as I puffed my cheeks.

"Not sure," he answered in a strained voice, standing tall and grimacing with his eyes closed as he placed his interlocked hands behind his head.

"Hang on," called a voice laced with intended comedy from the walkway behind us. I hadn't seen him, but Neil must have come out of the nearer stairwell as we passed and witnessed our sprint finish. He placed a finger to his ear, eyes vacant as though he was listening to some unheard transmission, then stood straight and drew the outline of a box with his two fingers starting at the top centre. He put his finger back to his ear, playing the part well as he mumbled and nodded, pretending to listen to the report of the video playback from the imaginary fourth official.

"Leah… *wins*!" he announced, in some echo of an old video game that was probably older than me.

"Fuck off, fatty," Dan quipped at his friend in a way that wasn't at all unkind. Whilst seemingly offensive, the kind-natured insult was, I had to admit, factually correct.

In the years since we had first found Sanctuary and been forced to defend it against a small army, Neil had grown… *comfortable,* whereas Dan had lost some of his bulk and trimmed down to be much leaner than before. I'd changed too, but that was what Marie attributed to my hormones. I was taller, obviously, but I had grown hips and needed new body armour as my chest no longer fit the one Dan had looted for me back when I was a kid. I knew I'd changed, mostly because some people looked at me differently when I walked, especially in the shorts and vest I wore to exercise in the heat.

Neil was carrying a bottle of water, clear plastic and well-worn with a label long since lost to hands gripping it every day. Wordlessly, ignoring Dan's abuse, he handed over his drink to me and we passed it between us, taking turns to gulp down long pulls of the tepid liquid and wipe the excess from our chins. The fresh water was one of Neil's earliest projects in Sanctuary; one of which he was proud, and we were eternally grateful. Cold water in summer was something of a forgotten memory, as the sterilisation process used sunlight and large, clear vessels that I didn't fully understand.

I didn't need to, not really, I only knew that Neil knew how to do it and had taught a half-dozen other people who took their turns at providing the town with fresh drinking water. The kitchen used a supply straight from the river that ran from the cliffs above our town, and they boiled it before cooking the food.

"Anyway," Neil said, "I was looking for you."

Dan looked at me, and I looked back at Neil.

"Which one?" we said in near unison. "Jinx," we said in stereo again, bumping fists tiredly as we always did when we voiced the same thought.

"Both," Neil said, smiling at us in that kindly uncle way.

"Urgent?" Dan asked, bending at the waist and leaning on his knees as he still tried to reclaim his breath. In contrast, maybe because I was seventeen and he was nearly forty, I was recovered enough to stand straight and just breathe heavily.

"I don't think so," Neil said, taking back his nearly empty bottle and drinking the last bit we had graciously left him, "otherwise Victor would've said something last night."

"The Wizard," Dan quipped, making me smile.

He always referred to Victor as the wizard in the tower, as he sat in the highest room in the town at the top of the central keep and worked day and night on his *l'encyclopédie* to complete his life's work of our skills as a kind of manual for human survival. He had even recruited a young French woman who could sketch with a skill unsurpassed among our people, adding detailed drawings to his words, and the tombs of knowledge extended to almost six packed volumes, each with a detailed reference section at the end.

"Indeed," Neil said, changing into another accent without explanation as often he did.

"Okay," Dan said, "shower and breakfast first."

"After we've finished," I said, smiling wickedly up at him. His face dropped.

"Not swimming," he complained, "I hate swimming."

"Trust me," I said, waving a goodbye to Neil before I turned and jogged to the far end of the walkway, hearing Dan's still-laboured breathing as he kept pace behind me. I heard Neil raise his voice again from behind us.

"Round-ah two… *fight!*" he called after our backs in the same video game voiceover.

Dropping down the staircase at the far end, far slower this time because running down uneven spiral staircases hundreds of years old wasn't for the faint hearted or the sensible. I waited at the bottom, seeing Dan emerge carefully a handful of seconds after I did, then we jogged down to the small beach and stripped off our running shoes and socks at the stone walkway before running barefoot across the wet sand. The tide was out, making our protected bay seem much smaller than it was at full flood. Our run was a little over a jog, but still a maintainable pace without burning out our muscles. Reaching the far end and climbing carefully down the rocks, we stepped into the clear water, both of us shuddering and Dan making a small, high-pitched noise as his waist met the cool sea water.

"Giggle band!" I announced in a sing-song voice, knowing that he would be smiling at the joke behind me without having to look.

True to his word, Dan was not a strong swimmer. I hadn't been, but over the last few years I had crossed the bay at least twice a week in the warm weather to strengthen my skills through trial and error and replicate what I had seen on TV back in the world. I swam in a relaxed freestyle, keeping my head out of the water as my sodden ponytail slapped from side to side. Beside me, Dan swam like an old woman. It was a curious mix of breaststroke and an intermittent doggy-paddle that he used to apply a burst of speed when needed or when he felt anxious that he was sinking.

Reaching the end nearest the town, hard under the walls of the ancient stone keep which formed part of the walls, we rescued our footwear and padded barefoot back into the castle to wash and dress before finding ourselves a breakfast of fresh bread, fish, eggs and fruits.

Now I was never a fan of fish, seeing as it smelt bloody awful, but a few years living in a fortified coastal town where the staple diet came from the sea, I had learned to love it.

Well, maybe *love* wasn't the right word, but I ate it. Some days we had bacon, but as the population of pigs still hadn't yet grown large enough to slaughter a few of them on a daily basis I had to make do with what there was.

I exchanged smiles and nods with the others, answering their polite greetings in both French and English as the town was truly becoming bilingual by then. Those who didn't speak French or English as their native languages usually used English, or a curious mix of both. Now, my French wasn't great, but I had picked up enough to at least be polite. Dan, despite his normal attitude towards foreign languages being to speak English in a loud, slow and ultimately condescending fashion, had taken to the language far better than expected, even being able to hold simple conversations in the native tongue. Marie was the same, her fluency lending her an air of being almost local, in spite of never having learned French, but instead picking it up by spending time with Polly, who had relinquished the leadership of the town willingly to them not long after Sanctuary had been defended against Le Chasseur and his Legionnaires. Marie split her time between caring for their son, Leah's much younger brother, and maintaining order of the town's economy as it was.

We were happy. We hadn't fired a shot in anger since the last captured attackers had been rounded up and executed by firing squad far away from the sensitive souls of the peace-loving civilians inside the safety of the walls, and everything just somehow worked well, with everyone pulling their weight for the greater good. I had to admit that it even worked better than our first home since everything began over five years before, back when we lived in caravans in a supermarket car park and when we subsequently took over the beautiful old manor house that was strangely marred by being a prison. Those days, indeed those places were long gone now. Lost to history and memory.

Our happiness was tainted by Victor's news, however, because it seemed that some of the surviving humans - after the global plague had claimed the lives of ninety-nine people out of every one hundred - still wanted to fight.

WORTH THE RISK

"Ah, *entrez* please," Victor said, whipping off his round spectacles which hadn't been in place when they had first met. The task of recording the skills of humanity by hand had obviously taken a toll on his eyesight.

"May I offer you a drink?" he asked politely, rising to gesture at a pewter tray and a selection of bottles.

"It's ten in the morning, Victor," Dan said carefully, not wanting to insult the man, but wanting to convey that hitting the high-proof alcohol before midday was unbecoming of them.

"It is?" Victor asked, his face registering surprise until he looked at the bright sunlight coming through the open shutters to his room. "Of course it is. I apologise. Some coffee, perhaps?"

I opened my mouth to accept, stopping before I could utter a sound and frowned at Dan who had just declined for us both. Ignoring it, I concentrated on what the man wanted to say as, from the look of him, he hadn't slept much recently.

"Of course, to the reason for my summoning then?" he asked, sitting in a battered leather chair and smiling. "We have received a message, a voice message from a nearby place by radio."

"Saying what?" Dan asked.

"Offering trade, mostly."

"Mostly?" I asked, sceptical of the academic's lack of detail.

"Yes," Victor said with a slight hint of discomfort, "they appear to have been having some problems with local bandits and the like, but I do—"

"Maybe it would be better if you let us hear the message instead of telling us?" Dan asked, hiding his annoyance and leaving out what I knew he wanted to add; the man was dressing it up to be something different to what was actually said.

"Yes, here you go," he said, picking up a piece of rough paper from beside him and handing it over. Dan had hoped that a voice recording had been taken, but seeing the scribbles in what looked like Spanish, French and then English made it clear to him that he wouldn't have understood a word of it anyway.

The paper, evidently having been screwed up at some point before it was retrieved and flattened out to allow the unused side to be scribbled on, read haltingly.

"I had to have it translated from Spanish, or at least the Catalan dialect," Victor said, trying to excuse the lack of accuracy and proper grammar. Dan grunted in answer and not even I understood whether it was a negative or a positive grunt or just one of acknowledgement that the man had spoken. The last few years hadn't helped his interpersonal skills much. He had never really clicked with Victor, thinking the man a little strange having never worked a day in his life but spent it studying all over the world until he was a font of knowledge which was all but useless in the cold light of the post-apocalyptic day.

Looking at the handwritten translation, I stored up my questions until I had finished reading and fully absorbing it.

"Hello to all who survived God's plague," it began.

Great start, I thought, *let's bring religion into this when it was humans who did it to themselves.*

"Warm greetings from the General Council of the Principality of Andorra. We seek anyone near to us for trade and to offer aid and assistance. We have goods available for trade and wish to establish contacts. Thieves"—this word had been crossed out in French above it twice—"have attacked us, but our valleys are strong."

Dan read it again, his lips moving and his brow furrowed, before handing me the paper and leaning back in thought.

"What's the confusion over *thieves*?" he asked suspiciously.

"It is an approximation. The word did not directly translate as such," Victor explained wearing a pained expression.

Dan grunted again in bland acknowledgement. I read it over again, before offering the quick version as I understood it.

"So," I began, "there are survivors in Andorra, wherever that is, and they want to make friends and trade with anyone, but people have tried to steal from them?"

"That's how I see it," Dan agreed darkly.

Victor saw the looks on our faces, clearly not understanding our multitude of problems that the message posed.

"Your hearts are not lifted by such news, no?" he asked uncomprehendingly.

"This is how I see it," Dan said, fixing the man with his most neutral look and explaining simply, "one"—he held up the thumb of his right hand—"we don't know if this message is genuine; it wouldn't be like it's the first time someone has lured unsuspecting victims into a trap. Two"—he held up the index finger—"we don't know what kind of *assistance* they're asking for and we aren't a charitable organisation. Three"—the middle finger flipped up to join the other two digits—"the 'thieves' mentioned aren't filling me with confidence. Have they been attacked? How many attackers? Are they well equipped? Well led? Organised? Are the people who sent the message geared for defence? Are we likely to get shot at for turning up on their borders?"

"Four, five, six," I added, flicking up three fingers of my own, "how far away is it? What is the route like? Are there others in between there and here?"

Victor took a breath, answering my questions first.

"It is roughly two hundred kilometres, and the route is a mixture of toll roads and mountain roads with two long tunnels in between." He paused, and I bit back my first hurdle about alternative routes as he went on to explain and nullify any interruption. "If those tunnels are impassable then the journey will be forced to go through Spain and add possibly another one hundred kilometres. The route can easily avoid any major towns, and we don't know of anyone between here and there."

That was maybe one positive, I thought. We had made contact with a lot of people all over the world and the radio equipment had grown with each scavenging run into the towns and cities within easy reach before fuel became a scarce resource. We still had plenty of diesel, but few of the vehicles were hardy enough to undertake such a journey given that the roads were falling apart and were overgrown in most places.

It really took the end of the world for people to realise how much nature wanted to blot out our presence.

Still, the distance itself was a problem. "Two hundred K?" I said to Dan, half in statement and half in question.

"Closer to one hundred and eighty," Victor said, receiving two glances and being ignored by both of us.

"A week on foot, at least, not counting detours and the mountains or the weather," Dan said, "a whole day in a vehicle if we're lucky and don't have to find alternative routes. Two, maybe three days there and back. Is that worth the resources for trade?"

"What of the trade caravans of old?" Victor interjected, interrupting our public but private operational planning brainstorming session.

"What? Horse and cart permanently on the road?" Dan asked with poorly hidden scorn.

"It is possible, yes."

Dan snorted softly to both accept and partially dismiss the idea.

"I'm not sure I like it," he said finally, "in winter it would be impossible. Isn't it a ski resort? That means snow, you realise?"

"Much the same as we get here," Victor countered, "only higher up, obviously."

"How much higher up? What's the elevation we'd have to gain?"

"Over two thousand metres," he answered in a deadpan voice, seeing both of our eyebrows raise in response.

"That's one hell of a drive let alone a walk if things go wrong," I said, playing devil's advocate even if I was starting to feel the familiar itch of wanting to get outside the walls for any kind of adventure, "but…"

Dan shot me a look, knowing that I was trying to find a way to go.

"But what?" he asked suspiciously.

"But I could do it in the Land Rover and be back in less than three days. Just to check it out," I said hopefully.

Dan stared at me for a time, one eye narrowing as he thought.

"It would use up a valuable amount of our remaining fuel," he said, "and I don't fancy much heading into Elne or even Perpignan for more to filter and use," he said, echoing a recurring conversation we had about the remaining refined fossil fuels. Neil was the closest we had to an expert in those things, and he was confident about using diesel after filtering it and pouring in additives to make it burn cleaner so as not to clog the engines up and break them permanently. His theory allowed that diesel could be used for another ten years, despite the common belief that it would be useless, just so long as the engines were driven carefully that was. The older and more *industrial* the vehicle, as he put it, stretched those odds out further still.

"But it's worth a try?" I asked, flashing him a hopeful smile which I knew he had to try very hard to resist.

"Let me think about it," he said, meaning that he wanted to ask Marie to tell him all of the factors he hadn't considered. "Can I keep this?" he asked Victor, taking back the paper and holding it up slightly. He nodded his gracious assent, winding Dan up further without realising it. He turned to me and said the words that gave my adventurous spirit more than a spark of excitement.

"Get a map, work it out, find a Spanish speaker and decide who you're taking. Then I'll decide."

I nodded, holding out my hand for the message Dan still held and turning to look at Victor who had already risen to shuffle through the papers on his desk and begin folding the map to the correct area.

"I'll catch up with you this afternoon," Dan told me, leaving the room deep in thought.

"We are here," Victor said, pointing at our tiny, enclosed bay close to the border with Spain, "and Andorra is… here," he said moving the pencil diagonally up and left on the map in a direction resembling west by northwest. "These are the tunnels, and the second one is just inside Andorra itself."

"Why is it Spanish?" I asked. "Why not French?"

"Ah," Victor exclaimed, happy to be able to provide a history lesson, "perhaps Polly is the better person to ask of this, but I know that this entire region of the Catalan is almost separate from both countries, not like the people are one or the other but that they are an… an *individual*."

"Okay," I said, realising that his answer didn't help at all, and looked back to the map.

"Only two roads in?" I asked.

"Yes, one south to Spain and one east to France," Victor answered.

"What do you know about the place?"

"Tourism mostly," he said, "a small population of under one hundred thousand people. Self-governing, although technically overseen by both countries in equal part."

"Resources?" I asked, trying to figure out what they could offer.

"Some crops, mostly tobacco I think, and some livestock."

"Did they have an army or anything like that?"

"This," he said, "I do not know. I shall ask word to be spread among the people for anyone who knows the valleys."

I nodded, scooping up the map and bidding him goodbye. As I always did when I needed another brain to bounce off, and usually before I took any kind of plan to Dan, I went to find Mitch and hoped to kill two birds with one stone.

He wasn't in their room, both he and Alita, the young woman who had attached herself to him before the battle for Sanctuary, being absent which wasn't surprising given the hot weather. He claimed that it was the Squaddie in him, but whenever the sun was out in force I seemed to turn my back and he was at least topless to soak up the rays. Worst case was finding him spread out like a starfish in what he sickeningly called his *budgie-smugglers*. I shuddered at that unwelcome thought and retrieved my dog before wandering down to the docks to try and find him.

"Nemesis, heel," I said, seeing the dog scramble to its feet in undisguised excitement.

Spark out to flat out in under a second, Dan always said that about Ash and his uncanny ability to be asleep in seconds and switch to full alertness even faster. His daughter was no different, other than the darker colouring and smaller size, but from the moment she had been given to me as a puppy I had trained her to be the equal to her father in every way possible.

Dan used to say that it wasn't the size of the dog that made it hit hard, but the speed. He joked, bragged really, that Ash was big *and* fast whereas Nemesis had to be taught guile instead of brute strength. She could track like a train, her nose gluing itself to the ground and following a scent like a bloodhound, and she could chase and bring down a man almost as well as her sire could. Where she was identical to him was in her loyalty, which to me was as unwavering as Ash was devoted to Dan. We both still worked each other's dogs, for their benefit as well as ours if we ever had to give commands to the other's sidekick.

At just over three years old she was fully grown and stood to my thigh with almost three-quarters the width across her back as Ash, and I was prouder of her than I was my battered, camouflage dappled M4 which I couldn't face parting with, even if there were brand-new HK416s in our armoury ready to be cleaned of the packing grease and used.

With Nemesis at my side, which I never got bored of saying, we walked to find Mitch to ask his opinion on how to impress my dad.

FAILURE TO PLAN...

I was lucky. Lucky that Mitch wasn't doing what he called 'rocking out' and was still wearing shorts at least. His skin had turned a rich golden brown, like tea stewed for too long, and that tan seemed to last him all year round so that when summer followed spring he only had to top it up instead of starting from scratch like many who had started their journey in the cold centre of England.

"*Hola*, Nikita," he said in an accent that still sounded unmistakably Scottish even when tinged with Spanish. Alita was originally from Spain but had travelled all over the world as a diving instructor, living on holiday resorts everywhere from the Canary Islands, Las Palmas as she called them, to Mauritius to the Caribbean and back to Southern France not far from where she was born near Barcelona.

"'Sup," I said, nodding my chin upwards and bumping his offered fist as I neared him. "Possibility of an Op," I explained, "could do with a second opinion for brainstorming it."

I could always be this blunt with Mitch and could always count on him to impart some knowledge to me. His life, or at least his previous life, as an infantryman had made him expect very little in the way of comfort in life, so he took it wherever he could and didn't complain when it was taken away. He was a joker, not quite as bad as Neil but then again nobody was as bad as Neil, but just like my dog he could switch on in an instant.

Okay, perhaps likening him to my dog isn't the nicest thing but...
well, the cap fits.

"Step into my office," Mitch said, indicating a patch of shade beside his sun spot just as Alita returned bringing two drinks. The glasses rang out with the tell-tale tinkle of ice cubes, a rare commodity given the low voltage supply of electricity from the far-off wind turbines and the individual setups using alternators from cars attached to large vehicle batteries. The latter, a trick we hadn't used before arriving in Sanctuary, supplied each individual room or house with a small supply of energy working much the same way as a car's engine had worked before with the belt charging the battery through the alternator. Only now instead of being powered by a moving combustion engine they were connected to wheels like children's toys, spinning either in the coastal breeze or else in the running water of the stream coming from the cliffs behind the town.

"*Hola*, Leah," Alita said, handing a drink to Mitch and smiling back at him to return his wink. "You have this one," she said in English, "I get more."

"Thank you," I said warmly, knowing that she would insist if I tried to vacate her seat and refuse the drink which had obviously been her own.

"So," Mitch asked, more business-like after a sip of his drink, "seven questions?"

The seven questions were the way he had taught me how to plan an operation and could be applied to pretty much everything that required forethought. It was an echo of the British Army that no longer existed but lived on through him.

"Situation?" he asked.

"Radio call from Andorra, two hundred K's inland. Offering

trade and reporting some hostile activity," I said.

"Task and reason?"

"Travel there, assess situation, possibility of trade and allies. Offer assistance if practicable," I answered, not realising how much I sounded like Dan.

"What do you need?"

"Vehicle, fuel, translator."

"Hmm," Mitch said, narrowing his eyes at me, "we have those," he answered. Covering questions four and five in one go, he asked, "When and where?"

"One eighty to two hundred K's west by northwest. Alternative routes requiring a further one hundred each way. Three days expected."

"Control measures?" he asked finally.

In answer I smiled wickedly and pointed at Nemesis who had found shade and was laid down panting. Mitch got the gist; the only control measure required was to deal with any threat harder and faster than they could deal with me.

"Okay," he said, sitting up and sipping his drink again. "Land Rover with the long-range fuel tank, diesel, a translator and one additional fighter unless the two are one and the same, route plan with alternatives, assess and return. Simple. Dan okay with you doing this on your own then?" he finished.

Now my hostility at being treated like a kid was long since passed, but it still bridled me to have to ask permission to go outside the walls. I volunteered to run protection on every trip going between the three settlements we regularly did trade with, one of them being our own inland farm where Mitch and I had witnessed the uncomfortable coupling of Ash and Nemesis' mother, and where we had first learned about their ingenious workaround using the alternators and batteries to supply electricity. I knew that everyone had to ask Dan's permission for any kind of mission, I mean the man *was* in charge, but it still hadn't dawned on me by then that I probably had it easier being his adopted kid than I did have it tough because of the same reason.

"He wants to hear my plan this afternoon," I said, only a trace of sullen teenager in my voice.

"Well it sounds like the objectives are simple," Mitch said, "you just need a fighter who can speak Español."

I nodded, knowing just who I could ask.

⁓

Because I had shit to do, and also because I was never really that hungry in hot weather, I skipped the midday meal when everyone took to the shade for a light snack and a break. Winter was different, but summer took on what Marie called the Mediterranean way and usually included a siesta for most people.

Over the last few years, since the aftermath of the battle had left us with dead to bury, wounds to heal and rebuilding to do, Polly had asked us – the fighters – to train a few people in our methods to a higher standard than the general militia training that most people received. Volunteers came forward, some from the farm inland and others already in Sanctuary, and they were equipped and trained from scratch. I could still hear Dan's *forget everything you think you already know* speech from day one.

The main reason for this swelling in ranks was to take the pressure off Dan, myself and Mitch, to be present for every supply run inland and to allow us a break from being on standby night and day in the wake of the attack when most people were still scared. It had taken us another half a year to heal; Mitch and Neil having been shot and Dan having been battered and sliced and blown up. I'd escaped relatively unscathed, only the chunk of rock slicing my cheek deeply left a mark and that was far better than the alternative of the enemy sniper turning my head into a gooey piñata. If I hadn't have crawled out under the tiny cover of the remaining parapet and got myself shot at, then we would have been overrun, but I had managed to get Mitch's detonator and call the ball for him to destroy the attack against us by what had been our own vehicle. I can still feel and smell the impossibly loud *crack* and *boom* of the two bar mines crushing the people and vehicles on the roadway.

In that time, the last of the Legionnaires had been rounded up, at least those who hadn't had the sense to flee far away as we assumed their leader had, even with an arrow stuck in him and a forty-foot fall off the ramparts of the Sky Fort. One of the people with them, however, wasn't a soldier. He was a Spanish boy of eighteen or nineteen, and he was kept by them as a kind of pet after they had slaughtered the group he was travelling with for refusing to contribute to their cause. He had begged for mercy when captured, and not being armed or dressed like the others his pleas were listened to. He was brought back to Sanctuary and stood a kind of trial like I had seen on TV way back when, and his story had been believed. He just wanted to survive, and now he wanted to be one of us. He had earned our trust and even shown a natural aptitude towards our profession, finding himself pulled out of militia training and elevated to the training ranks of the elite alongside his usual guard duties.

Rafael, or Rafi as he went by, was thin and fast but strong like a goat. Mitch said that most of the special forces types he had ever seen were more like him than big muscle men, that strength came more from willpower than from a gym, and Rafi proved himself capable. Seeing that I needed a fighter and a translator and taking three people just increased the odds of failure, and added another thirty per cent to our load, he was the obvious choice to come with me.

"Rafi," I called out after walking the length of the sea wall with another militia man I had grabbed to replace him, "I have a job for you."

"*Si?*" he said, a flash of white teeth in his olive face showing that he thought anything was better than guard duty on a hot day. He gave all of his food and water to the man replacing him, offering him a book to read which the man turned down as he was French and didn't grasp the language well enough to enjoy reading.

"*Si,*" I echoed, "come with me."

I took him back to the central keep, the thick stone walls instantly dropping the temperature as soon as we escaped the hot sun and walked through the communal areas until stopping at a table in the dining area and laying out the map. Looking around for one of the children who usually hunted in packs near to the kitchens, I snapped my finger at one of them and beckoned him over. Producing a brightly coloured wrapped sweet from my pocket I waved it at him enticingly, totally missing the irony of my actions. The scope of how bad it had looked didn't even strike me as I had offered these children to come and see my puppies when Nemesis was only a few weeks old.

"*Tu connais Neil?*" I asked in my poor French, hoping that he would understand my meaning and not just agree to anything to get the offered treat.

"*Oui,*" he said, his eyes never leaving the prize.

"*Va chercher pour moi,*" I asked slowly, guessing that my French wasn't perfect but hoping he got the point. I wanted the man brought to me and snatched back the sweet as he reached for it, adding, "*Non. Après.*"

The boy pulled a face but disappeared, chased by the others of his pack who shouted questions at him only to be ignored in case he was forced to share the bounty. In the week, those children would be in classes, being taught different things by different people for half of the day until they were released to learn the trades of their parents. It was what formed the basis of a kind of school system and ensured that the children didn't grow up feral. Waiting for Neil to be brought, I turned to Rafi and told him what was on.

"We need to drive to Andorra," I said slowly, keeping it as simple as possible as I knew he understood my hand signals in simulated combat better than he did my words. "Have you been there?"

"*Si,*" he said smiling, "many times. My father and his father went to there for buying their tobacco and brandy. They do not have the tax as we do Spain."

Good to know, I thought, *completely irrelevant, but at least he's been there.* I kept the sarcasm from my face, something I had only recently learned how to do, and went on.

"We need to drive there and speak to the people. They sent a message." I dug out the paper from my pocket containing the translated message and smoothed it down on the table. Rafi leaned over it, running his finger over the words until he paused.

"What is this word?" he asked, pointing to the English

translation from the French and Spanish before.

"Thieves," I said, "why?"

"This is not true Española," he said. "This *Catalan,* and this word does not mean thieves, it means how you would say a *highwayman.* A… a robber? On the road?"

"Great," I said, no longer keeping the sarcasm locked up inside, "let's keep that one to ourselves, shall we?"

Rafi smiled and nodded, making me suspicious that he hadn't really understood my meaning, but we were interrupted by Neil's entrance.

"Who disturbs my rest?" he boomed like some medieval monarch roused from his bed at an ungodly hour.

"Me," I said, "*siddown,*" I added with a smirk, making Neil pretend to jump to attention and hurry to comply. I saw the kid who had fetched him chewing on a mouthful as he waited beside me, knowing that the boy had already wrung some treat out of Neil, probably freely given, but waited to extract his promised reward from me. Not being of a mind to break my word to the young entrepreneur, I handed over the sweet and heard a high-pitched and rushed *'merci'* through his mouthful as he fled to defend his prize against the others who ran after him.

"We need the Land Rover," I said, getting straight to business, "and full tanks."

"Hey, Sarah Connor, how 'bout the fillings outta my fuckin' teeth?" Neil answered in an American accent, no doubt quoting some film older than me that I hadn't seen.

"Can you do it?" I asked, smiling but ignoring his attempt at humour to draw me in. He did that thing that he always did when

Dan asked him for something, wringing his hands and sucking in a breath through his teeth before finally releasing the breath and grinning.

"Of course I can. It's me you're talking to, kid."

I let the quip at me being a kid go. At my age I would probably have only just got my driving license, and that was if my mother had been able to find the money to pay for lessons. I'd been driving since I was thirteen, around the same time as I had been given my first Glock and a G36 carbine, so I'd convinced myself long ago that my childhood had drawn to a rapid close.

"Okay, thanks," I said, "ready for first light tomorrow?"

"Your will, my hands," he said, feigning a bow of subservience.

"You not even going to ask what for?" I said questioningly.

It was Neil's turn to smile.

"I assume because you and Rafi are driving to Andorra."

I said nothing, despite my mouth hanging open to form the question before I stopped myself. Not much got past Neil, who still hid a sharp intellect behind his jokes and impressions.

"Yes," I answered, hoping that Dan had already spoken to him to see if the obvious plan I was forming would be viable. I decided not to press any further, suspecting that he would report back to Dan what I said anyway.

"I shall take my leave then," he said rising. "I still have some rat-packs," he said, meaning the supply of British Army rations taken so long ago and likely still inside their best before date for a few years to come, "I'll leave them in the truck."

I thanked him, watched him leave the room, and turned back to Rafi where I traced along the route on the map.

"We go west, pick up the toll roads which should still be clear enough," I explained, "head north towards Perpignan but avoid the city, head west again through Villefranche and keep going to the Pyrenees and into Andorra."

Rafi nodded along as my finger traced the route, which my string-measuring technique had told me was closer to one hundred and sixty kilometres, even cutting out one of the tunnel choke-points by taking the winding mountain road instead and leaving only the main tunnel itself into the protected valley.

"If we can't get in that way," I said, "then we have to go back down and through Spain, adding another seventy-five or eighty kilometres to come in from the south."

"It looks good," Rafi said, smiling.

And it did. It looked good. And it looked easy. And it was completely wrong.

THE SIX P'S

"Allow me to lay some knowledge on you," I said cockily just over an hour later as I spread the map in front of Dan and looked over my notes hastily scribbled on the pad I had retrieved from my new equipment vest. When I had taken it off the stand Neil had built for me in my room it dawned on me that nobody had ever actually shot at me when I had worn it, and I couldn't be sure if that made it lucky or whether it was statistically due to be put to the test and prove its claim of being bulletproof. Shaking that away I had transferred everything from my head to the paper.

This was where I took different things from different people.

Neil always goaded me for being a mini-me of Dan, only with long hair, but I was very much my own person. I took military bits from Mitch, plucked a little of the coolness from Steve's head when he had first taught me how to respect a firearm and how to be precise; as a helicopter pilot precision had been something so natural to him that he took it for granted. From Dan I took a lot of things, like how to fight dirty to make sure I won. I took the little bits that everyone did really well and I made them my own, and for planning missions it was actually Marie who had taught me the best way. Mitch did his seven questions thing which was an army method, but that seemed just to help solidify the question in my head, whereas Marie's method helped me give the answers so that anyone could understand it.

Her way, and people often forgot that before she became our counsellor and leader that she was a professional investigator; a detective sergeant dealing with murders and things. She had researched, planned and overseen more operations, more missions, back in the world than most. Her way laid it out nice and simple for everyone to understand, and I hoped that it would resonate with Dan because he hadn't seen me do this yet. I think Marie liked giving me things I could use against him, maybe to take away some of that mystical hero aura that people thought surrounded him.

Walks around in a cloud of unicorn farts sprinkling rainbow dust everywhere, that one, Mitch often said of Dan when people seemed to idolise him. He was just a man, an extraordinary one, I'll allow, but all he did was think it through and execute it with precision and meaning. Maximum effort.

I cleared my throat.

"Information," I began, "is that there are survivors in Andorra. I presume you know the details and you don't need me to break that down?" I asked, guessing that he would have learned the detail of this tiny, almost unknown country which was one of the smallest independent states in the world.

He smiled.

"No, please lay your knowledge on me."

Bugger, I thought, but pressed on anyway.

"Small landlocked principality," I said, having only recently learned what that meant but not willing to let him know that. "Pre... *event* population was around eighty thousand but with a regular tourist attendance of up to ten times that number over a one-year period. Estimated survivor population given Emma's immunity percentages put the expected number of people there at one hundred plus. Predominant economical source was tourism, but exports of tobacco and some livestock, er…" I glanced at my notes as I'd lost my train of thought. "Geographically it's a bowl surrounded by impassable mountains. Two roads in, one east and one south. They have made radio contact requesting trade and have stated that they have suffered thefts. Now," I said, looking up and fixing him with an intense look, "translation issues have been raised to say that *thieves* may not be accurate as the Spanish and Catalan dialects can differ. A more correct assumption is that they mean *highwaymen.*"

I knew I'd struck a chord there and hit on something he didn't know because he couldn't hide an emotion on his face if his life depended on it. It was like he'd just smelt one of Ash's silent farts in polite company and was trying to pretend it hadn't happened.

"Intent," I went on, seeing the corner of his mouth prickle upwards as he finally recognised that I was using the police format for giving a mission briefing. "The intent is to travel there and open a dialogue with the survivors. The message was directed from the General Council, which is what their form of government is called. From this we can assume that they have established a form of co-operation or hierarchical command."

Dan was impressed, even though I still stumbled over the word that Marie had given me.

"Method," I said, glancing back down at my notes, "Land Rover with the extra fuel tank is available and the route planned. Myself and one other to act as interpreter if required, who also doubles up as trained."

"Rafi?" he asked, no doubt having either seen us together that day or else one of his little spies had told him. It didn't matter; Rafi was the obvious choice. "He's about your age, isn't he?" Dan asked me, not even bothering to hide the lift in his eyebrows.

"Four years older," I said, "almost twenty-two."

"The route should take a day unless detours are needed due to blocked roads. There is enough fuel to do the trip at its longest including detours without having to find any more."

I looked at Dan who just nodded, telling me that either he had sought out Neil or else Neil had found him and told him what I had asked already. Thick as bloody thieves they were, despite constantly ribbing each other whenever they spoke. They had been that way ever since they'd found me, and I was proud to be one of the very first few still alive who had started our little group.

"Full personal loadout," I went on. "I want to take a *four-one-seven* too," I said, meaning that we would both be fully armed but that I wanted to take one of our bigger calibre HK417 sniper rifles too, which was the bigger, meaner brother of the gun that Dan carried now. His was the short-barrelled version, the CQB which someone said was the gun that had shot Bin Laden. That was back in the world where I'd never seen a gun, let alone owned a few.

"Admin?" Dan asked, prompting me to move to the next section of the established briefing order. I ignored it.

"Five days rations each," I said trying not to show any annoyance, "full BOBs. Dog food for me. Ability to survive without scavenging if we had to walk back."

He nodded, evidently happy that I had considered the worst-case scenario.

"Risk assessment," I said as I looked into his eyes, "risks are road conditions and hostile action. I'll drive carefully and avoid people with guns. Communications," I went on before Dan stopped me.

"You don't want to take anything heavier?" he asked, one eyebrow up a little.

"Like what?" I asked.

"Like an AT4."

That surprised me. I knew we had a few, and I guessed that Mitch probably visited them from time to time in private, but I'd never used one or even considered learning how. Blowing shit up wasn't my thing; it was Mitch's.

"Anything requiring that kind of firepower," I said carefully, sensing a trap, "and I'd be looking to withdraw. There's only two of us so not enough to use flanking manoeuvres. I'm not looking to tangle with anyone."

Dan nodded, happy with what I realised was the correct answer. "Comms?"

"None to speak of really," I said, knowing that the CB would be useless after about ten kilometres from Sanctuary because of the high peaks. "I was thinking of trialling one of the pigeons for an SOS?"

Dan nodded, shifting in his seat. "Good idea. Take two though in case one doesn't make it back. If you get in the shit just release them and we'll follow your route in force."

My turn to nod, my mind being forced to consider failure and risk.

"Human rights," I said as I tried not to smile. Marie had been laughing when she told me this part, knowing that Dan would find it funny. "I don't foresee any collateral intrusion on the rights of

35

people not directly linked to the operation," I said, parroting what Marie had written down for me and keeping a straight face, "and all relevant sections of the European Human Rights Act will be carefully considered before any of those rights are engaged."

Dan stared at me, a smile beginning as he spoke. "Leah, I fully expect you to engage and breach Article Two should you feel the need. If you meet anyone willing to do you harm and they don't want to tell you the information you want, then you bloody well engage Article Three."

Okay, smartarse, I thought to myself, *you've got me there.*

He knew he had me, probably as certainly as he knew that Marie had helped me with the wording of the last bit. He held up his thumb again like he had when we spoke to Victor.

"Right to life," he said before holding up another digit, "and freedom from torture."

"So... I should kill people and torture them?" I asked, sensing another trap.

He shot me a shocked look.

"No! Not unless you need to, but what if you do have to?"

"Do it like you mean it," we chorused, bumping fists again as we both called jinx for the second time that day.

~

I spent the rest of the daylight getting what I needed together with Rafi and Nemesis flanking me. I went with him to his quarters, shared with a few other young men of the militia in a room with roughly constructed wooden bunks. The others in there smirked and tried to embarrass him at being picked by me, which I ignored because men are just big silly boys and aren't worth acknowledging when they snicker and giggle about girls. A soft snap of my fingers brought Nemesis to my heel and she let out a low, throaty growl before I loudly admonished her, although gently, telling her that the silly men don't mean to be rude, but they aren't capable of good manners and that she should bite any of them.

The snickering stopped abruptly after that and a few of the others found that they had somewhere else to be.

I helped Rafi empty out his backpack, finding it too small for the job so I used my eyebrows to suggest that someone else lend him theirs. He ended up with a hardy black canvas-style bag with tactical loops on, not too dissimilar to my own one but a little bigger. I helped him pack it, tossing out the things he didn't need. One of those items was a roll-on deodorant and shaving kit, and I saw the horror on his face at the thought of not being groomed in the presence of a girl.

"Trust me," I said, "after three days in a car in this heat with a dog, we'll both smell bad."

We didn't need to consider food and water as I knew Neil would load the truck with those things. We'd have to transfer that into our bags before we set off, because there was no point in having a bug-out bag if you had to pack it before bugging out.

He carried a sidearm, a mass-produced Glock as they were so widely available to European law enforcement and military. I carried the same one and knew there was a reason why they were so popular. They were easy to use and handle for a sidearm and were relatively simple to maintain.

"What about your main weapon?" I asked him.

"I have been trained with the H&K," he said, his accent forcing me to hide a smirk.

"Good, follow me. Nem!" I snapped, waking the dog up from where she had helped herself to a vacant bottom bunk.

One of the benefits of being the daughter of the town leaders, as well as one of the trusted lieutenants along with Neil and Mitch, was that I had both keys for the armoury. Only four of us could access the guns alone whereas the militia had to have two people present who had a key to one lock only. It was the safest way to prevent anyone getting their hands on the good stuff without us knowing about it, and Dan was ever suspicious of people who lingered too long near the heavy door. Dan probably knew that Mitch's room was a small armoury in itself, but he kept them locked up tight too. The sidearms that the militia carried when on guard duty, only a few at a time, were handed from person to person when they took over the watch.

I opened the door, unlocking one heavy mechanism at a time, and pulled it open to flick on the light and smiled as it sputtered into life. Stacks of looted 5.56 ammunition stood tall to my left, with racks of new HK416s sporting different attachments. There was still enough daylight left to sight one in, so I took one of the ready guns, the ones not smeared with packing grease, and looked it over.

"Holographic sight," I told Rafi, seeing him smile widely, "line up the red dot on what you want dead." I handed him the gun, first showing him that the breech was empty and patting the empty magazine housing. He held it comfortably by the foregrip and trigger housing, making a show of keeping his finger away from the trigger to demonstrate the discipline he had been taught. I liked that.

I took a baker's dozen of loaded magazines and put them in a bag as I left him holding the rifle. I took a Glock and another half-dozen loaded mags to put them in as well, pausing to add another one for luck before I handed Rafi the bag and ran my hand over the old MK14 and newer HK417. I picked up the HK, pulling back on the mechanism and smiling. I took four magazines for that, more than enough to do a lot of damage, and popped two of our remaining flashbangs in the bag. Flipping off the light and seeing Rafi scurry to follow me out of the door I locked it up and led the way back to the keep.

Taking the bag and the 416 from him I said, "I'll keep these until tomorrow." Mostly as Dan wouldn't approve but more because I knew they would be playing with it all night in their little barracks if he kept it and I wanted him alert after a full night's sleep instead of dying from a stray bullet negligently discharged by unpracticed hands.

"See you at dinner," I told him before heading for my room.

ON THE ROAD AGAIN

Now I didn't think for one second that Dan was just letting me run with this. I know he'd done his own plan, checked it against mine, probably spent all night picking apart both plans until he had boiled it down to what he thought could work.

And then he just trusted me.

I didn't want to think it, I certainly didn't want to give voice to my opinion, but Dan had softened since Marie had the baby. He was running around and jabbering away with both French and English words now, always up to something and never seeming to grow tired, but his birth had somehow changed Dan. He wasn't quite so rough and ready any more, somehow. He wasn't the physical presence in the room whenever he walked in and he didn't intimidate people, whether he meant to or not.

I knew he had been through enough before. How he had come close to the edge and been knocked out or beaten up or shot or blown up or stabbed and should have died twenty times over in the last five years but somehow, he always came out the other side. The battle for Sanctuary, along the healing and the aftermath, had left him exhausted. He had changed after that, and with a new baby he withdrew from his chosen role. He blamed his injuries to begin with; asking others to organise a guard and take a watch when he would have volunteered whether carrying an injury or not.

He was different, and I suspected that he had lost his edge. That was fine, understandable even. He'd got us this far, solved the existential crisis of humanity and led us to safety and a solution to our continued existence on earth. As far as career highlights go, he had done enough.

By the time my brother was a year old, Dan had started to make a reappearance. He began exercising and working Ash. He wore his weapons again and moved with purpose, and spent long hours talking with Marie and Polly until the expected happened and she stepped down to leave them in joint charge of the care of Sanctuary.

The mundane day-to-day, the training of the militia and the selection of leaders among the others, fell to Mitch and Neil. And me.

I was up early, doing the old trick of drinking an extra two bottles of water before sleep and waking up to a nagging bladder. Not as accurate, but just as effective as an alarm clock. I walked Nemesis up to the parapets and watched the daybreak over our bay having missed the sunrise, but watched the line of glowing orange creep down from the watchtower on the opposite side until it hit the level of the cliff it sat on.

I wasn't hungry, I never was when it was a morning like that, but I forced myself to eat and went to get ready.

I brushed Nemesis, which was a far easier task than Ash because of his thick double coat. Her fur was darker, with patches of brown at her paws, belly and muzzle, and the short fur took the brush easily. Balling up the dead fur, I tossed it into the fireplace in my room as the last few years had taught us all never to waste any resource no matter how small and seemingly inconsequential.

I pulled on my black combat trousers, made of a lighter material and designed for hill walking in fair weather, and the new pair of breathable walking boots which I had only recently broken in. Knowing the weather would be warm, I finished the outfit with a vest top with wide shoulders that wouldn't rub on my equipment. The boots and top were my usual style noir, obviously.

I shrugged into my vest, black and heavily padded to absorb any impact to the ceramic plates front and back, and tightened it.

Like Dan, I was always messing with my kit and tweaking it out of some obsession to find the perfect loadout or through simple boredom. A Glock went into the holster stitched horizontally on the chest ready for my right hand to draw it. Under it sat two spare magazines and beside that were four loaded magazines for my carbine. A small sheath knife sat on the front of my right shoulder and a larger one on my back. As excessive as that might have seemed, I still carried more. A rig attached to my left thigh and connected to my belt with a large clip held two loaded magazines for the 417, and my right thigh held the Walther with the suppressor I had borrowed from Dan about a year before and never got around to handing back. That gun fitted my hand better than the Glock did, but having only two magazines for it I had to hold it in reserve as a secondary, secondary weapon.

Dressed for war, and feeling as tough as I looked, I left my room and headed for the courtyard near the gatehouse where Neil was fussing over the Land Rover's engine bay as the engine ticked over to warm up. Rafi was lounging near the tailgate. He had already separated the food and water into two piles, filling the remaining room in his bag with half.

I passed the bag of weapons over to him, unslinging the 417

from my back and laying the long rifle across behind the front seats. He loaded the Glock and holstered it at his right hip before taking the 416 and resting it in the passenger footwell. I finished loading my bag and shut the back doors, turning to find a small farewell committee waiting for me near the open driver's door.

Victor was among them, strange for him as he rarely left the tower, and in his hands was a wooden crate with wide slats. Inside, I knew, were the two homing pigeons which had been reared as a hobby of his and had all come back when they were put to the test.

"They already carry an SOS message," he said, "so just release them if you need help."

I nodded my thanks, watching as the crate was shrouded and placed behind the front passenger seat. Marie hugged me, as did my little brother, who didn't seem to understand the significance of the farewell and ran off to play. I looked around but couldn't find Dan. Neil spoke to me, going over the details of the vehicle and the fuel which I already knew, and he knew I did, he just wanted to speak to me a little longer before standing on the sidestep and leaning up to kiss me on the forehead.

"I've got your route mapped," he told me, reiterating that he knew the roads we planned to take and marking the alternative routes in a different colour. The map we took was unmarked and still folded to the original creases, that way nobody could find or capture it and know our origin. Operational security, no matter how relaxed we had become, was still key.

Just as I thought Dan wouldn't be coming to see us off, he emerged with Ash and Mitch and both were dressed in boots, trousers and T-shirts under their equipment vests. Both were armed, maybe not as heavily as I was, but both were clearly going outside

43

the walls. Ash jumped in, Nemesis immediately licking his face and bothering him as he looked for a comfortable place to settle down and look out of the windows. My heart dropped slightly, thinking that they had decided at the last minute to come with us until I realised that their bags were of a size to sustain them for a day and not three.

"Drop us off near the split?" Dan asked, meaning to let them out in the low valley before the road leading away from Sanctuary forked north and south west. The lower road led to the inland farm and the two obviously planned a visit.

"We'll walk back tonight when it's cooler," Mitch added with a smile.

I sucked in air through my teeth, mimicking Neil whenever he was asked if something was possible. "Not sure we've got room," I said goadingly.

"Well if you didn't take up the whole back seat with a cannon then you bloody would," Mitch said as he climbed in and rested my 417 upright in the footwell to settle himself down. He wound down the window and rested the barrel of his rifle on the edge as though it was the most normal thing in the world. Rafi was already sat in the front seat and evidently unsure whether he should climb down and offer privileged position to the men behind him. But as neither of them gave him a look or spoke to him other than to offer a greeting, he stayed uncomfortably where he was.

The half-hour drive to the split was uneventful. I'd wound down my window, partly because the sun was already growing hotter and making my skin prickle with sweat under the heavy vest, and partly because I'd grown too big to drive the Defender without having to put my right elbow out of the window like Dan always did.

Some questions were aimed at me and Rafi, mostly to check that we had the right answers to hand and were probably designed as reminders for what Mitch called 'actions-on'. This was not a new concept to me and both men in the back seat knew it. Actions-on for an ambush, actions-on for a vehicle malfunction, for a puncture, for a blocked road, for discovering other people and how to make first contact. I let Rafi answer some, the easier questions which they knew I knew the answers to, and was happy with what he said.

I had to admit that he was a good-looking young man. He was a shade taller than me, wide in the shoulders but slim and toned like a swimmer with short, jet black hair and a quick smile. His olive skin only seemed to darken slightly in summer whereas I went from deathly pale to tanned in response to the seasons. I was almost eighteen, and Rafi was only a little older. I tried to push those thoughts aside and concentrate on the road which was more of a pitted stone track than the smooth tarmac it had been when we had first driven down it years ago; back when a young girl had walked towards the ancient gates of Sanctuary with her arms held wide begging for their assistance.

All around me I saw the passage of nature reclaiming what people had taken. The raw materials harvested from the earth had been refined and shaped and changed to form the straight lines and uniformity that nature abhorred, but everywhere those straight lines existed greenery attacked it slowly, insidiously, bringing it down to degrade and be recycled. Trees overhung the road in places and half the time I was driving off-road in two worn tyre tracks, but those tracks were caused by the horse-drawn carts travelling almost constantly in the warmer months between Sanctuary and the five other places we regularly did trade with.

Being effectively a fortified fishing village, our boats went out and hauled back more fish than we could consume with the couple of hundred people living inside the safety of the walls. This surplus was never wasted, and the teams of men, women and children met every returning trawler with shirt knives and waterproof aprons, some fashioned from whatever worked and others being custom made for the task back in the world, and the fish were gutted and cleaned. Some of those went to be used, some frozen, and others dried in the sunlight to be packed in crates of rough salt reclaimed from the sea water. That sea salt plant was another of Neil's ingenious plans, and the flat rooves of the town buildings were all laid out with shallow trays which were tended by many hands to bring the buckets of sea water up to evaporate in the bright sunlight and the remaining salt harvested.

Even the guts and wastage never got simply discarded, and whatever wasn't used for bait for larger swimming quarry, like some of the fish heads, went to the pigs who thrived on a diet of fish guts and food scraps. The chickens were much the same, recycling our food waste into fresh sources of protein in the form of their eggs.

The pigs, primarily bred for meat but still not a large enough population to use up too often, formed a large part of our little ecosystem, as much as my own abilities to fight and defend the people and to train the next generation were a valuable part of the wider organic machine.

The farm where Mitch and I had visited on our first trip outside the walls after recovering from the insane and unexpectedly violent passage across, around and through the continent, had grown and thrived well, with more people being required to live and work there. Neil had spent an entire summer there, coordinating the building of better houses and sanitary systems, even adding plans for a waterwheel and a mill which served to grind the corn into flour for our bread. Another version existed in Sanctuary, although this one had been a museum piece that was refurbished just enough for a small donkey to plod in boring circles and power the stone as it rolled over the crop.

I had spent time there too, along with Dan, and had worked on the defences as a small wooden palisade had been erected and a gate guarded night and day. Those defences could easily be overcome by just two of us, but it was designed as a show of strength as opposed to standing up to any real defence. If they were besieged, then the pigeons housed there would be released to bear messages to Sanctuary and bring forth a mighty vengeance on anyone seeking to take what wasn't theirs. In reality, the wall stood primarily to keep predators and vermin away from the crops and livestock.

Just as we were, the farm was producing more than it needed so they traded with the other places in our small network of Southern France and the north eastern coast of Spain. Whilst they had been dependent on Sanctuary for a few years, the farm had emerged as a settlement in its own right which cooperated with us for mutual benefit; we supplied arms and training and a steady supply of fish, promising to offer aid whenever they required it and in turn they provided us with fresh food and a small force of seasonal workers to boost the fishing fleet when their productivity wound down in the colder months.

Arriving at the split between the two roads, which was marked by a disused building having been patched up and repaired as a trading post, I pulled the truck to a stop and slipped it out of gear.

"See you in a couple days," Dan said, leaning forward to give my shoulder a squeeze before giving Rafi a light punch on his right shoulder and saying, "keep them safe. On day four, if you aren't back, I'm coming anyway."

Rafi assured him that he would, allowing his nervous tension to pour out as over-eagerness, which made Mitch chuckle. The two men climbed down, Ash's head popping up from the rear section before he responded to the single word from Dan and scrambled over the seats to follow.

"Stay," I added, seeing Nem's smaller head rear up also thinking that she was to stay with her sire. She shot me a look, head slightly cocked, and I reminded her that she was a good girl. The doors shut, and she climbed over into the back seat to sniff at the long rifle occupying the seat, happy to look out of both sides of the vehicle and enjoy the breeze from the open windows.

I watched as Dan turned back to me, nodding and smiling, before speaking to the guard on the trading post and shaking his hand. I slipped the truck back into gear and rolled away just as the meeting outside my window evolved to produce cigarettes and exchanged news in French. I smiled, driving away with the poor accent of Dan still echoing in my ears.

"Okay," I said, passing the map from my door pocket to Rafi, "follow our route in and keep me posted."

"What does this mean, keep you posted?" he asked, his finger tracing the route from home to the post.

"It means that I want you to say where we are, and what's coming up," I told him. I had given him a map after the evening meal, telling him to study it and learn it because he wouldn't have instructions the following day.

"Like the rally driving?" he asked with a smile I didn't see as my eyes were on the road but could hear in his voice.

"Like the rally driving," I agreed, half expecting to be told of a ninety left ahead.

We drove in silence for the first few hours, me keeping my eyes on the rough road and my thumbs outside of the wheel, him glancing up and down between the map and the road signs as we made our steady progress.

We passed through a few villages and two larger towns, all of them picked clean long ago and marked with white crosses on the doors to signify that there was nothing of value left inside. Picking up the toll roads I was able to gather more speed as the wider expanses of empty tarmac and concrete had fared better through the winters since all maintenance had suddenly stopped. The droning noise of the chunky tyres began to rattle my brain after a steady hour travelling at over fifty, and I could tell from the agitated body language of my navigator that he was feeling it too.

"Let's give Nem a break," I said as I pulled into one of the many overgrown rest stops beside the road, not saying that it was the humans who were struggling with the uncomfortable inactivity of a long drive that they were unaccustomed to. We stepped out of the truck, stretching and raising our weapons to make sure that nobody occupied the area, and as I sat on a concrete picnic bench with my feet on the seat to relax Rafi asked me a question.

"Why is your dog called this?" he asked, watching her relieve her bladder in a squat.

"Nemesis?" I asked, seeing both of them look at me at hearing the name. "She was the Greek Goddess of vengeance. She weighed your deeds and decided on how much fortune you deserved."

"She is vengeance? Like the deliverance of fate?" he asked. "My religion would say that this is divine providence," he explained, the

English words uncertain on his tongue.

"God's will?" I asked, feeling that the conversation was getting a little deep so early on into a long journey.

"Yes," he said, smiling that I had understood him, "I like your dog."

Somehow sensing that she was the subject of discussion, she padded towards him and nuzzled his hand held at his side. He recoiled slightly, unsure of the big animal, so I told her to sit. She sat, glancing only once at me before she turned to look at him expectantly.

"Go on," I reassured him. "She won't bite you unless I tell her to," I added with a playful smirk.

Rafi kept his eyes on the dog, slowly reaching out his hand to smooth down the fur on her head as she sniffed at him for any trace of food. I called her back after a while, seeing him flinch slightly as she moved fast.

We went into the small, low building separately as one of the benefits of using the toll roads were that they all had eco-toilets which didn't rely on running water. Re-emerging into the light, I went back to the truck and saw Rafi turn to toss me a bottle of water. I caught it as I walked, not breaking step, and opened it to drink a few pulls before lobbing it back to him. He kept his eyes on me, catching it low with his left hand on instinct and smiling despite himself at the cocky display.

Now, I didn't know if it was being raised by Dan, or whether Rafi was just impressive in his own right, but I couldn't help feeling a little flutter of excitement when he did that. It was stupid, and nothing to do with the mission, so I hid my blush and tucked an errant strand of hair behind my ear.

"Let's keep moving," I said, climbing back behind the wheel.

MOUNTAIN ROADS

I loved to drive, always had from the first time when I was only just thirteen. It gave me a sense of power and freedom, and always impressed other people because I was good at it. I knew that was down to Dan too, because he had taught me the dark arts from his experience of car chases and using three vehicles to force another to stop by boxing them in and ramming them off the road. I'd done that once, and for no reason I could understand I told Rafi the story of Dan finding Emma and me using the truck we were actually in to clip a car into the central reservation and kill the driver. I told him about the score mark on the roof above my head where a bullet had missed my head by inches. I left out the other details, like me shooting the passenger in the leg and then helping Dan torture him.

A girl has to have some secrets with a boy.

Rafi responded with a story of his childhood, obviously not as violent and war-like as my own but had taken place when he was about the same age.

"My brother, Mateo," he said laughing at the memory he hadn't even recounted yet, "when he had his first car before he even had his licence for driving, he took me out when our parents were away for a night and he was to be watching me. He not stopped in time and crashed into the walls. I remember he was so scared of what our father would say that he cried all the way home with only one lights at the front." He paused to chuckle again. "When our parents returned, we had told them a story of how we were playing in front of the house and fell against the car to make the damages…"

"And they fell for that?" I asked, explaining because I could see I had used a term he didn't understand. "They believed you?" I racked my brain, trying another way. "*Vraiment tu les as fait marcher?*"

"They did," he said with a wistful smile, "I knew later that they did not, but I think they were just happy that we stuck together in our lies."

He lapsed into amused silence, and I felt suddenly bad for him.

"I'm sorry," I said weakly.

"Why are you sorry?" he asked.

"Your family. Your brother…"

"My brother?"

"Yes," I said, "it must have been hard losing someone you were close to." I went on thinking of my own little brother so long put from my memory.

"He is not lost," Rafi said, "he works as a fisherman in the town!"

"Oh," I said, feeling foolish, "I… I didn't know."

"It is nothing," he said with a wave. "Turn left ahead onto the D612."

"How long for?"

He paused before answering.

"Err… For many hours, I think, until we reach the foothills."

'Many hours' was no exaggeration, as the roads were terrible in places. Twice I had to resort to the dried earth and cross drainage ditches beside the road and avoid blockages. One of those seemed deliberately placed, with the degraded tyres and rusted bodywork of cars lending the impression that the barricade was created by people. On that occasion I reversed the car back a hundred metres and deployed us on foot, creeping up the ditches to the blockage and scanning the area, but if that barricade was intentional then it was abandoned long ago.

We stopped for lunch after the road began to meander like a river, switching back and forth as we climbed further on each straight stretch until we found a wide bend overlooking the lush, green valley we had climbed. We ate from the foil bags of the remaining ration packs and I had to show Rafi how to add the water to the clear bag and heat the contents with the sachet of chemicals. He was intrigued by it, mesmerised almost just as I had been when I first ate them so long ago. I had learned to hate them after a while, even forcing myself to chew down the stodgy mess of the menu options I couldn't stomach in place of starving and growing weak. I enjoyed a vegetarian all day breakfast, my absolute favourite, cold from the packet with the spoon from my bag and washed it down with more water.

I liked Rafi, more and more with each mile I reckoned, and part of him reminded me of Steve. The old pilot would hold a comfortable silence for hours, only occasionally talking when he had to or when he remembered something of value to his company. Rafi was like that; he kept his eyes on the map and the road signs as well as looking out for any potential danger along our route. He would sometimes tell me more about what he and his brother got up to, painting the picture of a pair of tearaways who were fiercely loyal to one another, and I found myself responding with my own tales, although I realised that I had very little of interest to say from before Dan and Neil found me.

We rested a little longer in the shade of the truck before I forced myself to get moving again.

"Would you like me to do the driving?" he offered, making me frown. "It is okay if no."

"Yes," I said hurriedly, realising that he had misunderstood my frown, "that would be good."

I pulled myself inside the passenger seat, M4 rested out of the window on the sling over my torso and map over my knees. He drove carefully, crunching the gears occasionally until he grew more accustomed to the individual driving experience that was a Land Rover Defender. I even gave him careful tips, passing on the skills from Dan to Rafi as he navigated the ever-increasing rock falls before the landscape plateaued and fell away again. Another hour took us further to the west and climbing once more as the scenery changed to a rockier look when we ascended into the mountains proper.

~

"Eyes up," I said, leaning forward in my seat and slowing the truck after taking the wheel at our last stop, "looks like a police post."

"It is," Rafi said. "It is the French border where police and customs make searches."

"Looks abandoned," I said hopefully, slipping the key out of the ignition and opening the door quietly to slide down. I brought my weapon up, leaving the door open for Nemesis to follow me, and heard the muted click of Rafi shutting his own door as quietly as possible. My peripheral vision caught him taking in a full three-sixty as I moved forward with the dog at my left heel and my body crouched over my carbine. I reached the door of the building, effectively a single room with a roof that extended far beyond the walls like a fuel station, and glanced through the grime-covered windows.

Empty.

Empty and ransacked, by the look of it.

"The police here," I asked Rafi, "what guns did they carry?"

"The small machine guns," he answered. "The ones taking the same bullets as these," he added, tapping the Glock on his hip.

MP5s then? I thought, doing a tactical assessment that our own weapons carried a heavier projectile over longer distances. The place was long since inhabited, so I led us back to the truck and started it up, going through the last few turns on the mountain road before a small complex opened up ahead of us.

"It is like a small town there," Rafi said as he pointed. "I know because they have a McDonalds there."

I smiled in spite of the heightened tension at being near to our objective, but there was something about the place that unsettled me. I couldn't place it, and there was nothing I could see to support my feelings, so I stopped and switched off the engine to listen. Rafi said nothing, simply watched with me until he finally broke the silence.

"I can see nothing," he said softly.

"I don't like it," I said, fighting the urge to press on and reminding myself of my promise never to ignore my gut feeling ever again.

A few times Dan had come too close to not returning to me because he'd ignored his feelings, but those times he had ignored Ash as well. I shot a glance at Nemesis who just returned my look. She didn't stare or focus on a direction, nor did her ears twitch at the suds my own couldn't detect. I said nothing, just started the car again and pulled slowly forward.

CHOICES

Now, I didn't know it at the time, but the little town we had by-passed was where the General Council sat back when the world was still overcrowded, and where the public library and shopping mall were. There was even a hotel there. What I also didn't see was that there were actually three ways into Andorra, the tunnel and the road to the south, but also a mountain road that wasn't clear on the map but passed over the peak where the tunnel had been dug through the rock and joined back up with it on the other side just past the toll booth.

Rafi didn't know this either, because he had always visited via the southern road from his own country, and we opted to take the direct route.

The tunnel was long. I mean *really* long, like I had never been in a tunnel that long ever. With the lights off it looked like a big, black semi-circle of a mouth yawning at me and just daring me to drive inside. Not wanting to look scared in front of Rafi I drove in, flicking the switch on the steering column to turn the headlights on. The truck used to have those lights that were always on, but Neil had seen to that years ago which is why the car always showed a little warning light of a bulb to signify that they were out. It still had the main lights which is what illuminated the way ahead. As soon as we drove in the temperature dropped by a good eight or nine degrees and the smell was damp and musty like it never really dried out. I saw Rafi shift in his seat and shift the grip on his weapon; the map folded back to its original creases like I'd told him to and explained why.

If we'd have taken the mountain road I don't know what would have been different, but I still kick myself for driving in blindly.

I'd glanced at the mileage clock on the way in, illuminated in a dull greeny-yellow when I had turned the lights on, and counted up one point seven miles of progress through the darkness before we saw the daylight again having passed only one landmark near the halfway point of an abandoned van.

We were met at the far end by two men, both holding a long shotgun of the law enforcement type and not hunting weapons, so I slowed to a stop a good twenty paces away. I left the engine running, growled a *stay* to Nemesis, and slid out again to bring my carbine up into a low-ready position. Rafi did the same on the other side, not fanning out away from the truck like I did and staying on the same line making me rebuke myself again for not teaching him to get clear of vehicles in any kind of contact unless you were forced to use the engine block as cover.

I stopped, leaning into my weapon slightly, and called out to the two approaching men.

"That's far enough, stop," I said loudly, hearing my commands echoed in Spanish from Rafi. The two men stopped, looking between themselves and us before one of them answered in Spanish.

"They say that they mean us no harm," Rafi translated, "that they live here and do not know who we are."

"Tell them we heard their radio message," I instructed, "that we came to talk."

The two men rattled off a short conversation amongst themselves before one went back into the toll booth and picked up a handset. I longed to use the scope to see what he was doing, but that had the unfortunate look of taking aim on him, so I kept my nerve and my gun barrel low. I stayed in the low-ready with my safety off and my index finger held out straight along the trigger guard should I need to open up. Noises around me sparked my interest, that of birdsong and other small sounds that threatened to take away my total concentration, but the man came back out and spoke to his friend.

"The leaders say you are permitted," Rafi translated, "but we must leave our weapons here."

Well, I thought, *fuck that in the face with a chair.*

"Tell them we will leave our rifles in our vehicle and that's the best they can expect," I said, hearing the authority in Rafi's tone as he relayed the words. The man went back to the phone, waving his arms this time as he spoke before coming back out and sounding a little more annoyed.

"They say you cannot be permitted," came the translation, "not unless they know we are not the invaders from the south."

"Tell them," I snarled, already feeling too exposed to weapons fire and the early evening sun, "that we are from the French coast. Tell them that we are not from the south and that we are here to discuss trade, just like their message asked."

Another exchange in Spanish, another phone call from the booth.

"They say we are to wait here," Rafi said, "and someone will come to speak with us."

We waited. We waited for almost ten minutes until my nerve

was about to break and I was thinking of getting back behind the wheel and driving off to abandon the fool's errand of helping someone. My wanderlust at wanting to be outside the safety of our walls had already been satisfied and the return journey would see to the remainder. If these people were so twitchy, not that they were much different in Sanctuary, then Sanctuary wouldn't want to do business with Andorra anyway.

A car drove up the hill from the beautiful valley below. A black Mercedes of all things, a large one with blacked-out rear windows and chrome alloy wheels. The car stopped at the toll booth and a woman climbed out wearing boots, jeans and a shirt under a gilet which she zipped up despite the heat. She walked straight past the two shotgun-carrying guards and waved one of them away as he spoke with her. She paced straight towards Rafi which pissed me off no end, making me flick the safety on and walk to intercept her.

"I'm Leah," I said, holding out a hand and barely disguising my passive-aggressive hostility, "we heard your radio message about trade."

The woman stopped, stared at my hand then glanced between Rafi and my face.

"I apologise," she said in good but accented English, "I made an assumption."

"Don't worry about it," I said with a smirk, "a lot of people have underestimated me."

I tried to carry off the same arrogance that Dan did when he met people, only from me it sounded a little too sarcastic sometimes. The heat and the wait had tipped me over the edge into a little aggression, so I tried to dial it back.

"What's got you so paranoid?" I asked.

She seemed to relax slightly, her small frame and short, grey hair not detracting from the authority she leaked into the atmosphere.

"I am Carla Sofia Rovira," she said grandly, rolling so many R's into her name that she sounded like an engine revving, "and I am the head of our General Council. Please, come and speak, but I have to insist that you leave your weapons behind."

"Thanks," I said, "but I already told them that we won't go anywhere unarmed. We learned lessons the hard way."

Her eyes narrowed at this, no doubt assessing how sincere I was and searching for some form of compromise.

"We shall talk in there then," she said, indicating the booth. I nodded, turning to Rafi and asking him to stay outside.

I followed Carla inside and lent against the counter where I could still see the truck and Rafi. He was walking towards the other guards, his gun held low and his trigger hand up in greeting. I bit my lip at this, but let it slide to save face with this severe sounding woman.

"So you got our message?" she asked without preamble. "Which one?"

"How many did you send?" I shot back, my arms folded across my chest.

She seemed to hesitate before answering.

"We sent messages about trade but have since asked for help in lifting a blockade. This is why we are careful about who comes from the tunnel because we have had people who are not interested in trading but instead seek to take over our country."

It seemed more than a little ludicrous to me that someone could take over a country, even one this small with only a few roads in and out, but I let her speak.

"We have over two hundred people here," she went on, "mostly locals but many who were here on vacation and some who have come since from other towns and villages on both sides of the borders. We had a…" She hesitated again. "A *problem* with someone who used to live within our valleys. He has since returned to the head of a band of bad people and we are trapped inside."

I frowned, speaking before I had thought through my response. "We saw nobody as we drove in," I said, "I would have noticed."

"Trust me, Leah." She smiled as she used my name, no doubt trying to soften her words with the charm of a politician. "They are there. Anyone we have sent out to seek help has not returned. To the south they have set up camp across the roads and filled it with old cars so that we are behind a wall. They raid us, taking people and things, and we cannot stop them."

"Don't you have any more fighters?" I asked, flicking a hand towards the two men who were now smoking and speaking with animated hand gestures with Rafi outside.

"These men are not fighters," Carla said sadly, dropping her head fractionally as she spoke, "they are mostly from jobs in tourism as most of us where. We have no army, no police left now that Tomau was forced out, and I fear we will not last another year before they take over."

That was a lot of information to take in, so I stayed silent a moment. As I expected, she filled the gap as she had more to say than I did.

"Tomau was a good man for many years," she said, "he was the only man of our police force to live after the plague, but he sought blood and did not agree with how I and the other council members ran the towns."

"What happened?" I asked, hoping she would keep talking and give me more time to think.

"He…" She swallowed, then raised her head to look me in the eye. "He executed a man accused of stealing. There were no witnesses to the crime, and no justice was served by a trial. He just decided to do it himself and claimed that he would not work to keep a man alive in prison to do nothing but eat the food others have grown. The townspeople rallied and forced him out, making our decision impossible. We could not imprison him or kill him, so we marched him to the southern road and told him never to return."

"But he did," I guessed, "and he brought friends."

"Yes. They began in spring, but it is getting worse each day. I fear we will not be able to resist them when the snows come."

"How many and how well equipped are they?" I asked.

"Twenty or more at the southern road," she answered. "I do not know how many on this side, but I think less, or they would have blocked the road here also."

I leaned back a little, taking it all in and looking for solutions to the problems. Alone, I could use the 417 and drive them away from the southern road with relative ease, unless they had their own counter-sniper which was highly unlikely but hunting down the others would take more than just me and Rafi.

"We could help," I said after a pause, "and we could open a trade route afterwards."

Her eyes met mine and narrowed.

"You two?" she said, "you are not enough to stop them."

I fixed her with a look, and that look conveyed that despite my young years I was a hardened warrior who had a skill set beyond the understanding of most people. Some were farmers or fishermen or politicians, but my trade was hunting and killing when I needed to.

"We are more than just two," I said, "and do you know what a force multiplier is?"

The look on her face stayed vacant to show that she didn't.

"I'm worth ten civilians given a shotgun and told to keep guard on a road. I could've breezed in here so easily you would never have known about it. I could have stopped in the tunnel and killed your guards from half a mile away; double that if I had come in from the mountain road. *I* am a force multiplier, and I'm not even the best we have. Trust me when I say we can take these people out."

I finished, leaning back and cringing at how bloodthirsty I had sounded so I tried to soften my words.

"We are peaceful," I said in a gentler tone, "but everyone who has tried to take from us is dead. Now, what can you trade with us after it is done?"

Carla explained that they had adapted to grow fruits and vegetables as well as rear cattle. Instantly I cast my mind back to when Dan and Lexi had found a farm near our old prison home and swapped the cockerels and bulls to keep the animal's breeding lines healthy. I asked her about pigs too, which was a clear option open to us. It didn't sound like a monthly thing, but a yearly exchange was definitely on the cards. I promised to return with news, hoping that the news would be a force of us ready to use the remaining summer to drive off the thieves.

"Please," Carla said, "stay with us tonight and leave in the morning. You would be our guests."

Not relishing the thought of travelling in the dark, and even less enjoying the thought of sleeping overnight in an abandoned building in the open, I agreed. I went back outside to retrieve Rafi, who had somehow managed to become best friends with the two men in a few short minutes and told him to stand down and get back in the truck.

"We are staying?" he asked.

"Overnight," I told him, "I'll catch you up on what she told me later."

"I already know about Tomau and the others," he told me with a smile, "so we are to help them?"

HOSPITALITY

True to my word, I had agreed that we didn't appear among the Andorrans as warriors, so I left my vest and carbine in the Land Rover along with the 417. Rafi did the same, but both of us held on to a sidearm which didn't go unnoticed but at least we weren't the only ones to be similarly equipped. Over dinner, a rich Catalan dish which tasted of tomatoes and beef, they told me that every household had been required by law to possess a firearm and be called upon to defend the valleys as part of a militia. There was an army as such, but it was just a few people who undertook ceremonial duties and the police force had consisted of only a few even before it happened.

We ate, drank a little even though I was sure not to have too many glasses of the wine they brewed, and I reminded Rafi not to get drunk. He failed, and although not falling down he had taken enough drink to make his tongue loose and I was forced to kick him once under the table when he described the layout of our town. He seemed to realise what he had done and tried to excuse his lack of awareness by saying that he hadn't told them where it was.

"A fortified town on the south coast of France?" I asked him quietly. "How many places like that do you know of?"

He took my point, keeping his mouth closed on matters that pertained to our home after that. I saw him pour water into his glass instead and steer clear of the wine.

An older man, with red cheeks and kind eyes came over to us and asked a question in such rapid language that I couldn't understand a single word.

"He asks if we smoke?" Rafi translated.

Now, despite Dan having almost permanently had one hanging from his mouth for most of the time I had known him, he had always forbidden me from trying it. Being a teenager and not liking anyone telling me what to do I had obviously rebelled but found that although I liked the smell of it, the actual act of smoking didn't agree with my lungs. I liked to think of myself as just a passive smoker and tried to convert that to words that Rafi could explain.

"I like others smoking," I told him, seeing that he understood and listened to his rapid exchange with the man. He smiled, beckoning us to join him outside.

"Please," he said, "come."

We were handed a small glass of something questionable that emanated a sweet vapour and were cheered by the small collection of townspeople invited to the meal. Outside, the man offered Rafi a cigar from a small wooden box which he puffed on for nearly half a minute to get it burning. I found that I didn't enjoy the smell of cigars as much as I like their smaller cousins, and just lapsed into a comfortable silence as they babbled to each other animatedly.

"It truly is a beautiful place," a woman's voice said from behind me in the doorway. I turned to see Carla leaning against the frame and staring past me at the glow in the evening sky. "The most beautiful place on earth."

"You're from here?" I asked, looking to make conversation.

"I was born here, but my parents came from a village called

Escaló in Spain, where they sold their hotel and moved here. It was the best thing they ever did, and I studied English to bring more of your people here for skiing vacations."

I nodded slowly, not having much to say about her family's good fortune.

"It's been a long day," I said, starting to make my excuses for wanting to get away from the small crowd of people and get back to my dog who had been put in the room I was given.

"Of course, I will see you here for breakfast before you leave tomorrow?"

I nodded, shooting Rafi a look and heard him thank the old man graciously for the cigar before he did the same with Carla for the food and hospitality. He jogged to catch up with me, cigar still smouldering in his hand.

"Did you enjoy the food, Leah?" he asked, giving off a sense of increased bravery.

"I did," I answered, "did you enjoy the wine?"

"I did," he answered, "and I apologise for my words. I did not mean to anger you."

"I'm not angry," I said as I opened the door and felt the dog snake past my legs before closing it again. "I just don't know these people yet and I'm hardly going to give them my PIN number."

Even in the gathering dark I could see his face screw up in question.

"Never mind," I told him as I set off again to walk Nemesis up the road a little, "just don't be hungover tomorrow morning because we have a long drive back."

"I will not," he said, "Rafael does not get hangovers."

Rafael, perhaps in karmic punishment for referring to himself in the third person, groaned heavily when the ham and eggs were placed in front of him at breakfast. I took my time eating, enjoying his discomfort which luckily didn't last long as soon as the food took effect on him. He seemed refreshed when we strapped our gear back on, shaking hands with those who had risen early to see us off.

I shook hands with the stern Carla again, promising to be back with help.

Firing up the Defender and sending my dog in over the seats to settle behind my own, I beeped the horn twice to the small gathering who waved in my mirrors as they grew smaller. Slowing to give a nod to the two men, different ones this time, on bored-looking duty at the booth we drove into the tunnel, my mind already on the discussion to convince Dan to get involved in someone else's battles for the value of a little trade. I say that, because my mind wasn't fully on the road ahead.

Had it been, I might have noticed that the van, the only vehicle abandoned in the tunnel on our way through, was facing a different direction from when we had passed it the previous afternoon and that it was much closer to the further end. As soon as my brain had registered it, the van shot forwards to block our path and I stamped down hard on the throttle to try and beat the ambush.

Rafi gave a shout; an incoherent yelp which both registered shock and fear and somehow conveyed a warning to me, but it was too late.

The van hit us on my side near the front wheel, forcing the Defender over to scrape along the left wall of the tunnel and shower bright sparks in through the open passenger window. The wing mirror disintegrated on that side, and a terrible wobble and grinding noise forced me to a stop. I flew from the vehicle, showering shards of glass from my equipment and hair, I hadn't even realised my window had been smashed, not even having time to snatch up my carbine as I reached back inside, because a fist hit me in the back of my head and bounced my face off the door pillar. I dropped to my knees, trying desperately look up through blurred vision, and reached for a weapon with clumsy hands as a snarl erupted and my attacker disappeared under a bolt of black fur.

My head rang, from both the crash and the punch which still made my legs unable to respond, and I glanced up to see Rafi slumped in the passenger seat with blood pouring from a cut on his head. A scream, deep and full of terrified pain, was cut off abruptly from my left where Nemesis had crunched the throat of the man who had hit me.

That'll teach the fucker, my brain told me helpfully, *now get your bloody gun.*

Reaching back up to the cab for my M4 which I'd laid over the dashboard, I was forced to throw myself back and scramble along the concrete surface to the front of the engine because shots had already started pouring in towards me. I heard glass smash and the whine of bullets in the air punctuated by the hollow *thunk, thunk, thunk,* of them penetrating the thin metal body of the truck.

"Heel!" I yelled groggily, feeling my dog climb over me. A stolen glance past the damaged wheel and risking the incoming shower of bullets showed shapes pouring from an access door built into the wall of the tunnel. I replayed what I had seen in that split-second, my brain running the footage again slower so that I could count six, no *seven* people, all shooting.

My chest heaved, and my head swam as it threatened to fade into unconsciousness. I faced at least seven people with only two sidearms versus their heavier guns, and my only other option was ahead of me. I was less than twenty paces from the exit of the tunnel, the bright sunlight beckoning me like some kind of afterlife, and I carefully weighed my options.

I experienced what Mitch called 'bullet time'.

The way your thoughts in a contact came so fast that it was like the world moved in slow-motion in comparison. I considered my choices, holding them up in my mind against the facts I knew.

Rafi was injured, possibly dead and certainly unable to get out and run.

I was outgunned, outnumbered, and I knew I had little chance of winning any contest with these people; this ambush was well planned and well executed.

I also knew, because the ambush was well planned, that there would, without doubt, be a cut-off force out in the open. My only hope of escape and life was that the cut-off force was either late or wouldn't be a sniper with any kind of skill. In the space of two more ragged breaths, I ran.

Bullets sang as they bounced off the ground and curved walls. I screamed at Nemesis to come with me, hoping more than anything that she emerges into the light with me unscathed, and tore headlong out into the open where I turned a hard left to get out of sight of the guns behind me.

Break the line of sight, a voice in my head lectured, *find hard cover and remember: cover from view is not cover from fire.*

Was that Steve's voice? Dan's? Was it Rich?

I stumbled on a rock and rolled over the hard ground, pitching into the legs of a woman. I was right about the cut-off force, and luckily right that they were late to the party and that gave me just enough time to get into the open. Nemesis hit her before I could look up, and I only knew it was a woman from the tone of her screams as the dog chomped hard on her forearm to take her off her feet and roll away. I got to my feet unsteadily and didn't see the man with her until he reached out from my right side and grabbed the grip of the Glock holstered on my chest. He must have thought me dazed or had underestimated me because of what he saw.

Unthinking, reacting only on instinct and years of practice at weapon retention, I clamped my hand down on his, forcing it onto the gun and preventing him from pulling it free. I planted my feet, reached further up the arm with my left hand, and rammed my hips and body back into his to spin him over me.

He landed with a heavy thud flat on his back and I drove a knee hard into his solar plexus as the gun came free in my hand. His face registered pain and shock, his hands up in desperate surrender to show me his open palms, then total and utter abject fear as both of my hands settled onto the weapon and he recognised the look in my eyes. I fired twice, both bullets smashing through his face and rendering him unrecognisable in an instant. I stood, staggering slightly as I called Nemesis away. The woman cried and whined as she rolled around in the dust cradling the ruined remains of her forearm, then she received a trio of 9mm bullets.

Two in the chest, one in the head.

"Heel," I gasped at my dog, before half running and staggering as fast as I could into the cover of the nearest trees.

TIME FOR BED

"*Maman?*" called a soft voice from the doorway. "Their bath is getting cold."

"And that's all you're getting for tonight," Leah said from the chair, groaning again as she stood and shooed the complaining boys off the rug and towards the door, "your cousin is waiting for you to have a bath. Now go, you both smell terrible."

Both boys erupted into complaints and whining sounds in unison, waking the dog again and sparking another round of exhausted grumbles. She held up both hands in surrender just like the man she killed in her vivid memory had done.

"You want to have a cold bath?" she asked them in a menacingly mocking tone.

"But this isn't the story you told us before," Jack said, his small brow furrowed as he tried to reconcile what he thought he knew with what their aunt told them now.

"Perhaps not," Leah admitted, "but I don't think I told you how the next bit started, not properly anyway."

"Will you tell us more tomorrow?" he asked hopefully.

"I will," Leah said, seeing the look of determination set on the young boy's face. Once he had been promised something, he would not let it rest until that word had been fulfilled. He was very regimented in that sense; his personality saw things as one or the other. As black or white. As right or wrong, and in contrast it seemed as though his younger brother existed in the grey areas, as he always pushed the boundaries and looked for the hidden meaning in everything. Even at their young ages, Leah could see that these two were like chalk and cheese, and their vast differences would lead them to bicker and fight constantly, yet they were totally committed to one another.

They may fight like they hate one another, but if any of the other children threatened them they would combine to fight the common enemy with a fury unmatched by even the older children.

Leah looked at Peter, his eyes already promising a lack of resistance to sleep, but Jack's eyes looked away in thought as his eyebrows met in the middle.

"But you said that you went with Grandpapa when you went to Andorra for the first time," he asked her, "not with Rafi."

"Tomorrow," she told him with a sense of finality, pulling herself out of the chair and herding them towards the door with her hands, "go and wash, and come and see your auntie in the morning."

They went, following their cousin from the room after saying their goodnights to Leah and her old dog, Ares. She stood watching the door after they had gone, allowing herself a small moment of nostalgia as her mind had been taken back over twenty years.

Twenty years, she thought, *twenty-five since I first got here.*

Most of her life. She rarely thought about the times before, and those memories were snippets of a past she had forgotten as mostly irrelevant. She did not shed tears for her mother, for her brother or any others that she knew and loved before the sickness swept away most of the human race in a blink of an eye; those tears had long since been cried.

Marie told her that it was her age, as well as her temperament, which allowed her to do what she called compartmentalising. It made sense when she explained it, telling her that she had shut away parts of her mind and memories and feelings as though they were packed in a box and stored in the dark; she could only find them again if she went looking for them and rummaged around in the dark until she found them.

The problem with that, Marie's voice echoed to her from memory, *is if you go looking without a torch, without someone to guide you, then you don't know what you'll find.*

So Leah hadn't looked. She kept the thoughts from her past in layers, and only exposed the top few that bore no emotion so that she could show others and not be upset. She did that throughout her life, keeping things stored deep down inside and ignoring them so that they didn't hurt her because she could not afford the time to deal with the troublesome feelings that threatened to put her off her game. She had people, lots of people, relying on her.

"Come on," she said to the dog, seeing it struggle to its feet with another grumble. She was waiting for the next litter of puppies to wean before choosing one and training it, just as she had done with Nemesis before, and Ares' mother before that. She knew the old boy was beyond effective now, but she never could bear to part with her dogs and ended up with two generations of Ash's proud lineage sleeping in her room at a time until the older one finally drifted off in their final sleep.

The dog got to its feet, walking stiffly after her as its aching joints woke up, and shook off the fog of slumber. She walked through the corridors of the keep, pictures and paintings created by the town's inhabitants, both living and dead, adorning the walls. She saw a few people. All of them smiled in warm deference at her which she returned. She had been the sole leader of Sanctuary for seven years since Dan and Marie had retired to enjoy their last years with grandchildren and relaxation after a life spent battling. It had been longer still since she had been promoted to become the tip of the spear and took the place of Dan who seemed to have lost his lust for conflict after the passing of Ash.

She still relied on them to impart wisdom and knowledge but had evolved as she always did to find her own unique way of doing things. Hers was trust and delegation, as she couldn't physically be everywhere at once and know everything. She also didn't know enough about the individual trades and skills of the town, so she had followed Neil's advice and always found someone who did before making decisions.

Neil had always said of management, that if you didn't know the job of someone working for you, then you had no way of knowing if they were giving you honest answers and estimates. If she tasked someone to conduct a mission, to be a Ranger of Sanctuary, and they presented her with a plan, then she could tell in a heartbeat if they were lying to her or themselves. When it came to water desalination or sterilisation, or the parts required to fix one of their ailing boat engines that yet still had life in it, then she was forced to either accept the word of the people or have a trusted second opinion.

This style of delegation made her popularity rise further still, and ushered in a generation of trust and cooperation that hadn't been seen before. That wasn't to say that she criticised Dan and Marie or Polly, not at all. In fact their stewardship of the town had seen their people through the fall and the period of war and danger that had followed. Humanity, as Dan liked to say after his third drink, had a habit of trying to wipe itself out.

Leah disagreed. She believed, deep down, that the vast majority of people were kind and decent. The problem came when there was one person who wasn't, because they often made enough noise for ten of those decent people and were followed by the weak who used cruelty as a shield against the harsh reality of life.

That said, when they did encounter people like that, she was sure to kill them instead of sitting them down and discussing their feelings.

As she walked slowly through the courtyard and out past the stable block where grass had grown beside the livestock pens, pausing every so often for her old dog to sniff at something before arthritically lifting a leg to mark it in what Neil had always called 'checking his emails', she thought about one such cruel man and the weak people that he had gathered to his cause.

TOMAU

Tomau Codina had never really been happy. He had been born and raised in the stunning and affluent tax haven nestled in the valleys of the Pyrenees Mountains. His parents, both workers in the tourist industry which accounted for much of the revenue of Andorra, had never set their sights high enough in his opinion. He had been schooled there, even attended the new university there the same year it had first opened and had left after graduating with dreams of foreign adventure and glory.

His plans faded away to nothing when his mother fell ill and had stayed in the family home until she died a year later. His father, a man he saw as weak, could not accept the loss and drank more than he ate until he faded away a handful of years later. By that time, he had joined *El Cos de Policia d'Andorra*, the Police Corps of Andorra, after being on a waiting list for selection. While he waited he trained to become as physically fit as possible and held a dull job in retail where he was forced to bow and scrape to the foreign tourists who treated his country like a resort.

The police force, comprising of less than five hundred people and less than half of those being actual officers, grew tiresome for him as he had been posted directly from training to border patrol duties. Searching cars in and out of the natural choke points of entry into the valleys was fun to begin with, but he found himself longing for excitement. He spoke with his commanding officer, submitted his request in writing, and took a six-month break from his career to join a charitable program building schools in Western Africa. That time had humbled him in many ways, but when he returned to his home with a renewed sense of worth he soon fell back into a dark mood. His father had been fired from his job and sat in the dark at home drinking, and he was placed back on border patrol duties where he faced the same daily boredom as though he had never even been away.

He began to vent his frustration by conducting almost constant 'random' checks on cars, forcing the occupants out with the threat of violence if they didn't comply and finding any reason to make arrests or seize their property. This got him noticed, and not in the best way, so he was moved into investigative policing in the area of drugs and exploitation. He enjoyed this for two years until boredom set in once more, and he fixed his sights on promotion which saw him rotate a year in all departments until he changed his mind after being seduced by the heroism of an incident.

He was working in the community role for one of the seven parishes when an incident involving a worker at the hydroelectric power station had been declared a hostage situation. The man, gone insane by all accounts, had taken his gun to work and held his supervisor captive. Tomau had been lucky enough to be placed near to the action on the inner cordon, and his eyes grew wide in awe of the small team who advanced to end the situation.

The *Grup d'Intervenció Policia d'Andorra,* or GIPA, stalked past him in full SWAT loadout with the badges of the diving eagle emblazoned on their shoulders. He had never seen anything like it in real life, in fact in his lifetime the GIPA had rarely been called out to such an incident, and from that moment he was in love with the idea of being one of them. In the aftermath of the incident, which had resulted in the man being arrested peacefully with no loss of life, he had sidled up to two members of the group and asked how he could join.

"You are in luck," one of them told him, eyeing his strong physique, "we will have an opening in three months when our boss is promoted."

Tomau returned to his commanding officer and submitted his application, passing each form of test required of him and facing down three other contenders for the available spot in the physical tests which were the final hurdle. He aced them, even shooting with a one hundred per cent accuracy score, and was admitted to the elite.

The next year was spent on training for various situations, something which the team did amongst themselves, and was interspersed with other duties like prisoner escorts and the execution of raids to support the investigation teams. At the peak of tourist season, they rode around the small towns in the valleys to snuff out trouble before it erupted, but the thing that Tomau found here that he hadn't found anywhere else was acceptance; he was part of something special.

But he grew bored again in his years doing the same things, and when he had elevated himself to become the third in command of the GIPA, the world ended. Of the GIPA, of the police force entirely in fact, he was the only survivor of the plague that swept across the world. His career aspirations dashed against the rocks, Tomau found a new niche to carve out for himself and became the protector of the survivors. A kind of government re-established itself, with new members of the General Council being voted in by the survivors, both native and visiting, and order began to take hold once more. The survivors had condensed into two of the parishes to prevent them being spread out, and organised work to strip the other towns of resources and to lay the dead to rest. Their small agricultural sector grew with as much land as possible being reclaimed to plant crops and raise livestock, and when forays outside of their valleys were required it was Tomau they called upon to keep them safe. Over the first year, many had come to the country and were welcomed, but with each person passing through the borders unchecked, Tomau grew ever-increasingly suspicious.

He made no attempts to hide his sullen discomfort from the council, which consisted of only three people, and when he found one of these newcomers in an abandoned parish checking houses for new clothes, he dragged him to their town square and executed him for theft to serve as a message for anyone who did not abide by his laws.

The townspeople were outraged, and he was stripped of his weapons before being locked in a room whilst the council decided his fate. They bowed to public opinion, agreeing that to execute the murderer would make them as godless as he was, but agreed that they could not keep him there as a prisoner.

They exiled him, providing him with food, a vehicle and his weapons as they released his bonds at the southern border with Spain. He was told never to return, and he didn't. Not for three years when his return sparked fear among the peaceful people of Andorra.

THE DAY-TO-DAY

Leah rose early as she always did, fighting her way free of the sheets as her dog slept with all four paws in the air and his tongue lolling from his mouth as he snored, and dressed. She picked up her battered gun from where it rested on the hooks by the door to her room and woke up the animal to follow her outside.

She responded to the greetings of the people, smiling as she always did at the growing population who felt safe and happy under her leadership, and exercised her old friend with a walk on the ramparts as was her morning routine.

The day was spent listening to news and reading the reports from the other settlements allied to her fortified town. They too flourished under the protection of Sanctuary, but she claimed no fiefdom over them; they were their own people who could call on hers for aid should they need it, but she had no plans to build an empire.

She ate, she exercised, and she took her daily tour around the town to check on the two militia sentries; one on the gate and one on the sea wall. She had relaxed their duties after she had taken over, explaining the reasons to Dan nervously as she listed her thoughts. He was fine with it, happy even, and she had changed the two twelve-hour shifts into three eight-hour shifts running six until two, two until ten, and then ten until six to start the cycle again. This required more people, but she employed Marie's help to generate a shift pattern that allowed those on days off to still do other jobs and have time to themselves.

The only sentries she didn't visit daily were the three young men who manned the watchtower. There had been a woman posted there, but the enforced closeness had led to an uncomfortable situation that needed resolving. That woman still served in the militia but was far more comfortable in the town where the abnormal jealousy didn't affect her. Leah visited every month with the supplies, inspected their weapons and spent the day talking with them. Ares could no longer make the climb, as much as that pained her heart, and she looked forward to the time when her new puppy was ready to be outside.

She saw her friends, both new and old, and kept a schedule in her head as to who she was due to see.

That day was a Thursday, so that meant crossing the harbour to the seaward side of the town and talking with the old soldier. Despite the warm weather of spring, Mitch was sat under blankets as he never seemed to be able to feel warm any more. He had never been one to complain, saying every time she visited that he was no stranger to the three boys of Mr and Mrs Death.

"Cold, wet and hungry," Leah chorused with him, making them smile every time. She didn't know if Mitch was fully aware of the passage of time any more, but Alita cared for him with an adoration that warmed her deep down. Theirs was a companionship that never seemed to be publicly affectionate, but Leah sensed the deep bond between them.

She left Mitch, walking back to the castle via the only section of their enclave to be levelled and green. The pigs, chickens and horses were well-tended, and the house nearby had the door ajar, so she walked inside and called a greeting as she did.

Both Paul and Lexi, scarred and broken from the unthinkable torment their minds and bodies had been put through, lived a quiet and peaceful life often far removed from the company of others. Leah had offered them the watchtower years back, but neither seemed to hold any love for their former roles and craved peace instead. It was understandable, given how they had come to be there.

She found them both on hands and knees tending neat rows in the rear garden, pulling out small weeds by hand and gently ripping away foliage when they found them wilted. They tended their vegetable patch lovingly, and each day in the good weather they could be found sat side by side on the sea wall with long cords dropped into the ocean for their daily catch.

She would never insist that they join the others for the main meal, never remove their free will to be left in peace, and was sure to see that they had what they needed.

They had paid their price, and Leah was happy to let them retire in quiet companionship.

The evening meal was fish and potatoes, with fresh greens from the last shipment from the farm which had arrived the day before. She never sat apart from the others, never sat in the same spot and always made herself freely available to anyone and made sure that she wasn't surrounded by a clique or an entourage that could dissuade anyone from speaking to her.

After the meal, she found her two nephews and asked them if they wanted to resume the tale from the previous night. The boys agreed enthusiastically, and Leah's own daughter brought them to her room where a small fire burned to ward off the evening chill.

"Now," she said to them as she settled back into her armchair, "where were we?"

ESCAPE AND EVADE

It was Steve who had first explained to me what that was. Having been a helicopter pilot in the Royal Air Force, a concept that I had to explain to many people, he was at a heightened risk of being shot down in enemy-controlled territory. Being a pilot and an officer, he would likely have been tortured for information and intelligence, so he had been trained to escape and evade capture.

His training had been done not far from where I was born and where Dan had first secured the weapons that had kept us alive. The weapon I carried had come from there, as had the ugly shotgun I had inherited. He had been dropped off in the middle of nowhere along with two other RAF personnel, given only a map with rendezvous coordinates, and had to evade the hunter force. He told me that they used a different army regiment each time, and Mitch had even been part of that force once upon a time, but the worst ones were either the Parachute Regiment or the Rifles. There was a fierce competition among those men as, apparently, they claimed to provide the best recruits for the special forces regiment who ran the training as directing staff. Their own hopeful recruits were on the same exercise, as that was part of the selection process.

The second part of that training was when they were captured, which they always were even if they made it to the very end without being detected, was what he had called RTI, or resistance to interrogation. That was where they kept you in the dark or in the bright light, so you couldn't tell if it was day or night. Where they scrambled your brain with loud static or white noise or thrash metal, and where they forced you to hold painful stress positions until you collapsed. They didn't attach electrodes to your nipples or anything, not that they told me anyway, but Steve always said that whatever they put him through would only be a taster of the real thing.

None of that really made any difference to me, despite Dan's training that I should always have my BOB, my bug-out bag, with me because I was well and truly fucked.

I ran hard through the woods, just putting distance between me and the ambush as fast as possible in a straight line before turning a sharp right and maintaining the pace. I turned right because, in my head, it was the direction of home and safety and the road I had travelled in on, but in truth I had strayed too far north.

My brain went around like a washing machine on a high spin cycle and was a combination of the fear and panic mixed with the throbbing agony I felt from my skull.

I ran as hard and as fast as I could, only afterwards guessing that I must have ended up a couple of miles away from the road in deep woodland filled with evergreen trees which littered the forest floor with soft, dry branches. It was like I was a mouse under a massive concentration of Christmas trees. When my body finally gave out, I slumped to the ground and banged my knee hard against an exposed tree root, hissing and cursing from the pain as I rocked back and forth gripping it. Nemesis, never leaving my side, nuzzled her face into mine. The blood had dried in places, lending her snout a darker look than normal, but when she licked me I was left with faint traces of pink-tinged saliva on my skin.

"Good girl," I crooned softly at her, "you're a good girl."

She gave a high-pitched whine in response, which sounded every bit as hollow and alone as I felt. I hugged her around the neck, closing my eyes tightly and breathing raggedly as the guilt hit me. I replayed the ambush again in my mind, assessing it and looking for ways to blame myself for what had happened.

Rafi was most likely dead, or the best-case scenario saw him locked up somewhere, stripped of his weapons and equipment and left without medical care that I was sure he needed. He hadn't looked good in that one, tiny snapshot I had of him in my head but as my breathing began to slow so too did my sense start to return.

"It was a cut to the head," I told Nem, "and we all know head injuries piss with blood and look worse than they are. It's a capillary bleed, most likely, so it'll look worse than it is…"

She didn't respond. She just sat back and whined again, fidgeting her paws as though she reminded me that we had to keep moving.

"I know, girl," I said, "just give me a minute."

I forced my breathing to slow, knowing that I had already used up all of the calories I had taken in that morning on the insane sprint to safety. No sign of any pursuit had reached me, but that didn't mean they wouldn't be looking for me, especially after I had killed two of them in as many seconds. If that was me, I'd hunt the bastard who killed my people down like an animal.

I did the top-to-toe survey, focusing inside my body as I tried to assess any damage to me that the adrenaline had masked. I got as far as my head, and the pain was intense. I had lumps on the back and the front, and I re-evaluated what had hit me thinking that a fist would have felt so sharp. The lump on the front was caused by the solid construction of the Land Rover, but I forced myself to check the rest of me. My torso heaved to suck the oxygen back in, and my legs shook from the exertion and chemical fear. My arms were marked with cuts from the branches I had fled through even though none of the small slices bled or had been noticed.

Fight or flight. Well I'd done both and I was utterly burnt out.

I'd figured out that I wasn't badly damaged, even if I was going to have the mother of all mild-concussion headaches sometime soon, so I turned my attention to my equipment. Nemesis whined again and struck the pose as though she was going to bark, but the long hours spent training her not to unless commanded paid off. She was looking at me and not the woodland, so I guessed it was just her impatience and not a warning.

"In a minute," I mumbled to her.

I laid down the Glock beside the three full magazines and the Walther beside that with its two. I checked with my hand that the large knife was still on my lower back and that the smaller one was on my right shoulder, and I ignored the spare magazines for my M4. The loss of that stung me deeply but getting angry was just a waste of time. I emptied out my other pouches and found the flint and steel, lighter and cotton wool in the tightly wrapped bundle which could be used to light a fire. I had a small torch, four heavy cable ties and field dressings and a compression bandage on the back of my right shoulder, and I used a single antiseptic wipe to clean the scrapes on my exposed skin.

What I didn't have was any food or water. When that hit me, my mouth suddenly screamed that it was dry, and my throat felt like it was closing up. I knew this was my mind reacting and not my body, so I forced a swallow and made myself think.

This is day two, I told myself, *I'm probably six days from home if I have to walk, but Dan will be coming on the fifth day. I can't stay here.*

And I knew I couldn't, but I vowed to be back.

We set off, following the contours of the ground towards the lower part of the forest for two reasons: One, I knew I had driven uphill towards the tunnel so uphill from where I was had to be the wrong direction. And two, water had a very natural habit of being found in lower ground instead of on tree-covered hills. We both needed water, so we headed down.

I had no idea how I had run so far or so fast from the gunfire and the concrete without losing my footing as the forest floor was almost slippery underfoot and covered in exposed roots that could easily turn an ankle and break a bone. Nemesis stalked beside me, silent but obviously nervous as her worried glances up at me sought constant reassurance. I had to remind myself that she was still a young dog and had never been truly tested before, unlike her father who would take all of this in his stride and simply perform until it was time to eat and sleep.

I stopped after another ten minutes as the foliage changed ahead. Thick bramble bushes and deciduous trees emerged from the woods in different colours and made the smell of the land change. I knew we were heading towards water in some form, even if it was under the ground, because those kinds of tree wouldn't grow higher up. Forcing our progress to slow as we picked our way through the thorns that threatened to hook my clothing I paused again.

"Hear that?" I whispered, seeing Nemesis cock her head at me and shoot out her tongue to lick her snout.

"Water," I told her, pressing onwards until the faint noise

became a bubbling stream over jagged rocks. Nem went in, standing up to her soft belly in the water as she lapped at it greedily, and I crouched down to cup my hands and drink handful after handful of the cool, clear water until a sound made me react so quickly that I almost pitched forwards into the stream in my haste to draw the Walther from my right thigh holster.

A vehicle groaned and revved as a lower gear was selected, and the only sound heard above that was the running water and the low growl coming from my dog who still stood in the stream but had turned her head towards the noise. Her nose was pointed further right than the fat suppressor on the barrel of my gun, and as I trusted her hearing above my own I adjusted my aim to face towards the unseen threat.

"It's okay, girl," I whispered, slowly rising to my feet and stalking downstream on the far bank, "come."

With her at my heel I crept forwards, both of us dressed in black and blending into the shadowed woodland, until I could see the metal barrier up ahead and above me to prevent any cars from crashing off the road.

Tense seconds ticked by as the engine noise grew in intensity until I was rewarded with a flash of a truck passing by from right to left; the brief sight held in my mind until I had assessed it.

Pickup. Two in the front and one in the bed. Armed.

I had no chance to see this and recognise it as the truck passed, but the mental image stayed long enough for me to pick out the details. The only weapon I saw was a long shotgun, a tactical one like those the guards in Andorra had wielded with evident uncertainty, and I doubted I could win a toe-to-toe fight with these men if they were all similarly armed. A pang of angry loss at my M4 and 417 being in the hands of these bastards was pushed back down as unhelpful and irrelevant as I told myself to work with what I had available.

I had found the road, which was good, but they were hunting me along it and that was bad. I would be forced to stay in the shadows and that meant travelling twice as slow as walking on the tarmac. I waited for five minutes, then ten, but the truck didn't reappear on a return journey.

"Come on," I said softly as I turned to walk parallel to the road and make some progress at least. My mind ran at breakneck speed as I considered all the options and choices.

If it was me, and someone had escaped my ambush on foot, especially given that there was only one god-damned road out of the area, I would send a cut-off force down the mountain and blockade the road to wait for them as the rest of my force drove the quarry forwards to them.

That left me with two choices initially; move forwards with only sidearms and no supplies or transport, or go back up the mountain and get back into Andorra to relative safety and the hope of calling for help. Option one was fraught with potential dangers, the worst being a likely unavoidable conflict with superior numbers with bigger guns but going back became more dangerous for others. Dan would be following our route after four days, which meant that if I couldn't get back in and send a message to Sanctuary then he would be walking into an ambush without warning. I couldn't let that happen.

I pushed forwards, stopping when the pain in my head became too bad and I was forced to rest. Even though we were under heavy tree cover and shielded from the sun which was already high in the sky and beating down, the heat under the leaves was almost unbearable. I pushed further back into the forest, climbing higher until I found a shaded patch to rest. I closed my eyes, meaning to rest for just a while.

I woke to a growl from Nemesis. Suddenly awake with a gasp and a moment of confusion, I held my breath and listened. I couldn't detect anything that she could, so I rubbed my face and grimaced at the renewed pain in my skull as I climbed back to my feet.

I ran the image of the map through my head, luckily still there in parts from the hours I had spent planning the route. The road home went east for a long while before it met a junction, from what I could recall. That road split off north while the road I needed to take went further east then turned south to drop out of the mountains. If I was in their shoes, that would be where I would place the ambush. Determined to get away and prize open the jaws of the trap I was in, I moved off with violence in mind.

It took me over an hour moving carefully through the forest until the low growl rippled from Nemesis. I quieted her with a hand, knowing that the growl was for my benefit and not her losing any kind of control. I inched forward, getting closer to the road with every gentle movement until I could make out a break in the foliage to signify where humans had carved a slice out of the mountain for a road. There was no barrier here, and I was eventually rewarded with a view of a straight, white line.

"Down. Stay," I whispered, hearing her settle down to wait in silence and knowing that her eyes would be glued to my back.

Another few feet forward and the white line morphed into the front wing of the truck I had seen pass earlier in the day. I couldn't see anyone there, so I waited.

Movement shifted, and the vehicle shifted under the weight of a person readjusting their position. Cigarette smoke drifted towards me, snatched away by the breeze as soon as I had detected it. Faint noises that bore the pattern of speech reached my ears, the words undecipherable but the sound obvious to me. It was neither English or French, the flow was wrong, but they were definitely speaking out loud to one another.

Fools, I thought before correcting my attitude. Three amateurs with guns could kill me just as easily as experts, even if they had set up a straight checkpoint and not an ambush.

I would have blocked the road and made it look like the truck had crashed or broken down, I thought, *then put the men in the woods either side of it. Right about where I am now, actually…*

That thought made my heart stop for a moment, the sudden fear that I had been the one to underestimate an enemy could mean that a gun was pointed at my head even now. I relaxed. If they knew I was here, they would have made some kind of move by now.

The sun was still high, no doubt making the interior of the truck an uncomfortably hot place to be. I knew one of them at least was there, but the other two were still unaccounted for and I wouldn't be able to make any kind of move myself until I had a clear line of sight on all of them. Inching backwards I retrieved my dog in silence and spent a further painfully slow half an hour creeping further down until I was parallel with the truck.

Only when I was sure I had the upper hand did I show them what they had done wrong in trying to trap us.

BREAKING OPEN THE TRAP

Having set my mind to the more personally dangerous course of action, I made sure to keep my head and do the job properly. I waited and waited, eventually being rewarded by movement off to my left as one of them stood up from the shade of a tree to stretch and unzip to piss noisily against a tree. I was close enough to smell it but was careful just to screw up my nose and track the movement with my eyes. He finished, calling something out in a language I didn't speak to the others which prompted a responding chuckle of laughter. It didn't come from the truck, so in doing that he had given away the position of the third one.

I tensed, squeezing the ergonomic grip of the suppressed Walther in my hand and forcing myself not to act yet. I ran through how it would go down.

Stand up, weapon up, move forward and put two in the driver. He wouldn't see it coming. Turn left and put two in the joker, switch a one-eighty and drop laughing boy.

Too risky, I told myself, not knowing who held the shotgun I saw. If it was Joker then I had a chance, but if it was Laughing Boy I could go down blown to pieces by the heavy lead ripping into me. If I chose to take them down in the opposite order I face the same problem.

So I waited some more.

It wasn't long before I was rewarded, when a burst of static came from the open window of the truck. The one in the cab picked up a speaker mic, answering, "*Si,*" as the others contracted to hear the transmission. Now was my chance, and I took it.

Rising out of the foliage and turning my body sideways, I gripped the gun with both hands and took three fast paces forwards. I stopped, focused, and squeezed.

Pft pft, pft pft, pft... pft.

The weapon cracked off in my hand as I fired a double-tap into the shaved head of Joker before switching the barrel to aim at the stunned profile of Laughing Boy. I put two into him just as fast, both entering his skull just above his left ear as I concentrated on the shocked look on the face of the driver. He had the mic raised to his face and held it a hand's breadth away from his mouth. I saw the decision, the pre-tensing of the movement as though I could see the impulse travelling slowly from his brain to his hand and click the talk button.

My first shot was a snap reflex, taking him in the left side of his neck as the bullet scored across his skin and shattered the glass of the partly-open window on the far side of the car. Registering that he could still activate the radio and scream a warning I moved the barrel a centimetre up and left and fired again.

That last bullet shattered the front of his skull and left his forehead a gory ruin. I breathed two hard breaths, repaying the debt I owed my body for holding my breath as I fired, and relaxed. I stepped forwards, gun still up as I glanced down to check my footing to climb up onto the road, and only then did I realise I had fucked up.

I had dropped three of them in under two seconds, an impressive feat really, but my brain registered that I couldn't see the shotgun. Neither Joker nor Laughing Boy held it, and it wasn't in the cab. Just as I was looking for it, I heard it.

It was one of the most unmistakable sounds I have ever heard, and in the echoing confines of an overgrown mountain road it sounded as though he had racked a cartridge into the chamber as we shared the same elevator. He roared a challenge, half fear and half adrenaline, as he rose up from where he had been sitting on the far side of the truck, no doubt slumbering in the shade of the wheel from the hot sun. My eyes stretched wide in fear, a weird sensation to feel when you're certain of your own imminent death, and as he rose into sight I sent the message down to my legs to give out. I dropped like a stone, hitting the ground hard with my left shoulder as I brought the weapon to bear. An explosive *boom* rang out over me, peppering the inside of the truck bed with the pellets as the barrel was depressed to try and track my movement.

As I hit the deck my hand pushed out in front of me as I kept my elbows tucked into my sides. It was the close-quarters method I had learned, keeping the gun in both hands high against my chest and knowing that my target would be directly in front of wherever my body pointed. I saw feet, or boots to be specific. They were the kind of slip-on tan building boots that people wore, and something sparked in my mind screamed about the steel toe caps. I quick-fired the last four shots in the magazine until the slide locked back. I didn't freeze, instead I dropped it where I lay, and half rolled to my right to give my arm space to draw the Glock from my chest before rolling back, searching for the target.

Which was gone.

Fuck, my brain screamed, *fuuuck.*

A crunch of boot on broken glass sounded from ahead of me, and in that instant, I knew he'd chosen to run instead of fight.

Amateur, I thought again. If I was in his shoes I'd be moving and pumping another three-inch cartridge into the chamber to dismember whoever had attacked me. *But then again, a lot of people weren't me.*

I rolled, scrambling to my feet and slipping on the blood of Joker as I rose to point the Glock through the open passenger side window.

"Don't," I snapped as fiercely as I could with my voice quavering from the adrenaline. He froze, half in the vehicle. I could feel the cogs ticking over in his brain, hear him figuring out if he could escape, could move the body of the driver and start the car and drive off, could bring the shotgun to bear. And then I saw the realisation on his face when he knew he could do none of those things. I had the sights of the gun lined up right on his mouth as he faced directly towards me. He was six feet away, and a squeeze of my finger would destroy all brain function before he even registered the muzzle flash.

"Don't," I said again, lower and more menacingly. "Heel!" I shouted, bringing Nemesis stalking from the trees as his confused look registered the dog. The look on his face told me that he hadn't been expecting that, that he had been told to look out for a woman, not a silent killer with a big, black dog at her side.

"Gun down, now," I said.

"Nnn… No parlo…" he stammered.

"Put. The Fucking. Gun. *Down!*" I snarled, making each word nice and loud so that he understood me, lifting my gun slightly to make it clear. The shotgun clattered to the ground and his hands came up in surrender. I twitched the barrel to the right, telling him I wanted him to walk around the front of the truck. No translation was needed as he started to edge around never taking his eyes off me.

"Watch him," I muttered, trying to hide my cruel smile as Nemesis paced forwards with her head down and her teeth bared. Her snarl also needed no translation, neither did the small yelp of fear that came from the man.

"Down," I told him, "on your knees." The movement of the gun again made my intentions clear. He babbled in rapid Spanish, or at least what sounded like Spanish to me, and I made sure he was facing Nemesis as I walked behind him. The babbling sounded like a repeated prayer and didn't seem to be directed at me.

Good, I thought, *appeal for divine intervention.*

I holstered the Glock as I whipped one of the four thick cable ties in a loose loop. I pushed his hands down to his waist, muttering a word to Nem to make sure she had his full attention, and pulled them tight to zip his wrists together.

"Up," I said, dragging his clothing to make him stand as I drew the gun again and rotated the barrel to the left before jabbing it into the sweat-soaked material of his shirt between his shoulder blades, then twisted it back to the right to snag the material around the barrel. He wasn't going anywhere with the gun pressed into his spine and the fingers of my left hand digging into the collar bone in search of the pressure point buried there. I walked him to the back of the truck, taking my left hand away to flip down the tailgate, then leant him over the back. I drew in a breath, pulled the gun away and held it up high to smash the butt of the weapon into his head once, twice, then a third until he went limp. I didn't think I'd knocked him out, not properly, but he was half insensible to make it easier to tip his legs up and roll him inside. He winced and whimpered as he rolled over his bound hands. I climbed up and flipped him over again, cable-tying his ankles together after slipping off the thick boots and then connecting the two restraints together with a third strong binding. Having hog-tied him in the back and hearing him moan and mumble to himself I climbed down and shut the tailgate.

"Don't want you rolling out, do I?" I said conversationally to him. I retrieved the Walther and reloaded it, then picked up the shotgun he had carried. It was dirty, clearly not maintained lovingly and probably passed from person to person. I couldn't find any spare ammunition for it which further annoyed me at the irresponsible way some people treated their guns. I guessed this one had been looted from some police supply somewhere, probably from a place like the border post, and I was reminded just how much easier it was to get your hands on any kind of military or police-spec weapon pretty much anywhere on earth apart from back home in the UK. I dragged the dead driver out and searched his pockets, finding nothing of worth, then checked Joker and Laughing Boy. The passenger seat of the truck held water and food, all looted with long dates or else already past the recommended use-by, and nothing homemade or grown. These men were pirates.

There was water, two big bottles of it, and I drank some before pouring more into my hand for Nem to lap up. She left a greasy film on my hand by licking me, so I leaned into the truck bed and wiped it clean on the man's shirt.

"Hup," I said, holding open the passenger door for Nem to jump in then went around to sweep the shards of shattered safety glass off the driver's seat. The truck had a column-shifter which I wasn't familiar with, but I got it started and drove forward with the wheel hard over to begin an awkward thirty-three-point turn in the narrow road and weave my way back through the bodies to head down the winding mountain roads. A glance at the fuel gauge told me I had a quarter of a tank, and although I couldn't know how much that would give me I knew it wouldn't get me home.

"We'll be walking some of the way, girl," I told Nemesis. She gave a grumble in return and licked my right elbow.

"*Hola?*" the radio crackled after a few minutes. I ignored it, letting them repeat the word a few times with gathering annoyance before it went silent.

Let them go and find the bodies, I thought, *that's five of them down and one missing. Hopefully that will give them an idea of what is coming for them.*

I drove carefully, keeping the speed comfortable and the revs low to try and conserve as much fuel as possible. If I'd had a manual I would have coasted out of gear and controlled my descent with the brakes, but I had to make do with what I had. I kept glancing in the rearview, waiting for my prisoner to regain his senses but he didn't pop up. After an hour I grew a little concerned that I'd hit him once too many times and my conscience forced me to pull over and check him; it was one thing to kill someone who was going to kill or capture you, but another for a restrained prisoner to suffocate or bleed out.

I didn't have to worry. He was alive and awake, with wide eyes staring at me when I peered over the truck bed. He spoke to me again, pleadingly from the tone of his voice, but I ignored him and went to get back in. I paused, asking myself why I really had brought him with me and deciding that I needed him alive to answer questions. I reached back into the cab for a water bottle and dragged him half upright to pour some of the warm fluid into his mouth before pulling it away and dropping him back down.

"*Gràcies,*" he said weakly, repeating the word twice more. I ignored him, climbing back behind the wheel and driving off again. I drove until the sun began to set and decided that I didn't want to be trying to navigate in the dark in an unfamiliar vehicle without a map and running out of fuel. I'd tried switching off the engine on the longer, straighter sections of downhill road but with the engine went the power steering and I almost crashed as I fought the heavy wheel against its annoying tendency to pull to the right. I guessed it must run the power steering off the engine and not the electronics, which annoyed me.

I made it out of the mountains and the foothills before the fuel warning light came on, and I rolled into the nearest village to park the truck nose-in between two other vehicles before getting out and scanning over the barrel of the Walther. I parked like that intentionally, as Dan always said that vehicles looking ready to go were always a dead giveaway that people inhabited an abandoned place.

Nobody came to investigate the sound of my engine, and everything about the place told me that it was abandoned. Where I had stopped was well beyond our usual range for scavenging, so it was unlikely that anyone had even been here since everything changed. I tried doors until I found a small bar. I knew I wouldn't be getting any sleep, but I needed to get off the road until daybreak. I returned to the truck and dropped the tailgate to drag the man out by his feet which made him squirm and plead loudly.

104

"Shut your mouth," I snarled at him, "just shut up."

He understood.

I drew the blade from my right shoulder and the noise made him wriggle again and whimper until he felt the bonds at his feet cut and stopped moving.

"Out," I said, sheathing the knife again and drawing the Walther, "walk."

He walked, turning once to open his mouth and try to speak but the twitch of my gun barrel stopped whatever thought he had before it came out. I walked him into the bar and pointed him towards a padded bench.

"Sit down," I told him, watching him as he did as instructed before whistling for Nemesis to come in from where she was sniffing around outside. I shut the door and could barely see so I took out the little LED torch I carried, wound the handle on it a dozen times then flicked the switch to look for something, anything, to fill the silence. I found a few candles and set them on the dust-covered dark wood of the bar and tried to light them with the matches I'd found in the same place. The matches were dried out and the wood snapped in my fingers, so I tutted and used the disposable lighter from my vest. I slipped the heavy ballistic armour off, sighing as I did, and rested it on the back of a chair before walking behind the bar and opening the doors of the small refrigerators under the counter. I took two small bottles of beer, looking around for the opener before figuring out that they were twist-offs. I used the hem of my vest top to protect my hand and screwed off the lid with a small hiss before the tinkle of the discarded cap rang out on the floor. I took a sip, finding it still drinkable and far smoother and lighter than the home brew lager at Sanctuary. At home.

I opened the other one and took a straw from the glass on the bar, placing it in the neck of the bottle and sliding it towards my prisoner across the table he was sat behind. He leaned forward and took an awkward sip, his eyes still glued to me.

"*Gràcies,*" he said again, then tried another language as I didn't understand his words. "*Merci?*"

"You're welcome," I said in sullen English, not wanting to converse with him.

He took another sip and leaned back to breathe out with that satisfied *aaah* that just seemed natural after the first beer at the end of a hard day.

"What are you called?" he asked in English so accented that it took me a moment to understand him.

"Don't worry about that," I growled, trying and failing to intimidate him like Dan would have, "just drink your beer and shut the fuck up."

He gave an amused shrug to show that he expected no less, even if he didn't understand my words he understood my tone. That didn't dissuade him enough though, evidently.

"You are angry that they try to make catch of you?" he asked.

I said nothing, grasping instead at the 'they' part of what he said and guessing it was a translation issue. I couldn't let it go.

"They?" I asked icily. "You mean *we.*"

"No, is not me," he said adamantly, "these men, they are no my... *amics,* no my friend?"

I bit.

"You expect me to believe that those people weren't your friends when you were the only one with a gun?"

He shrugged, either because he didn't understand or else that he didn't care whether I believed him or not.

"Like I said," I told him, "just drink your beer and shut the fuck up."

I settled in for a long night with my back to the door and tried not to fall asleep.

DEAD MOUSE ON THE DOORSTEP

I woke with the dawn, which in that part of the world in the middle of summer was early. He was slumped over on the bench, breathing heavily in an almost snore, so I kicked the table in front of him and hid my smile as he sat bolt upright with a snort and dust plastered to one side of his face.

"Urgh," he moaned, "I must go…"

Yeah, I thought, *I do too.* How to manage this stumped me for a while before I just decided that I'd have to cover him. I walked him back to the truck and cut his bonds, stepping back and drawing the gun from my leg again. The threat was evident. He rubbed his wrists and stretched his shoulders and arms out.

"Hurry it up," I warned, seeing him put both hands up and turn away to the derelict vehicle beside the truck to unfasten his fly and give a loud sigh of relief before emptying his bladder. He took a long time and I had to admit that the amount his bladder could hold was impressive. He finished and turned back to me smiling with relief and gratitude. I stepped back and raised the gun slightly.

"Get back in," I told him.

"I no fight," he said, his hands up in surrender again, "I no fight you."

The way he said *you* as *choo* was funny, but I kept my face straight.

"Tough tits," I said, knowing that he would have to read my tone of voice for that translation, "get in." He sighed in defeat and climbed back in the truck. I used sign language to make him put his hands up against the bars behind the glass of the cab and whistled for Nemesis. She jumped up to skitter her claws on the plastic liner and I muttered for her to watch him. She switched on the growl and set her front paws wide with her head low.

"Is okay," the man said in fear, "okay…"

I ignored him, a little pleased with the fear my dog sparked in others, and used my last cable tie to bind his wrists to the grate and force him to sit up to face the direction we would be driving in. I didn't like him watching over my shoulder, but I liked the thought of him unsecured even less, so I guessed I just had to deal with it.

I left him there and went back into the bar to throw a few choice items into a bag I'd found, namely three bottles of decent scotch for Dan and Neil as I was never one to miss an opportunity to scavenge, and used the useless toilets there.

I went back outside and saw him wriggling his wrists until he heard my approach and went still. I climbed back up into the truck bed and gave another pull on the cable tie to cinch it up. Few clicks tighter. He hissed in pain but said nothing, evidently thinking it was fair enough as I'd blatantly caught him trying to see if he could get free.

I started the truck and coaxed it backwards out of the spot to pull the unfamiliar lever into drive, then headed out as gently as possible for the coast.

The needle registered just inside the red on the fuel gauge, and I had no idea if that meant there was supposed to be a certain amount left which I could correlate into kilometres but seeing as I reckoned I'd done two thirds of the journey before having to stop I had hope yet that I could make it back to Sanctuary without having to resort to walking.

Within an hour I started to recognise the roads and reckoned I knew the way back, but a good few miles short of the trading post the engine spluttered and coughed.

"Shit," I snarled, earning a sudden alertness from my dog who scuffed my arm with a big paw. "It's alright, girl," I said, "we can make a few more miles yet I reck—"

The engine coughed again and cut out, rolling to a creaking stop after fifty paces as the fuel had run dry at the foot of an incline.

"Cancel that," I said, picking up the two full water bottles I had found at the bar and climbing out to abandon the truck where it had stopped.

I repeated the routine of getting Nem to watch him as I cut his hands free and covered him with the Glock as I was close enough to home to not worry about my shots attracting attention.

I made him climb out and carry the bag as I gestured him to walk ahead of me, the shotgun in my hand.

"We…" he said questioningly, clearly unhappy at the thought, "we walks?"

"Yes mate," I snapped, "we fucking walks. *Watch him!*"

Nem's sudden and unwanted attention made him almost start jogging. I walked behind my prisoner come pack mule as the sun beat down on us, the gun held relaxed across my body. Friendly territory or not, my eyes still scanned the surroundings for any threat as Nemesis kept a close eye on the prisoner after I had called her back to heel.

It took close to two hours, meaning a distance of just over six and half miles by my usual pace, until the trading post became visible through the heat haze.

I almost cried with relief when I saw it, and it was all I could do not to run the rest of the way until I realised I was too exhausted and it was much further away than I thought.

"This your houses?" he asked tiredly, squinting his eyes against the bright sunlight.

"No, dickhead," I said, "it's not."

He half turned to look at me, getting the gist but trying to understand my sarcasm.

Good luck with that, matey.

The guard at the trading post saw us coming and wandered into the road when we were far enough away for me to just about make out his face and held his gun low. I knew they wouldn't be expecting anyone on foot from this direction, and I hoped it would be someone who recognised me.

It was. I knew the man as Roland, a man originally from the farm who had shown an aptitude for guard duty by staying alert and being friendly. He volunteered to live at the trading post with another couple of men, one of them being from Sanctuary.

"*Leah? Qu'est qui se passe?*" he asked, wanting to know what was going on, his eyes casting suspicious glances between me and the prisoner.

"*C'est une longue histoire. Je dois envoyer un message au*

111

Sanctuaire," I responded, telling him that it was a long story and that I needed to get a message to Sanctuary. He beckoned me inside.

"*Prisonnier,*" I told him, pointing at the man in answer to the question he seemed to want to ask. He looked at the man who smiled at him.

"*Hola,*" he said, being ignored by Roland who puffed up his chest and set his mouth into a grim mask of disapproval.

I went inside, happy that Roland could watch the man as he would be more exhausted than I was having not eaten for a day and dehydrated along with me clumping him on the head a few times. I pointed at a bottle of water and the old man behind the counter passed one to me with a bowl for Nem. I thanked him and poured out the water for her which she started lapping up greedily before I'd even finished pouring it. He passed me another one and I chugged it straight down before asking him in French to get a pigeon ready and give me a pen and paper. I scribbled the note hastily.

D.
Bring vehicle to trading post
ASAFP.
L.

I handed over the message and watched as the old man rolled it tight to slide it into the tube on the struggling pigeon's leg. It was old-fashioned, but it was effective. The bird could get to Sanctuary faster than I could drive there, so I was satisfied and relieved to sit in the cool interior of the high-ceilinged building and wait. Roland brought my prisoner inside, demonstrating his alpha male status as he pushed him ahead of him. I tossed him another bottle of water and he thanked me again, earning a suspicious glance from Roland as to why I was wasting water on a prisoner, an enemy. I told him, "Article three: prohibition of inhumane treatment," and saw him frown as he didn't understand the relevance of the words.

"*Il ne peut pas parler s'il est mort,*" I explained, seeing that Roland understood that the man couldn't be questioned if he keeled over from dehydration.

Thirty minutes of strained silence later and an engine note pierced the air, so I climbed to my feet followed by Nem who struggled awake to pad out of the door. The engine revved, being driven hard as I heard the tyre bite into the gravelly dust outside as it skidded to a hurried stop. The sound of a door opening and closing reached me as Dan flew from the small van as soon as it reached a stop and he ran up to me firing questions the whole time as Ash bounded out to circle the area with his nose to the ground until Nem ran to him and the two froze in a locked sniffing contest.

"Relax," I said, "I'm not hurt but you need to listen first and ask questions after."

He nodded, his mouth set firm in anger at the risk I had been in.

I told him about getting there, how it was uneventful and how we were stopped at the border or just inside to be accurate. I told him about the setup of the place and what they offered and what problems they had encountered. He listened with obvious impatience and paced distractingly as he fought against himself to not interrupt and let me get the whole story out.

"We left after breakfast and got ambushed in the tunnel," I said, seeing his nostrils flare with a righteous fury that threatened to boil over as he glanced between me and the man he didn't know. I suspected he knew the answer to that particular question but didn't want to act until I had told him the rest.

"The Defender got trashed, front-offside wheel was knackered. Rafi was out from a head injury and I got hit in the head with something." I waved him away as he tried to fuss at my skull and look for injuries. "Nem took him out but when I tried to get Rafi they started coming out of some kind of access door and laid down fire. I ran for the exit of the tunnel but ran into a cut-off team. They were behind schedule and both went down, I—"

"How?" Dan asked, unable to contain himself.

"Nem dropped a woman with an arm takedown and a bloke tried to take the Glock off my chest. I locked him up and took him down before I put two in his head. She got the same."

"Then what?" he asked, his pacing gathering enough speed to wear a rut in the floor as he shot vicious glances at my prisoner with enough venom to make him back up to the wall.

"I ran. Straight into the woods before a direction change. Spent most of the day trying to get down the mountain paralleling the road until the first junction where there was another cut-off force."

"And?" he snapped, misdirecting his anger at me which I ignored.

"And I stalked them. I only saw three with one weapon so when they bunched up to hear a radio call I took them out with the Walther. This one," I said, gesturing at the terrified prisoner, "missed me with this"—I hefted the shotgun—"and I took him prisoner along with their truck. It's less than ten miles back up the road. Had to stop for the night about ninety K's away and almost made it back before the fuel ran out."

Dan stared at me for a few seconds before turning to regard the prisoner in concerning detail.

"*Hola?*" he tried weakly before flinching as Dan took two fast steps towards him.

"Hola your fucking self," he snarled, sparking Ash to step forward and regard the man for the first time. It was not attention that seemed friendly.

Seeing the two dogs side by side I realised just how bloody big Ash was, and if Nem was a killer then Ash was death incarnate.

Dan seemed ready to set Ash on the man or else pull his limbs off by hand and beat him to death with them with all the fury of a father cornering his daughter's ex-boyfriend after a bad breakup. He controlled himself and instead whipped out his own cable tie from his vest and grabbed the man's shoulder to spin him around and bind his wrists.

Other than a hiss of pain as his hands seemed to turn purple with the pressure he said nothing, demonstrating that he could read a situation and at least had the sense to try and stay alive.

"Let's go," he said. "You're like an unruly cat…"

"What's that supposed to mean?" I moaned.

"I let you out, and you bloody well bring me back a half-dead mouse to drop on my doormat. Let's go."

THE ART OF INTERROGATION

"You talk to the fucker," Dan snarled at Mitch, who knew better than to take it personally, "I'm too angry."

Mitch sighed, biting back the quip about it being his day off in light of the seriousness.

"What are you doing?" he asked me.

"I'm going to find Rafi's brother," I said, seeing both of their eyebrows raise, "I need to tell him what happened. Don't start without me… and if you want Alita then I need her first."

There was a pause, both men coming up with questions which they bit back given the resolved look on my face. It was my responsibility to inform his next of kin that I had got him killed or captured, and it was my responsibility to make the promise to his face that I was going back to bring him back his brother, or if the worst had happened then his body for a proper burial on the cliff overlooking Sanctuary.

I rehearsed it my head, trying out different words in different combinations until I settled on something that didn't sound like I was asking him to feel sorry for me. If he had any sense, the purple welt on my forehead and the scratches on my arms should tell him that I didn't run away without getting involved at least.

I found Alita on the way, sitting in the shade near her place that she shared with Mitch by the harbour. It had been the dive centre way back when, and Alita had just stayed there out of a sense of familiarity and converted it into a home.

"Can you help me?" I asked her, seeing her eyes roam over my visible injuries.

"Aye," she said in her curious Spanish/Scottish accent, having learned most of her English from Mitch which was a separate language in itself.

"Do you know Mateo? Rafi's brother?"

"No, what does he do?" she asked, knowing that the best way to track down one of their number was through their trade.

"He's on one of the fishing boats, I think," I told her, replaying all of the information I had gleaned from talking to Rafi.

"Let's away then," she said, mixing the highland colloquialism with her accent.

We walked a short distance to the place in the harbour that smelled of fish guts all year around. It was where the trawlers unloaded and was arrayed with flat tables with lips where the fish were gutted, cleaned and sorted. There were stacks of crab and lobster pots beside an old woman who had done the same thing even before the world went sideways. Alita spoke to her in a rapid conversation that sounded like Spanish but used words I didn't understand. It translated intermittently in my head to French words, but I retreated inside myself to think and try to make sense of the conversation.

"We are in luck," Alita said, "his boat came in last night and are not due to leave until after evening meal."

I nodded, thanking the old fish woman in French for her help, and followed Alita towards the houses nearer the sea wall where half of the fishing boat crews lived. She asked a few people if they knew Mateo, following their directions to a faded, yellow-painted house in a terraced row. He seemed to have been napping, likely having been awake in the night on board his boat.

The look on my face and my nervous presence told the man enough, and his face of warm but confused greeting dropped as he looked at me. I took a pace closer to him and held out my hand.

"Mateo, I'm Leah."

"Hello, Leah," he said before giving the rest of his answer in Spanish. He saw my uncomprehending face and looked to Alita to ask a question. Alita didn't relay this to me but answered. I made out the words English and French in the reply.

"Is my brother okay?" he asked in accented French, a look of worry creasing his brow.

He was the wider, stockier image of his younger brother. Just as quick to smile, under different circumstances I imagined, and with just as much expression on his face. I sighed, sucking in a breath and drawing myself up formally to take responsibility, and glanced to Alita. I wanted to explain in English to use the words I knew best instead of running the risk of not giving enough detail in a language I had yet to master. I knew there was a risk of Alita miscommunicating, so I kept it simple.

"Rafi was in the seat beside me," I explained slowly, "and we were ambushed – attacked – by people as we left Andorra." I paused, waiting for his face to register the translation. He listened to Alita but never once took his eyes from my face. "He was unconscious, and they started shooting at us." I glanced at Alita as her hands told the story alongside her words. "And I managed to escape, but *I promise,* I'm going back to get him."

Mateo listened to my words, looking right into my soul to gauge my sincerity.

"He lives?" he asked haltingly.

I swallowed hard before answering, unable to tell a lie or even sugar-coat the truth. "I... I don't know, but I'm going to bring him back one way or another," I promised.

Mateo thought for a long moment, his fingers picking nervously at his lips as his eyes looked at nothing on the ground, until he took a sharp breath in and looked up to rattle off an emphatic and impassioned speech to Alita. She watched him, muttering in English out of the side of her mouth as she translated.

"He says he wants to come with us, he says he believes that you did not abandon his brother, but he wants to be there to bring him back. Whether he yet lives or not."

I hid my sigh, only able to promise that I would pass on the request and support it. I knew I wouldn't be running the return mission, because the risk I had been in had angered Dan to such a rage that I had seen rivalled only once, and then he had burned a barn full of people alive.

I still shuddered at the thought of that, at the brutality we visited on the evil bastards who had killed Joe and hung his body from a streetlight. They had all died, and I was as responsible as everyone else for the violence we inflicted on others that night, but afterwards I was haunted by the screams of those burning and choking people. Their screams merged with the howling and snarling of the pack of wild dogs even now, years after both terrifying incidents, and although I made a promise to myself to always be aware of the limits of what would keep me human I was pretty sure that Dan's enraged state held no such upper limit.

Mateo followed us back to the keep, quietly refusing the request to stay and wait for an answer, and I slipped ahead of him to get to the interrogation and hopefully avoid having to keep him away from my prisoner. I was saved that task by Marie, who had been waiting and suspecting she would have to intervene ever since Dan returned like a raging toddler unable to calm down. I told her who Mateo was, but she already seemed to know. She always seemed to know. She took him aside and offered him comfort, speaking in French in a soothing tone.

I walked into the small, empty stone room near the gatehouse where he was still bound and had been forced to his knees. Dan stood over him, still tense and seeming to be fighting his urge to reformat the guy's face. I glanced at Mitch who just nodded a serious look to me. That nod and the look on his face told me everything I needed to know.

Don't you worry, Nikita, it said, *I won't let him lose his shit.*

Alita followed me inside, placing a cautious hand on Dan's shoulder and snapping him out of his trance. He looked at me, then at Mitch, and left the room.

Now this wasn't a new concept to us, but it *was* new in the fact that we had never interrogated a prisoner. Everyone who had wandered up to our gates, or who we had found on supply runs or just on the road had been subjected to a kind of entrance interview. We couldn't just let anyone in to live among us and the vulnerable people inside our walls, so we had rehearsed our classic good cop, bad cop routine and all taken turns to be the sullen one whose job it was to seem unconvinced to let them stay.

I went first, choosing to be good cop, on the basis that I had killed three of his buddies and battered him a little, so if he thought

I was the good one then he should be scared to death of Mitch. I cut his bonds and handed him a bottle of water, smiling a little as though I felt sorry for him. He gasped, muttered something in Spanish and rubbed at the swollen flesh of his hands. He looked up at me and returned my smile.

"*Hola,*" he said again.

"Tell me your name," I told him, hearing Alita's voice sound softly behind me.

"Rocco," he answered, smiling again.

"Don't fucking grin at her you wee shite!" Mitch snarled as he pushed away from the wall and shoved his face down into the man's until their foreheads rang together with a *clunk.*

Bad cop established, I pushed Mitch away who pretended to obey and backed off balling his fists.

"Tell him I'm sorry about that, but if he doesn't answer my questions then I won't be able to keep him safe," I said to Alita with my eyes still boring into him almost pleadingly. She rattled off the translation and I saw Rocco's eyes flicker up to Mitch and back to mine.

"I need to know how many people are in his group," I said softly, seeing his eyes switch to Alita before returning to mine. He gave an answer as the smile returned.

"He says," Alita began, clearing her throat and sounded annoyed, "he says you have pretty eyes."

SMACK!

Mitch launched away from the wall again and clapped an almighty slap across the right side of his face sending him backwards so hard that he rolled over to come to a rest facing the other wall. I had seen him do that before, even taken the piss out of him for it, but he was adamant that if he had to rough someone up then a slap was the best method short of waterboarding him. He maintained that if he wanted to knock him out then he would punch him, but some good, hard slaps around a man's face had the psychological effect of beating him badly without actually shaking the brain and risking damage.

Rocco gasped and lolled his head in shock at the speed and savagery of the slap. It worked, because he instantly stopped trying to hit on me and switched to a new tactic.

"He says he does not know," Alita translated his rapid babble, "he says he is small man in group and is not told these things."

"That's not true, is it?" I asked as I cupped his chin softly and lifted it to meet my gaze, "because if you weren't that important then how come you were the only one out of four to have a weapon?"

He waited for the translation, his eyes darkening as he considered my logic. He said nothing instead.

"Let's start again shall we, Rocco?" I said as I stood and leaned against the wall. Mitch sidled around the room and stood behind him in his blind spot, making him cringe away from the next strike that he wouldn't be able to see coming.

"How many in your group?"

He said nothing, squirming to try and see over his left shoulder whilst still maintaining a watch on me.

SMACK!

He pitched forwards to land on his face and rubbed desperately at his right cheek where the full swing of Mitch's hand had connected. Mitch rubbed his hand too, and I was pleased to see that he seemed to take no pleasure in inflicting pain on someone else.

"Too long," Mitch growled, "fucking answer her."

Alita spoke rapidly, pleadingly to him as though she wanted the violence to stop. Although a timid woman by nature she had a core of pure steel, so I knew she was just messing with his head to try and push him down the path of talking.

"How many?" I asked again.

"*Mil*," he growled, smiling at me.

"He says a thousand," Alita translated.

I doubted that, as did Mitch who stepped up his game to speed things along. He hauled Rocco up bodily, slammed him against the wall and hit him with a hard left, right low in his abdomen. He made that awful croaking noise a person makes when their diaphragm goes into spasm and they can't breathe. Knowing that Rocco wouldn't be able to speak for a few minutes we left him there in the foetal position as he retched and gasped in breaths.

We reconvened down the hallway out of earshot with Dan. Marie still spoke to Mateo soothingly, one arm on his broad shoulder as the reality of his brother's fate finally hit him.

"He's playing silly buggers," Mitch said, "thinks he's a hard man."

"We don't have the time for this," I said impatiently, "we need to know everything he knows."

"Dog?" Dan suggested.

That could work, I thought, recalling how effective Ash had been as Dan's bad cop when our home had been attacked and I had killed their leader as he ran from the destroyed vehicle convoy that Neil has shredded with the machine gun.

"I'll do it," I said, "give me Ash as well."

Dan looked at me, glanced to where Marie was unaware of the conversation.

"Do it," he said quietly, snapping his fingers to bring his dog from the shadows where he lay down. I did the same, hearing the clatter of claws on stone as both dogs padded towards us.

I opened the door again, saying nothing as I called the dogs in and closed it after Alita entered. She kept herself well away from the dogs as she knew what was coming and tucking herself into the opposite corner from where Rocco was huddled. His eyes grew wide as the dogs sniffed at him, keeping his hands away from them and trying to shrink away.

"Watch him," I said in a flat tone.

Both dogs switched it on in an instant, dropping into low poses and snarling as though they were possessed. Ash, by far the veteran, showed his daughter how it was done as he lunged forward and snapped his teeth at the whimpering man.

"*Watch him,*" I growled, hearing Nemesis' bark echo in the empty room and drown out the shrieks of fear from Rocco. Ash continued to lunge forwards, bouncing onto his front paws and rearing back onto his hind legs to gather the momentum for the next feigned attack. Rocco buried his face into the wall, tears streaming down his dirty cheeks as he sobbed.

"Tell him," I said loudly to Alita, "that if he doesn't want to see what they do next, then he needs to answer my questions."

She raised her voice, telling him what I wanted her to. He yelled and begged, that much was clear, and I called the dogs back. As soon as they had stopped snarling I heard an argument going on outside the door and rushed back outside to see Marie rearing up on her tiptoes in Dan's face, clearly unhappy at our tactics.

"… out of bloody order," she snapped, "this is *too far.*"

"It's done," I said, hoping as all teenagers did that their parents would stop arguing.

Marie scowled at me, turning on me for my turn.

"And you!" she whipped at me, "*you* are better than this."

I put my head down and let her berate me, taking the tongue-lashing that I probably deserved, but it wasn't worth arguing back that some rules were worth bending when someone's life was at stake.

None of us noticed Mateo slip into the room as Marie tore a strip from all of us. He had taken the key out of the old lock and the first we knew of what he was doing was the mechanism clicking over to lock him in from the inside.

"Fuck it," Dan growled, immediately raising his boot and slamming it hard into the old wood. It didn't budge, despite him being the victor of countless battles between himself and locked doors. He kicked it again, harder this time, to no effect. Mitch joined him as Alita shouted for Mateo to unlock the door.

"Back up," Dan yelled as he drew the Walther from his vest.

"No!" I yelled, putting my myself in the way knowing that he would fire. "It's too risky."

Dan regained his senses in time to know he would probably hit one of them, when a foul scream of agony tore the air inside the room and made us all freeze. A pause sounded before another scream reached us, this one devolving into a desperate sob which undulated until the door lock snapped open and we piled inside.

"He talk now," Mateo said, turning over a small knife in his hands with a blade that had evidently been sharpened so many times that it was just a whisper of steel.

As one, we looked at Rocco who held his groin with both hands. Dark red blood stained his hands as he sobbed and his legs seemed unable to stop his bare feet from dancing on the stone floor.

"What the fuck did you do?" Mitch asked.

Was that a hint of admiration I heard in his voice?

He spoke to Alita, who stared at him with her mouth wide open.

"He says," she stammered, "he says he slice on his…"

"Oh for fuck sake," Marie said in exasperation turning from the room and shouting for someone to fetch Kate.

JAWS 3

Rocco hadn't been castrated, despite what Marie feared. Mateo had just run the slim blade across his balls to part a few layers of skin with deft skill, but promised to skin him alive staring with the rest of his sack if he didn't tell him what had happened to his brother.

The beating had scared him. The dogs had terrified him. But the threat of dismemberment at the hands of the brother of the man they had captured had seemed more of a promise.

Mateo had apologised to us, assured us that he was never out of control, and had handled the rest of the questioning under close supervision after Kate, our ever-ready but constantly annoyed paramedic had staunched the bleeding and put three stitches into a body part she was squeamishly unaccustomed to handling.

Dan called a team together, more of a posse if I was honest, and planned to make the return trip to Andorra at the next dawn. I was going, that was without doubt, but Neil and Mitch had assumed they were involved also and I wouldn't say no to that. Word had spread quickly, with people clamouring to volunteer. I had placed a call on the radio to the watchtower, asking for one of the young men by name. I told him to bring his rifle and prepare to be away for a few days.

I admit, I had a little flutter of excitement about him. Lucien

Dumas, who Dan always insisted on calling *Dumbass* in an American accent. Mitch and Neil laughed when he did it, even Marie thought it was funny, but I had no idea what old film they were copying. One of the reasons they teased me about him was because he had some kind of effect on me and I blushed whenever I was around him. He was a couple of years older than me and had been a boxer as a child. He didn't have the squashed face of one, in fact I thought he was pretty with his ash blonde hair falling in waves over his cheeky smile. He had volunteered to be part of the militia after we had arrived at Sanctuary and shown a natural ability to shoot well at distance. I had only found out he was a boxer when Henry, the daft boy who had stowed away with us from our home back in England, tried to show his superior size and strength to the smaller boy by beating him up in front of everyone, no doubt because he thought that would get my attention, and had ended up unable to land a single blow as Lucien had danced around him and pounded the fleshy boy into tears. He had smiled the whole time, even helping the boy up after he had humiliated him. Henry, the sting of shame on his face, had moved to the farm then where he remained, growing bigger and stronger but still not able to remove the pain of defeat.

I had insisted that Lucien go to the watchtower, mostly because he had the attention of any woman remotely near his age and I felt something that was worryingly like jealousy.

Now, despite what I might feel about his cheeky smile and the glint in his eyes, I needed a shooter. I saw him jogging down the long cliff path, rucksack on his back and the only remaining HK417 in his hand, then turned away from the ramparts where the radios were under the cover of a shelter constructed by Neil, nodded to the woman of the militia who watched over the gate and went to the dining hall where the planning meeting was called.

Dan, Marie, Neil, Mitch, Alita and Mateo sat at the table, with three of the militia who Mitch had hand-picked. I agreed with his choices, knowing the two men and one woman to be reliable and steady. Anyone likely to be enthusiastic to go into conflict was a liability in my opinion.

"…need more fuel," Neil said, "so we'll have to go almost as far as Perpignan to pump some out. Leah?" I lifted my face to his gaze. "That truck of theirs, you said it had a radio in?"

"Yes, short range only and probably made worse by the mountains."

Neil nodded. "We'll refuel that and take it, so that's our second vehicle. We'll have to cram into the first two and send the others back after we've siphoned enough tanks or pumped out a fuel station." He looked at Dan who took over.

"From what the prisoner has told us," he began with only the subtlest of glances at Mateo, "we are facing a force of almost fifty. Some are armed, and some are trained. Ex-police or similar. They've blockaded the southern road to Spain, but their leader is with the majority of their forces at the French border. Leah?"

"It's just inside the border," I said, "there's a checkpoint which looks abandoned, and a small town before the road into the valleys. There's a tunnel, which is where they ambushed us, and a mountain road over the top. I haven't been up there. I would guess they are in the small town before the tunnel splits from the mountain road."

"That's what the prisoner said," Dan interrupted. It worried me that he kept calling him *the prisoner*, doing what Marie called dehumanising, "and that's where they're keeping Rafi."

The confirmation that Rafi had at least been alive when the cut-off force had been sent to try and net me was a blessing which both soothed my conscience and tempered my resolve to go back and get him.

"Did Rocco," I asked, reminding Dan that the prisoner was still a man, still a living human being despite the company he kept, "say why they had ambushed us?"

Dan fixed me with a look, making it obvious that he would rather have discussed that part in less open forums. He was still angry, still boiling from the rage of my return, and I knew it was because he was blaming himself for not going with me or not insisting that we took more people. I had considered that too, having spent a quiet hour contemplating every part of the trip and trying to figure out what I did wrong and what I should have done differently.

I had come to the conclusion that having say Mitch and Dan in the truck when we had been hit would have had similar if not worse consequences; the passenger side would still have been pressed against the tunnel wall preventing a rapid decamp from the vehicle, the front passenger, which probably would have been me, would still likely have a head injury and be incapacitated, and the weight of fire coming against us would still have been too great to counter with the best-case three weapons returning it. The cut-off force comprising of the two now-dead people would have had time to get in place and we would have been pinned down and forced into surrender or killed, and even the luckiest scenario in my head still had a fifty per cent escape figure, which would have also doubled the number of dead or captured and reduced our ability to return in strength.

These replays and scenario changes helped me come to terms with what had happened as, to quote Neil and everyone else who had coined his phrase, "What's the worst that could happen?"

Well, what happened was bad, but it always could have been

worse. It could have been Dan in the passenger seat and he could have died. The dogs could have been badly hurt. We could all have been shot and left everyone we cared about in Sanctuary never knowing why we hadn't returned.

"We don't have the numbers to have a stand-up fight with them," Dan said, bringing me back to the present, "so we will look to parlay first. That said, I have no intention of fucking about with these people. I propose this…"

Dan's plan, skipping over the part where we had to take a long detour to the north in search of additional fuel supplies, was to take two vehicles back into the mountains and for him and Mitch to go in under a white flag. He would ask for Rafi back, promise to stay away from their territory and give a false story about where we were from. That plan assumed that Rafi hadn't told them all about Sanctuary, which was a gamble as everyone spoke eventually, but the lie would be expected he explained.

That wasn't to say that the plan didn't involve fail-safes, which is why he had asked me to pick the best shot from the watchtower and dust off my old MK14. The watchtower was still very well equipped with high-powered hunting rifles which were more than capable of ventilating anyone foolish enough to try attacking our home, but when given the choice between civilian and military weaponry we both knew where our bets lay.

Lucien and I would be on the higher ground with a view to take out as many of them as we could if Dan gave the signal, much the same as when they had gone to what was now the legend of Slaver's Bay before they let me step up. Back then it had been Lexi and Steve who had been the shooters, and Neil had been hidden under an aluminium canopy ready to pop up and lay waste to the enemy with a machine gun, but we had to work with what we had.

Lexi hadn't held a weapon since her exhausted body and shattered mind had been returned to us, and Steve was busy running his own show back home.

No, I reminded myself, *this is home now; the others are back where we started.*

We would, if needs be, take the town and put a stop to the siege of what I had assured everyone were peaceful people who wanted no conflict. They were useful to our own continued survival, but that was jeopardised by a band of pirates picking off the weak and the innocent.

I knew where this was going, and it echoed Polly's and my own sentiments when we had been threatened by another group before.

We kill them all.

It was bloodthirsty, I knew, but what other choice did we have? Leave a hostile group with weapons and a mind towards piracy to hurt and exploit others? Run the risk that they will gather numbers and advance south? To attack the farms, the trading post and the smaller settlements we offered our protection to?

No. They had to go; or at least have every ounce of leadership cut from them so that they posed no threat of reorganising. I wasn't against the idea of letting the lower echelons live, as often these people were simply going along with it to keep living, but that always posed the risk that we would be responsible for releasing a wolf among the sheep.

Cross those bridges when we come to them, I told myself, *gain control first and clean up afterwards.*

One thing Dan said had penetrated my thoughts, infecting me

with a nagging doubt that trickled down my spine like a drop of rainwater that had somehow found its way inside warm clothes.

We don't have the numbers.

And we didn't, but that was what training and superior equipment was for. I had already proven that I was equal to four of theirs, although they were unaware and mostly unarmed. That wasn't to say that they weren't dangerous, but they were desperately unaware of the risks, and that spoke to their lack of knowledge and training. Even the other two I had killed, *we*, I should say as without Nemesis I wouldn't have made it out, let alone back in one piece.

Force multipliers, that's what Dan had called me and him and Mitch and the two dogs we used as warriors. Anyone could pick up a gun and threaten someone, especially nowadays when there was no law or risk of punishment and consequence unless you lived inside one of the enclaves of a real society as we did, but having the knowledge, training and above all else the discipline to use it properly then it stood for very little.

Not only were the three of us very well equipped, but we were hardened in combat and still lived despite the attempts made on us and the people we cared about. Our level of experience stood us apart and worth five or even ten untrained people in most circumstances. We had trained our own militia to a decent standard, but given that the supply of bullets was something we couldn't rely on for many more years it was only natural that very few of them had ever fired a shot in anger.

"What about another Thunderbird?" Neil asked hopefully, meaning to mount one of the two heavy machine guns we still had at our disposal in the back of a truck bed as something Mitch called a *technical*, but the once infantryman put that idea to bed immediately.

"Too finicky," he said, listing the reasons that he wouldn't want to have a plan based on the reliability of a very old fifty-calibre Browning. The construction and mounting of a gun onto a vehicle would take most of the following day alone, and that affected the timeline I wanted badly.

The meeting drew to a close as Mitch took the others who didn't have access to their own weapons to the armoury to be equipped. I knew him well enough that he would do the same as I had with Rafi and provide them with the basic weapons without the personal idiosyncrasies that we preferred. That thought soured me as my own weapon, one that had never left my side since before we even left our home country, was missing. No doubt taken and being used by one of the bastards who had attacked me. I imagined them fighting over it like animals, none of them possessing skill worthy enough to even touch the gun in my opinion, then I stopped myself because my imagination was convincing me that our enemy were thugs; mindless and ill-disciplined, and that potential underestimation could be a fatal flaw if they turned out to be otherwise. I shut that away, leaving myself with the hollow feeling of shame at having lost my weapon.

I took a seat as the others went away, finding myself in very familiar company among the core of our spear tip.

"So the plan is to get there then make a plan?" Marie asked Dan, annoyed to the point of near hostility as she always was when her man prepared to go stomping off like some Neanderthal and bonk other cavemen over their heads with his club.

"Pretty much," he admitted, "but without more intelligence then we can only guess. We can only make assumptions, and we all know what happens when you make an assumption, don't we?"

"Yes," Marie said tiredly, almost with boredom, cutting off the punchline she had heard too many times to laugh, "you make an ass out of you and 'umption."

Dan reached into his equipment vest, worn inside the walls as some kind of message that he was mentally preparing to go back to war, and pulled out one of the few precious packets of cigarettes left in the world and rose. I went with him, wanting to know his thoughts and hoping to hear reassurance that what had happened wasn't entirely my fault, and walked to the ramparts with our dogs slowly following up the stone steps. We walked on the ramparts under the sky which was already darkening from the invisible sun hidden behind the high cliff and the lonely but ominous-looking watchtower it silhouetted, and Dan smoked as he wandered in silence. I walked beside him, long ago having learned not to talk unless I had something to say or a pertinent question which couldn't wait.

"This could be messy," he said quietly.

"It already is," I told him, "and it wasn't our choice to make it like that."

He *hmm'd* in response, giving neither disagreement nor support to my sentiment before he changed the subject in his head and spoke to force me to catch up with the logical process I had been excluded from.

"Did you ever watch the *Jaws* films?" he asked without explanation as to why.

"First one," I said, thinking of the slow-moving rubber shark and terrible special effects that still terrified me and made me nervous of swimming in any water I couldn't see the bottom of, "why?"

"In the third one," he explained as he flicked the butt of the cigarette over the wall with thumb and forefinger, "there's this lagoon, like a water park and an aquarium in one place where loads of people go in summer. Well this big-ass shark finds its way inside the shark nets and they catch it. It dies, but the thing's mum comes looking for it and eats everyone. Can't remember how it ends, but I remember the feeling of dread when they'd pissed off the bigger shark. That's like this; they've made me very fucking angry."

With that he walked back to the stairs and I stayed on the ramparts.

I was pretty certain that, in all the *Jaws* films and despite the body count, the shark gets killed eventually.

WHAT'S THE FRENCH FOR
OO-RAH?

Anyone who had spent any amount of time with Neil knew his repertoire after a while. It went from him being laugh out loud funny in the first couple of years, to more of a pained groan whenever he cracked the same jokes now. He wasn't just tolerated though, he was loved and made the world a better place to be.

Apart from his ever-changing voice in whatever accent or impression he felt like doing, and the constant film references which I rarely understood, he was a born inventor and had never given up on anything that others had declared as 'fucked'. He even relished the thought of fixing something that had been branded as 'properly fucked', like it was some kind of personal challenge. I'd watched him once coaxing an outboard motor back to life, acting like an emergency room doctor on some American hospital drama as he feigned working on it desperately, telling his young French assistant to "Charge paddles to two hundred," before loudly declaring, "clear!" and pretending to zap it as it sparked and coughed into reluctant life. After that he had switched into Doctor Frankenstein himself and cackled that it lived, *it lived*, and drawing a small but bewildered crowd.

If I hadn't done what he was joking about for real on Jack, our grizzled old Irish goat of a friend who had lost his life before I had rescued Dan in the act of saving Henry's, then I might have found it funnier than I did.

Neil's ingenuity continued, perhaps even increased a few levels when everything from the old world began to slowly wear out and die off. Already, even by then, half of our fishing boats were powered by sail as fuel and engine parts were becoming too difficult to source. There were plans to refit and find more, but they would have to wait until the end of summer when the long days weren't put to maximum use gathering food.

I'd risen early, having not slept too much because my brain spun with all the what-ifs, and I put myself in the mindset of going into conflict. When I walked outside even before the sun was fully up, I found Neil in the cobbled courtyard near the gates with an improvised fuel bowser on the back of a flat-bed truck and a jury-rigged pump he had constructed from plastic tubes and what looked like plumbing pipes. He used a steering wheel from a car, old enough to not have an airbag, and tested it as I walked into the yard by spinning it around and around with one hand pressed over the end of the long tube. He stopped, pulling his hand away and assessing the red circle where the suction had proven to be working adequately, standing up straight to smile at me. I saw that he wore a bandolier of red plastic shotgun cartridges and had adopted the gun I had captured along with the prisoner. Apparently, it was a Benelli tactical, but the big boomsticks he favoured were never my thing. Too… *messy.*

I had Nemesis at my heel, fully refreshed as she clearly didn't suffer the same nagging doubts about her performance and what was expected of her like I did, and I was dressed in fresh clothing similar to the day before with my vest and loaded handguns and knives strapped to me. I had nothing in my hands, which was my reason for passing the courtyard on my way to the armoury and waved at the portly man as I passed. Nemesis ran to him without bothering to check for my permission and sniffed at him with her tail wagging as he ruffled the fur between her large ears and reached into the cab of the truck and came out with something which had been swallowed by the dog before I could see what it was.

I used my keys to open the heavy, old door and went inside. We had captured, looted and found various weapons since we had been there, but being something of a snob I ignored the weird and wonderful and finally relented in picking up one of the brand-new HK416s. I opted for the short barrel version of which we only had a few, and set to work with a multitool adding the things I wanted from a wide array of accessories designed to fit the universal rails on all sides of the short barrel. I used the last but two of the suppressors to lengthen it only slightly, adding the same flip down sight I preferred which could be pushed aside if the action was too close in to use the zoom part of the optic. With that small telescopic part aside, it left a holographic red dot which felt so familiar. Dan preferred the angular foregrip, but I liked the vertical version and held it onto the rail before attaching it firmly to be sure I had the perfect positioning as I pulled the gun into my shoulder.

I used a few magazine spacers and loaded them, effectively just a metal clamp that held two of the thirty-round magazines together to speed up reloading. I had one for my M4, guessing that if I needed to lay down more than sixty rounds so fast that speed-reloading was necessary then I was in a world of shit, but I wasn't in the mood to be guessing right then. I wanted to be prepared for all-out carnage in case I was ever caught unaware ever again.

I had to lay down a few shots to sight the optic and make a few tweaks, as I wasn't going outside of the walls having not test fired it, so I took a handful of extra five-five-six bullets and put them in a leg pocket ready to replenish the magazine when they were expended.

I took the rig on my left thigh and set it aside for Lucien, who still possessed our only remaining 417, and took a new rig before loading it with the three spare magazines for the MK14, the enhanced battle rifle I had brought from home, not even remembering when it had fallen into our loving arms. The magazines were annoyingly unique to each weapon, unlike the STANAG mags for the rifles and carbines, and only held twenty of the heavy 7.62 bullets which could kill after travelling a mile or more through the air. I knew I wasn't skilled enough to put a single bullet in the right place at that kind of distance; that ghostly skill took years to master at the cost of countless hours practicing and thousands of the bullets which we couldn't afford to expend on training. That said, inside of a half mile I could be fairly certain to hit what I wanted to, and things hit by seven-six-two weren't known for their habit of getting up afterwards. Ever.

I collapsed the extendable stock fitted to it and slung the gun on my back with its big optic resting beside the replacement bug-out bag I had packed with new equipment, pausing only to replenish my 9mm stocks from the magazines I had expended in my escape, before nestling the 416 on my body by the single-point sling so that it hung down slightly to the right of the centre of my torso. I went the other way along the stone corridor after locking up the armoury, taking the stairs at the far end to look out over the part of town that was uninhabited to pick a target inside of eighty paces. That was the maximum range I'd likely be engaging anyone with the short-barrelled gun, so I set the MK14 down to rest the foregrip of my 416 on the stone shelf and took aim.

The coughing spit of the round leaving the barrel sounded muted in comparison with the sharp crack that echoed back to me before the puff of dust shot up to the left and high of my target. I made two slight adjustments and settled in again to control my breathing and aim at the centre mass of the target, an ancient television set dumped on a patch of gravel which was of no value as be worth moving. It served a purpose now, as my next round scored a chunk of the old wooden veneer from the left side and shifted the set. Another click of adjustment saw my next eight rounds punch true through the glass and mess of wires behind satisfying me that it was accurate, and to be sure I picked the gun up into my standing position and held the foregrip tightly to hit it again three more times. I relaxed and dropped out the twin magazines to feed the gap where the spent rounds had been with the spares from my pocket, marvelling as I did how the barrel didn't feel even the slightest bit warm after being fired.

I liked that.

I met Adam on the ramparts above the gates on the way back and we talked briefly. He was to be left in charge of the defences in our, in *my*, absence and was dressed accordingly. He had been quiet recently, having spent most of the winter unwell with a mysterious bug that had affected a dozen people in the town, but the warm weather had revived him enough to regain some fitness. He was still very much the understudy of Mitch and had worked with him for the last few years to train the militia, but took his turn on guard duty as the others did.

I went back down the steps, finding a lot more people gathered in the courtyard and another vehicle behind Neil's fuel truck.

141

Nemesis bounded over to Ash who, seemingly less alert than his daughter so early in the morning, avoided her attempts to swat at him and turned his head away. Dan nodded at me, dressed in his full battle gear which had evolved just as mine had since we had settled here. He still carried the evil shotgun on his back, but the new vest he wore was a lighter tan than the old one and the elasticated sling the gun sat in was higher. The Walther still sat on the left side, with the front of his vest sprouting ranks of magazine pouches with open tops. A big knife with a pointed metal cone at the end of the hilt sat horizontally across the top of the chest, just as my spare Glock was holstered on my own. An elasticated rank of red shotgun cartridges offered a flash of colour to the scarred man dressed black and tan, and everything about him from the way he dressed to the air of coiled violence that radiated from him spoke volumes.

"Alright, fuckers?" Mitch said gleefully, appearing from behind me with his own individual weapon resting over one shoulder. He carried the same weapon as Dan, as me now I had to remember, only his had the longer barrel and a bulbous addition underneath ahead of the trigger and grip. That addition, trusted in the hands of nobody else, lobbed 40mm bombs. He was dripping with equipment, almost as extravagantly as Dan and me, and between us we looked like a bad Hollywood movie cast. Alita followed him, wearing walking boots and brown trousers of a light material under a polo shirt and a thick body armour, looking every inch the foreign correspondent in a warzone; she just lacked the camera crew following her for the exclusive.

Mitch saw my raised eyebrows at her appearance, unable to comprehend that she was coming when he was so fiercely protective of her.

"Best interpreter we have," he answered, "and besides, she

wouldn't stay behind. Believe me I tried." He sighed as though to indicate that the argument was temporarily forgotten, even if he had lost and didn't quite realise it just yet. He had equipped her with a gun, not surprisingly a Glock as they accounted for almost all of our sidearms, but the resolved look on her face made it clear that she was wearing it on her vest simply to stop Mitch moaning at her.

The militia members arrived at once and hovered near to Mitch who bent down to hand over a duffel bag to them. The two men and one woman took their rifles and handguns before dishing out the charged magazines until they were evenly distributed. They stood ready, as resolved as Alita and trying to appear for everyone to see that they were fearless in spite of their obvious trepidation at being about to head into conflict for the first time.

Two of them had been involved in the battle for Sanctuary and had been at the head of the queue of volunteers when we called for a standing army, however small, to be trained. Both Mitch, Dan and Neil had been badly injured in that desperate fight, and it fell to me to organise the defenders in the wake of the destruction wrought on us.

One man, tall, thin and miserable looking but transformed when he smiled, was named Jean. Beside him, golden hair falling over his forehead in waves over his piercing blue eyes and wearing a permanent look of confident amusement, was Lucien and beside him, Chloe. I smiled at Chloe, my eyes flickering towards Lucien and my cheeks flushed when he turned his smile on me. I pulled out the thigh rig with spare HK417 magazines and handed it to him without a word.

Chloe was ten years older than me, and at first, I didn't think I liked her. She constantly muttered to those beside her when I was giving instructions and teaching the small classes in the basics, and back then my French was almost non-existent, so I was forced to rely on Polly and Alita and a few others to translate my words. I got the impression that Chloe was constantly undermining me, commenting under her breath on every other point I made, and I was close to losing my temper on more than one occasion. In a rare moment of honesty, I broke down to Alita. I was still only thirteen then and cried because I didn't think they took me seriously. She hugged me and told me how wrong I was, because Chloe was helping to explain what I was saying to a man beside her.

"She hangs on your every word," Alita told me, "and I have heard her defending your age to them."

I changed my opinion completely at that point, spending extra time with her as my French developed over the subsequent years just as her English improved. She had a natural leadership quality which I liked, and despite the age difference she looked up to me and learned easily. It was no doubt that Mitch and Dan saw those qualities in her too, and she was one of the three senior members of the militia who whipped the others into shape when required. I wasn't surprised in the slightest to see her volunteering ahead of anyone else to be part of the rescue mission.

Rocco had been brought out, his hands now properly secured in handcuffs taken from a French policeman who had ceased to have need of them years before, and he was pushed towards the back of the van lined up behind the fuel truck. It was a sturdy thing, but I knew from having driven it that it was stripped out in the back and completely spartan. With two dogs and six people in the back, it was going to be uncomfortable. Dan saw my eyes lingering on the van and guessed what I was thinking.

"Another reason to set off early," he said, "is so that we get to Perpignan before the sun gets up too high."

"Shotgun," I answered deadpan, hoping that I would actually get away with it.

We gathered around. Mitch and Alita, the three militia fighters, me, Neil and his two apprentice engineers and Mateo hovering silently near the back, and all of us faced Dan.

"We're getting fuel, we're picking up the other truck, and we're going to get our man back." Murmured agreement met his words, spoken in rough French, which evidently wasn't enough.

"We're going to get our man back, and we're going to put a stop to the bastards who did this to us... let's do this."

"*En avant!*" Chloe shouted, echoing the sentiment as other voices raised in support.

MOTION LOTION PART III

Despite feeling pretty pleased with myself for calling shotgun, I grew guiltier with each mile that passed as the others in the back of the van would be getting more and more uncomfortable. It was still fairly good going on the road north after the trading post, as it was well travelled by another, smaller settlement, about fifteen kilometres towards the remnants of the city's outskirts. Trees hung over the road from both sides, but a kind of tunnel was left down the middle which is what our small convoy stuck to as we made decent progress. We bypassed the gap in the trees ahead to our left where the settlement was; a farm similar to our own sub-district where the surrounding houses in the town had been populated to form a group big enough to evolve their own leadership and routines of society.

I'd been there a few times, in fact I was there for the first meeting back when Polly was still in charge and when the settlement had only just been claimed or started or whatever. They were worried at first, I could see that from their terrified looks at our weapons, and they seemed to prepare to leave when we explained who we were and what territory we controlled. Dan asked why they were packing back up, and when Polly told him that they were scared that they had encroached he waved his hands for them to stop. I remember it well, because he only knew a handful of words and phrases in French at that point and relied on Polly to translate almost all of what he was saying to them as he threw in the words he did know.

He told them that we weren't there to drive them off our land, that he wanted them to stay and to visit Sanctuary and to trade goods and food and for people to come and go between the two places as they pleased, that we would provide help and resources to them because they were our neighbours. Their faces told me that everything would be fine, that they were and would always be grateful for the kindness and the offer of friendship.

I had asked Dan about it afterwards, teasing him gently about going soft in his old age, but he explained his logic and made me feel like a fool for not understanding it.

"They've moved in on our doorstep," he said, "there are enough of them to be a nuisance to us if they decided to be hostile, even if they don't look like being able to offer any real threat. If they see us as their help and protection, then they aren't likely to decide that we are a threat or a target. I was setting the tone," he told me in a voice that sounded like the lecture was drawing to a close, "and I think they will be our friends because of it."

"And what if they try to take what's ours?" I said, genuinely wanting to know how he would deal with the hand of friendship being bitten.

"Then I'll kick the shit out of someone," he answered bluntly, as though no problems had ever existed in the world that he couldn't solve with action.

They hadn't, obviously, and there had even been an exchange of people between the new settlement and Sanctuary as some of them were fishermen by trade and we had some with skills that could help them. It became so that there was weekly travel between Sanctuary and Les Vergers, or *The Orchards,* as they had become known.

Whereas the farm produced mainly potatoes and vegetables, The Orchards were in a sun trap and the groves of fruit trees were plentiful and needed no replanting, if not more than a little tender loving care, and their renewed productivity led to the trading post being established at the natural midpoint between the farm, The Orchards and Sanctuary. Refurbished, repaired and staffed by volunteers, the post signified something resembling the next level in rebuilding, at least to me, because it showed that we as a group were expanding and incorporating more people. They weren't necessarily *our* people in that they weren't living under our control, but they were part of our wider group and under our protection. It made me feel that the world was bigger than just our little group, and that made me happy.

Bypassing the road to that settlement, I fixed my eyes back on the road and switched on. It took us another forty minutes to reach the outskirts of the city, which always gave me a prickly feeling of malevolence. We had categorically avoided anything bigger than a small town since, well since forever really. The closest I had come to a city after everything changed back in England was when we got attacked by a pack of wild dogs, which probably had something to do with it. It was bizarre, because we – the *gunslingers* as Marie called us – were far happier in the dark countryside than we were anywhere near the concrete jungle.

We reached the outskirts and drove straight past the first two fuel stations we found, heading around the long loops of the exit roads to circle back onto a huge *hypermarché* where the fuel station bearing the same name stood at the far end of the car park. I slipped down from the passenger side, the right-hand seat as the van didn't come with us from the UK, and hugged the side of the van to the rear doors. They opened as I reached the back and I gave a low whistle to bring Nemesis to my side. Dan mirrored my movements on the opposite side as Ash circled twice and looked up at me before realising that Dan was out to play and bounded straight to his side as the better option.

We fanned out, having already planned and done this with some of the militia, knowing that they would be getting their guns up and creating an inner cordon around the vehicles. Neil and his two helpers were still in there waiting for us to signal them the all-clear. Dan and I jogged forward, eyes up and alert as though the concept of being attacked or ambushed for our vehicles and weapons was a normal thing.

It was, had been for years, but just because it was normal didn't mean it was right. I hated those kind of people, and as much as hated killing, I kind of felt like it fell to me to stop them hurting other people that couldn't fight back.

We moved in silence, as much as in that we didn't need to talk to each other to get the job done; not even to our dogs who were well accustomed to how we worked. Dan stretched out ahead, extending his lead by half a dozen paces to reach the door ahead of me. As we had so much backup, which we didn't usually have, Dan crashed straight into the door to the fuel station. And bounced back.

As much as I tried to, I couldn't help myself. I laughed so hard I couldn't even keep my gun up. He picked himself off the floor, glanced back to where the others were, and his face darkened as he knew that he wouldn't get away with pretending that hadn't happened.

"It's…" I choked, trying to stop myself laughing, "it's a sli… it's a *sliding* door, *dickhead.*"

I didn't hear what he mumbled, but the sight of Ash worrying at him as he stood set me off again, like the dog was scared that Dan had been hurt by something, and then back-pedalled a few steps to look up at him confused as he stood. Dan, still grumbling, dropped his gun to hang on the sling and pulled the knife from his vest before jamming it into the crack where the door met the frame. He wiggled the knife, not to try and pry the door open and risk snapping the blade but just to give his fingers enough room to gain some purchase. He set one boot against the frame, the muscles in his arms bunching up and his face turning red as the effort seemed to raise his blood pressure in an attempt to force the door open like he was some kind of organic pneumatic device. The door, even though it tried its best to stay seized firmly shut, creaked open a few inches and allowed Dan to get a firmer grip on the inside. It gave way more and he put his body in the gap and forced it the rest of the way. With an exaggerated breath out, he relaxed and stepped aside for me to enter first as I was fresh. Gun raised, knees bent and my breathing steady I stepped inside as that dank, musty air hit me. I had pulled up the bandana over my mouth before going inside as experience had taught me that I didn't want to breathe in the stale air of a building that had been sealed up tight for half a decade. The inside was only a small kiosk, not like the larger fuel stations back in England which were small supermarkets most of the time, and the only door led to a small store room and the passageway to the raised desk where the till sat under a layer of dust.

"Clear," I said softly, getting no answer to the obvious declaration from Dan who still covered the doorway. He went back over to the others, stopping halfway to wave Neil over. I heard the engine start as I scanned my eyes over the shelves which didn't seem to have been picked over, reaching down for a plastic carrier bag I threw in the cartons of cigarettes as I always did whenever I cleared a new place.

Everything we needed we had in fresh supply, but the cancer sticks he still couldn't give up were becoming pretty rare.

I went back outside, grabbing a packet of potato snacks and checking the back for a date before it struck me that I only knew it was summer, and I had to drift off deep inside my head to figure out that they were still good for a few more months. I threw in as many packs as the bag could hold and went back to the van to put the bag in the footwell beside my new kit bag. I found Chloe near the back chatting with Mitch and looked around at the other faces.

"*Où est Lucien?*" I asked, getting my answer in the form of a pointed finger at the large billboard and the ladder running up one of the large support legs. I saw the stationary shape of the sniper doing his job and muttered, "Good," in French.

It struck me that none of us had really ever sat down with the intention of learning the language, but having to explain everything and mixing English with French just kind of leaked in, like a kind of osmosis.

The sounds of Neil attacking the lock of the refilling pipes reached my ears and my eyes met Dan's. He nudged his head towards the main shop, a hulking building the size of an aircraft hangar, and I pulled a face and shook my head.

"No time," I said, meaning that we would only scratch the surface of a place like that unless we had bigger trucks and the whole day to attack it. He shrugged as though it was nothing.

"I got you something," I told him, "in the front of the van."

"Smokes?" he asked, an eyebrow raised in hope. I nodded, and he smiled, happy that someone had thought about him and grateful that he didn't have to appear self-serving by helping himself to a bad habit while others stood watch. He was funny like that.

Neil had dropped in the long, looped hose through the reservoir pipe and began to spin the steering wheel to pump the fuel. I watched as he turned it with enthusiasm and grew tired after less than a minute. Having shown his apprentices the way, he stood back and breathed hard as his expanding midriff had slowed him over the last few years. He wandered over to us, red-faced and sweating from the brief exertion, and gave his assessment of the time it would take.

"Give them half an hour," he said, "won't fill it up, just give us enough to brim the tanks and a couple of the jerrycans for you."

Dan nodded, his hands going to the pouch on his vest that carried his slowest killing tool, lighting one and leaning his head back to blow a stream of smoke upwards and not in our faces. The others huddled around, eyes aware and conversation hushed as we waited.

"That's enough go-*jus* I think," he declared finally, ending the safer part of our day.

Just over an hour back in the uncomfortable van saw us passing the trading post, Dan slowing to wave at the guard who had wandered outside in response to the sound of engines approaching. It was Roland, as it often was, and he returned the wave with all the self-importance of a man standing guard over his own small fiefdom.

The drive to where the battered, grubby once-white pickup was abandoned had been longer than I expected, showing just how exhausted I must have been when I had walked the man who had tried to kill me back towards the trading post. Fuel was siphoned out, topping off the van and filling the pickup's tank before making it splutter back to life.

Three hours after our early start, the fuel truck headed for home and we headed for the mountains. And for revenge.

I Spy

I led the way, driving the pickup with, of all bloody people, Lucien sat beside me and our long rifles creating a kind of barrier in between us. He had this annoying habit of keeping silent, which I usually liked, but he did it with a kind of smirk that drove me crazy.

I lasted about fifteen kilometres before I started shifting in my seat and huffing, which made him smile wider and stay infuriatingly silent. Another fifteen kilometres and I cracked when he chuckled to himself.

"What's so funny?" I asked him in English, forgetting to translate my thoughts as they came out.

"I do not laugh at you, Leah," he said smoothly, still smirking.

"What then?" I snapped back, returning his smile for some unknown reason and trying to wipe it off my face in case he didn't take me seriously.

"I was just remembering," he said carefully in English that was better than I recalled or expected, "when your boyfriend tried to show me how big and strong he was..." He trailed away to look out the window and chuckle ruefully again.

"He's not my boyfriend," I snapped, sounding younger than I was as he touched a raw nerve, "he never was. He's a dick."

Lucien burst out laughing, a melodic giggle with a hint of tenor that made my concentration waver from the road more than I expected.

"What?"

"What is this word, dick?" he asked in a tone that suggested he knew what I meant but wanted me to say it. I called his bluff.

"Henry," I said carefully, "is a cock. A penis. A bloody *bellend*, and I don't like him, and I was angry that he thought I was his... his *property* to be argued over."

Lucien thought about it for a while before answering.

"I apology," he said. I ignored the grammar knowing that I would be just as roughly translated if I tried to have the conversation in French. "I did not mean to make you angry. It is just that..." He paused, taking in a long breath through his nose and stretching his neck up in thought. I forced my eyes back to the road and away from the defined muscles in his neck. "It is just that he had... *raisons pour lesquelles*."

"Reasons?" I asked. "What reasons?"

"He heard me speak of you, and I think he try to defend you."

"Oh," I said, not sure where to take the conversation. Luckily, he pointed at a road sign ahead and changed the subject for me.

"That is the way to where I used to call my home," he said wistfully.

"Where did you live?"

"To the east of Le Mans," he said, lost in retrospection, "in a small town of little value. We were *les Sarthoises*," he said, pronouncing it *Sart-warrs*, "much as the people of Sanctuary and indeed of Andorra are Catalan. That is the language the prisoner has, Catalan, not Spanish."

"How did you get to Sanctuary then?" I asked, ignoring the information Alita had already given me.

"I was in Barcelona for a fight," he said, "my father called our home and my mother said she was sick. So was my sister. My father became unwell that night..." He trailed off, not wanting to go any further on the subject.

"I was left alone too," I told him, "I was only twelve."

"I was sixteen," he said softly, "I was in the summer after leaving school, and my trainer said that these fights in Spain would get me seen by the people in Paris"—he pronounced that in the true way— "and that I would have the chance to be with the Olympics if I did well."

"And did you?" I asked, feeling dumb but trying to roll with it anyway. He gave that smooth little self-depreciating chuckle again before answering.

"I did not have the chance, and there was almost nobody there to see. None of the Olympics coaches came. That was the same night that all was changed."

I nodded and drove in silence for a while. I tried to think of a way to fill the awkward silence that now echoed around the squeaky cab, and decided on a complete subject change.

"What did you do to pass the time on long journeys?" I asked him, a hint of conspiratorial mischief in my voice. "You know, to pass the time?" He leaned back a little, shifting his position for comfort before answering.

"We talked, we listened to music..." he said almost vacantly, "and you?"

"Same," I said, "and we played I Spy."

I kept my eyes on the road but could feel his amused gaze boring into the side of my head as he waited for the explanation. I decided to make him ask.

"I surrender," he said mockingly, "what is the *I Spy?*"

"It's a game," I told him, "we take it in turns. I find something I can see and tell you what it begins with, then you have to guess."

"Okay," he said smiling, "you begin."

"I spy," I said, drawing out the words theatrically like I was thinking, just as my mother had done when I was younger, "with my little eye... something beginning with... C."

"Are we to play in English?" he asked after a pause.

"Yes," I said, "my game, my language." He smirked with a mock huff.

"Car?"

"Yes. Your turn," I said with feigned annoyance having given him the easiest one I could think of as we passed a long line of derelict vehicles on my side of the road where they had been parked and never returned to.

"I spy with my little eye," he said, faster than I had, "something beginning with L."

I thought hard, seeing nothing obvious.

"In English?" I asked.

"Yes," he said, his tone of voice making it obvious that he was enjoying teasing me. I thought again, casting my vision out to the extremes of what I could see.

"Lights?" I tried.

"No."

"I give up," I said in exasperation.

"Leah," he said softly. I tutted, rolling my eyes at the simplicity of the joke at my expense.

"I see you. I watch you run sometimes," he went on, "you are fast."

I paused, not sure whether to feel creeped out or excited.

"Through your scope?" I asked. "From the watchtower?"

"Yes."

"So… you've been pointing a high-powered rifle at me?" I said carefully. He pulled a face as though he was only just considering this for the first time.

"Yes, but I have the safety on," he replied ruefully making me blush despite the breeze coming in through my window. I drove on in silence, not wanting to play I Spy any longer.

You can keep your bloody safety on, I thought, *and we can discuss that remark when we've finished the job.*

At the end of the long stretch that Rafi had told me would take a long time, I slowed before we reached the foothills, dabbing the brakes to roll the truck to a stop and pulling to the side of the road. Dan pulled up beside me, the passenger window open and Alita's smiling face looking slightly downwards to mine.

"The road gets steeper after this," I said, pointing out the obvious as the landscape about a mile ahead began to rise steeply, "and that's where I hit the ambush."

Dan, leaning forward with his left forearm resting on the top of the steering wheel, nodded and thought.

"Nothing on their radio yet?"

"No," I replied, "but I doubt it will work this far away."

"Okay," he said, his eyes looking ahead as he thought, "carry on, carefully, until we get to before where you ambushed them. Then I'll figure out what to do."

We drove, slower now because the winding roads were awkward and forced the speed down to be able to see around the switch-back bends, and because I half expected to meet resistance.

When I had reached the fork in the road where the very truck I was driving had been parked to cut off my escape, as though I would be dumb enough to walk along the only road off the mountain top, I almost missed it until the oily-black stains on the tarmac caught the sun. I stopped, crunching the selector up into park and switching off the engine before climbing out to raise my weapon. I moved four quick strides to my left to get my body clear of the vehicle.

Vehicles attract fire, my brain barked at me as though I ever needed reminding.

Lucien had done the same, breaking off right and settling himself into the foliage at the roadside near to where I had hidden to await my opportunity to take out Rocco's friends, the unfamiliar assault rifle in his hands as the marksman rifle was a hindrance in the close confines of the leaf-shaded road. Nemesis had bounced down from the bed of the truck, her claws clattering on the metal and the tarmac as she moved to my side, and the van rolled to a stop behind us before killing its engine.

I waited, straining my ears in the silence to filter out the natural sounds and force myself to detect any unnatural ones.

Nothing.

I waited for longer, but still nothing.

I rose, flicked my thumb up to engage the safety on the carbine, and walked back to the open driver's window of the van.

"A few K's ahead," I explained softly, "after the border post, the road drops down into a shallow bowl. The new town is there, and the road swings right to avoid it. The tunnel and mountain road split off there."

"Go ahead, slowly," he told me, "then stop before the town is visible. I want you and pretty boy up high before I go in on foot."

"What's the plan?"

He chewed the inside of his cheek as he thought.

"I'll offer an exchange of prisoners," he said cryptically, "and take it from there. You know the signal."

It was a statement, not a question, and I nodded before turning back to the battered truck.

We were heading back to Andorra.

THE HIGH GROUND

The border post was exactly as it had been when I had left it, with no sign of anyone using it for the intended purpose. We cleared it anyway, because it never paid to take chances or make asses of you and 'umption, and I led the way onwards and upwards.

Stopping well short of the crest of the rise before the tops of the buildings came into view, I swung the truck off the road and killed the engine but left the keys in the ignition. Someone would take over driving it, probably Neil if I had to guess, but that wasn't my concern any longer.

Lucien mirrored my movements, strapping his own weapon on his back in favour of the longer barrelled marksman rifles we now needed, and I pointed to the right side of the road. He understood and set off to make the climb out of sight there as I looked up at the left side of the road. I don't know if it was my imagination, but my side looked a lot steeper. I looked back at Dan who now had Rocco sat on the road in front of the van as the others fanned out to protect our staging area from any unwanted surprises. He didn't have Ash with him, no doubt forcing him to grumble as he stayed with the others. I didn't blame him; I wouldn't want Nem at my side when I was walking into a killing zone in case any stray bullets found their errant way to her unarmoured body.

I nodded to him, flashing two fingers like a victory salute before making an 'o' with my thumb and forefinger, having the nod returned on his serious face that seemed to brood darkly. Whenever he smiled, the vicious scar that had only now faded to a dull pink as it ran down his face from eyebrow to cheek seemed to disappear, but when his mood darkened the scar somehow took on another meaning and made him look menacing.

I set off, jogging up the slope with my dog picking her way almost daintily between the rocks, eager to reach the high ground and settle into a vantage point with the twenty minutes I had before he began his own journey.

I was sweating and breathing hard before I had even moved around the bluff of the rise to approach the direction of the town, and when the rooftops came into sight I ducked down until I could no longer disguise my profile. I dropped slowly onto my belly, crawling forwards on knees and elbows and wished I had adopted some protective pads for my arms. The knee pads did their job well, but I could feel the skin being worn away from my elbows each time they connected with the arid surface.

Eventually, uncomfortably, I reached a rocky outcrop that offered me a view of the road below while providing a small amount of cover from the direction of the town. Checking my watch, I saw that I had a minute before Dan would begin walking brazenly down the middle of the road. Nemesis was flat to the ground, her hind legs coiled underneath her as she was ready to spring into action if called upon, and I was happy that she had found some shade as her dark fur grew hot under the beating sun.

And I waited.

I scanned the opposite ridge, lower than my vantage point, until I located the long black barrel of Lucien's weapon protruding from a bush. I knew he would have gently cut away some branches to give himself the best cover from view and provide a clear shot, and I smiled at the thought of him doing it.

Focus, I told myself, *focus.*

Dan checked his watch, gave it another minute just to be sure, and told Rocco to get to his feet. Mitch flanked him, with Alita at his shoulder, and he exchanged a glance with Neil who would be left in charge of the others.

He marched the handcuffed prisoner ahead of him, not prodding him with the barrel of his gun as some people would do and kept a sedate pace so as not to expend energy unnecessarily. Alita, following Mitch's instructions, stayed behind him to keep her small body out of sight of their unknown enemy ahead.

He didn't glance up to his left or his right, wasn't so ill-trained as to betray their position to anyone eyeing his approach, but he knew that the two marksmen would be there, covering their approach like angels watching over them.

He stopped a few hundred paces from the edge of the town, near to where the road split to turn right and in view of the gaping, black maw of the unlit tunnel, and waited. If anyone occupied the town, if they had any sense at all, then he would have been seen by now. He waited five minutes, then another five.

Eventually he grew tired of waiting and rested the carbine on its sling to draw the ugly shotgun over his right shoulder.

"Cover your ears," he warned the others softly as he braced

himself against the expected recoil, aimed it at a patch of dusty ground off to their right, and fired twice as he let each shot reverberate massively around the natural acoustics of the area.

It worked; movement in the distance showed where people ran about near to the end of the town at the limits of the shadows of the buildings until they organised themselves. A contingent of three began to walk out of the light grey buildings, walking slowly as they went to investigate what had roused them.

Dan waited, unmoving and stoic as was his way, and by the time the people were close enough to make out any details he had hardened his exterior into the ruthless warrior he needed them to see.

The man at the head of the trio, advancing like a lead fighter pilot with his two wingmen flanking him, was tall and well built. His dark olive forearms were muscled, and he wore a gun on his hip, as did his companions. He stopped ten paces away from Dan and assessed him, his eyes flickering over the way he and the man beside him were festooned with weapons. He regarded their guns with a keen eye that suggested he knew what he was looking at, and only the slightest raised eyebrow responded to the fat protrusion under the barrel of Mitch's weapon. He tried to show no surprise at being called out from his nest to greet heavily armed soldiers. He leaned around, trying to see Alita with a smile that was less than friendly, and only then did his eyes land on Rocco.

His face darkened into a scowl that promised a retribution for failure. He held the handcuffed man's eyes until his hopeful smile dropped and his eyes went to the ground. Only then did he speak.

Dan didn't understand him, but he held his gaze all the same and waited for Alita to translate.

"He wants to know what you want," she muttered.

164

"Tell him," Dan said slowly as he fixed the man with a look not of threat, but of guarantee, "that I want to swap prisoners."

He waited for the words to be translated and called out from behind Mitch, seeing the man smirk and scoff as though the trade was an unwelcome one.

"Tell him that he can have his man back, and we get ours, along with his weapons and equipment." He paused for the translation to catch up. "And after that we will leave and not come back here."

The man took that in, scratching at a stubbled chin under suspicious brown eyes as he looked back into Dan's cold blue ones. He spoke again.

"He says he is Tomau Codina," she said, "and he is commander of this area. He says he has a hundred men at his words and wants to know why he would do a trading with you."

"Because," Dan said, investing a small amount of gusto into his voice and not bothering to introduce himself, "we have a sniper trained on him right now."

At that, the man stiffened slightly, and his hand fluttered as though he wanted to reach for his weapon but he stopped himself in case this intruder wasn't bluffing.

"You understood that well enough," Dan said, taking a pace forwards that the man mirrored, and drew himself up, "so let me be clear… If you want to live through this, then we get our own people back and we go our separate ways."

Alita still chattered from behind Mitch, translating the words anyway.

"Give us back our man and take yours, then we don't have to piss in each other's ponds again. Ever."

Tomau Codina smiled then and held up a hand. All eyes watched as he closed it into a fist and dropped it down.

Dan heard the bullet before the report from the barrel reached his ears. By that point he had ducked and spun away, but the sound of the projectile punching through flesh and bone was played in slow-motion in his mind as he rose to one knee and raised his gun to point it at the chest of the bastard, who was smiling and holding up his hands in a clear gesture of non-aggression. Dan didn't take his eyes away but spoke to Mitch by muttering his name.

"Both fine," he replied in a guttural growl, "they killed their own man."

Dan looked away then, off to his left where the broken sack of meat and bone lay bleeding out beside him, a huge, ragged hole sprouting from between his shoulder blades where the high-velocity round had blown him into oblivion.

"You see now, Englishman," Tomau with a heavy accent, "you have nothing to trade me for now."

Dan, for once, was shocked at the brutality of what had just happened. He opened his mouth to renew the threat of his own snipers when the man clearly had a ruthless streak of his own. The next words cut off any such threat anyway.

"My man has seen your sniper, and my next signal tell him to kill them," he said, seeing the logic flashing across Dan's face as he intercepted the thought with his next words, "and if I fall then he is to kill you also."

Dan rose, standing directly before the bastard and looked up into his eyes. The Dan of a few years ago would have the man beaten on size before he had slimmed down on a diet of fresh fish and produce, but he lost out on at least three inches of height which was a psychological battle of its own.

"You may go now," he told Dan, "if you come back here then I will be forced to kill you. This is not your territory."

Dan held his gaze for a moment longer, his mouth tightening into a grim line, then he turned and walked away.

SKINNING THE CAT

I saw the drama unfolding far below me, saw the prisoner drop long before I heard the report of the gunshot, and scanned the view through my optic desperately until I was sure that none of our people were hit. I watched Dan stand up into the face of the man before he turned and walked away, only then did I scan ahead for the shooter. I cut up the view of the rooftops into four segments, searching each one in turn until I found them. Lying flat on a rooftop with the long barrel of a rifle overhanging the edge I swallowed down my anger. The profile of the gun, I couldn't be sure at that distance but in my heart, I think I knew it, looked just like the weapon I had lost, had abandoned to these bastards, when I was ambushed.

I hoped that Lucien would be steady enough to hold his nerve and not fire until the others were clear as I kept taking my eye from the scope and slowly rotating my head – slowly so as not to attract the attention of the shooter – until I could no longer see Dan and the others.

Waiting longer, just to be sure, I settled in on the enemy sniper and prepared to take aim, but the bastard was up and moving; walking briskly across the rooftop to an access door to a stairwell. I settled in, preparing to make a difficult shot on a moving target, and squeezed off three rounds.

I snatched the shots, rushing them and not taking the time to readjust after each pull of the trigger, and all I served to do was make him duck and run for the door. He was gone before I could line him up again, so I switched my aim to the man who had given the command. He was gone, and I had missed my chance.

I shuffled backwards from the ridge, rising into a crouch where I ran as fast as was safe for the lower ground of the leeward slope, then straightened up and headed down. Lucien was there first, talking to Dan who I saw place a hand on his shoulder before turning away to face me. The gesture spoke volumes. *You did the right thing,* it said, *you were right to keep your nerve and hold your fire.* The look he gave me said something different.

"What happened?" he snapped as Ash joined him and looked up at me wearing an expression that bordered on judgemental also.

"I had a line on their shooter," I said, "but he was running, and I missed."

Dan breathed in, holding it before letting it out in a frustrated sigh.

"Okay," he said, "that's too bad." He turned away, evidently having forgiven me for attempting to gain a tactical advantage over them when he probably assumed I was taking pot shots at their leader, and called Neil.

"How's it looking?" he asked.

"All good," Neil answered, "just need the message writing on here," he said, pointing at the front of the stolen pickup. He had siphoned off as much diesel as he could, filling the jerrycans and decanting it into the van before refilling them again.

"What's the plan?" I asked Dan.

"We come at them from a direction they aren't expecting," he replied ambiguously.

Alita used a permanent marker pen on the dirty-white paint, etching a message in a language I didn't read, as Neil waited for her to get clear. He lifted the lever to put the driver's seat all the way forwards before bending down underneath the chair and fiddling for a while. He stepped back, moving slowly, his hands up as though he was frightened to move then shut the truck door carefully and nudged it to click home.

"Let's go," he said, climbing into the front passenger seat of the van. I climbed in the back, Nemesis licking at Ash's face as they tried to find space among the tangle of bodies crammed inside, and the doors were shut. The van set off, turning in shuffles on the narrow road, and we headed down off the mountain.

"My brother lives?" Mateo asked in English. I opened my mouth to speak, but closed it when I realised I had nothing to say and shot a glance at Alita. She answered him in Spanish, and I watched as his face fell into a resolved hope that Rafi still clung on to life.

We drove for just over an hour, and despite Dan not pushing the unstable van to any kind of speed the ride in the back was a stressful and uncomfortable one. The air soon felt thick and clogged with a lack of oxygen and I was painfully aware that my sweat had dried, and I suspected that I smelt a little funky. Even though Dan scoffed at me whenever he saw it, I kept a can of deodorant in my bag, but I could hardly dig it out and use it in front of everyone out of embarrassment. Luckily, just after I was planning on how to force a rest stop, the van slowed, and the engine stopped. I jumped out, Nem at my heel, and raised my new carbine after leaving the big rifle in the back of the van. I fanned out, clearing the area just as four others did the same to push out a cordon, and when satisfied that we were in an abandoned area I lowered my gun and went to get answers.

I pulled Dan aside, my face making it clear that I wasn't going to settle for another vague answer, and asked for an explanation.

"You said that the people in Andorra were blockaded from the southern road, right?" he asked.

"Yes…" I answered, drawing out the word suspiciously.

"So we hit that blockade, open it up, and come at those fuckers from their own backyard."

I thought about that for a second.

"And what guarantees do we have that they aren't already inside? That they aren't going to ambush us again in the tunnel or in the open? They have, or at least they've *said* they have more than we do, and thanks to me they've got a bloody 417 and someone who knows how to use it. How's that going to work?" I demanded almost angrily.

He grabbed my arm and led me away from the others in case my words infected them with doubt.

"What's the mantra?" he asked.

"What do you me—"

"What do we do when some fucker comes at us and threatens us?" he snapped in a low growl as he squeezed my arm for effect.

"We kill them," I answered simply.

"Yeah," he snarled, angry at the situation and not me, "we kill 'em all. Just like the King of fucking Wales, just like Bronson and his thugs, just like the ones who attacked the prison and just like that mad shit who tried to blow me up with my own friend."

And with that he walked away, leaving me with a nagging doubt that he wasn't in total control of himself.

I found a quiet corner to spray the cold chemicals under my armpits and down my back and chest, feeling fresher even if I was just masking the need for a decent shower to remove the film of sweat and dust from my skin. Feeling refreshed, as much as was possible in a deserted patch of nowhere, I climbed back inside the van and settled in for the long drive around the mountains and into Spain.

Tomau congratulated his sniper, a Canadian of all people, named Elias who had been swallowed up as part of the flotsam of humanity stranded far away from his birth country. The man had been a hunter and had expressed an ability in shooting at distance. The captured prize of the big military rifle found strewn across the rear seats in the ruined vehicle they had ambushed provided an opportunity for that claim to be put to the test, and the two of them had snuck through the tunnel before day break to rest on the cold ground far away from the entrance. As the sun rose, Elias took aim at the unsuspecting guard at the toll booth, and calmly blew his left arm off just below the shoulder. The man screamed fit to wake the dead, but such was the fear that the fatal shot had inspired that nobody dared come to his aid. His screams faded rapidly as he bled out, and the two retreated to the other side of the tunnel in triumph.

Tomau knew that the people of Andorra, *his* people, would eventually submit to his rule and such displays were a necessity if leadership is to be accepted without question. His Canadian had kept the rifle just as Tomau had kept one of the heavier assault rifles to replace the MP5 he had taken from a Spanish police station so long ago, and with the weapons rose their standing and reputation among the group. There were almost fifty of them, half of those armed with something resembling a decent weapon, and he allowed mob rule to establish its own hierarchy amongst the lower ranks, much as he had been forced to fight for recognition and advancement in his life before.

He organised a party to follow the intruders, to see them safely off his territory and see that they weren't loitering to make a foolish attempt on his town under the cover of darkness. The detachment was well armed and led by a cruel man who he had only recently rotated away from the blockade at the Spanish border as he was growing restless for action. Tomau wanted him closer to his sight so that no orders were given that he hadn't personally issued, as he suspected the man to be a candidate to overthrow him should he gather enough support.

They quickly found the truck thought lost when their own ambush was so poorly equipped and overrun, and he left two men to bring it back as he drove the lead vehicle down the slopes to chase off the foreigners. He had gone so far ahead that he didn't know what had happened to them until he returned and found Tomau stood near the smouldering wreck wearing a look of savage intent.

The message on the front of the truck was still visible, and bore the words, "Do not follow us."

The two men dropped off at the truck thought that they had got off lightly in the afternoon heat, and lazily opened the doors of the hot cab. Neither thought to glance inside, and had Neil known this he would have been annoyed at the efforts he went to making sure that the booby trap was well obscured from prying eyes.

As the man went to climb inside he found the seat too far forward to get his body behind. Reaching down for the release handle, he lifted it and slid it back, his eyes meeting his companion across the hot interior as they both heard a metallic sound and a faint *pop*.

The grenade, one of the few precious items deemed necessary to part with by Dan in return for the execution of his prisoner, had been firmly fixed underneath the driver's seat with a cable tie looped through the seat runner and the pin of the small bomb fastened securely under the old foam. When it detonated, which it did with a far smaller explosion than any inexperienced person watching would have thought, it blew the would-be drivers legs clean off at the knees and threw enough shrapnel into the body of the passenger to kill them both and leave their bodies to cook by the heat of the burning truck.

Tomau was savage, instantly demoting the man by taking the automatic weapon and spare ammunition from him before granting someone else the status of owning the weapons.

"Double the guard," he shouted as he climbed back into the passenger seat of the vehicle he had commandeered, "I want to be sure that these bastards do not return."

Invincibility Lies in the Defence

That was a strong belief, especially for those of us who lived behind walls impervious to all but heavy artillery, but what I saw through my scope looked almost too easy.

We had driven all day, reaching the southern border area under looming mountain tops to our right, stopping short as was sensible to approach on foot. The defenders of the blockade, the not-so-merry band of pirates sent to choke off their target from the south, were woefully unaware of any threat other than one they assumed would come from Andorra itself.

Perhaps they imagined some form of sally-forth to assault their barricade, some kind of uprising where the normal people brought their pitchforks against the guns of their besiegers in some desperate attempt to die as heroes instead of living like trapped animals.

Either way, not one of them was looking in any direction other than inwards towards the road they had cut. Lucien had come with me and Dan, another powerful optic brought to bear on the enemy which he didn't get to use as Dan had simply asked to borrow the rifle and not given it back. He raised his other weapon but stopped before bringing it to bear, realising that he did not have any magnification on the assault rifle. I half rolled slowly and unclipped my own, passing it to him one-handed so that he could at least see a little better than with the naked eye.

"I count eighteen," Dan muttered, his face screwed up as he peered through the sight. In contrast I kept both eyes open as Mitch had taught me to but came to a different conclusion.

"Seventeen," I said, "one went inside and came back out wearing a red jacket. It's not a new one."

Dan grunted to accept that, not that he would enjoy being wrong but that he had learned to trust my eyes as they were younger and sharper. We watched until the sun set, and fires were lit to warm them and bathe them in flickering orange light.

"The stupid bastards have literally set up camp on the road," Dan said, incredulity in his voice at the amateur hour he was witnessing, "no reserve base, no separate reinforcements, just... just a bloody campsite behind the barricade."

"Options?" I asked, feeling him stiffen in annoyance as he always did when I used one of his lines before he could say it. Spend long enough in stressful environments with one person and you develop a kind of pre-cognition about them, unless they've annoyed you so much you want to kill them, that is.

"Sniper OP," he said softly, "highest building to the right. Good elevation and not enough cover to get to the far side. Both of you up there. Main assault by vehicle after you start proceedings; shouldn't be too hard as they're not organised. I'll need to go in to clear out the buildings. Me, Mitch and two others; leave Neil with one of the militia with the non-coms back here."

Non-combatants, I thought, *was there such a thing out here?* I pushed that thought away as I ran through the simple plan, trying to find holes in it if I was one of the ignorant defenders who could seize opportunity to break the trap just as I had on the other side of these mountains. Dan didn't prompt me for an answer, he knew I would be thinking and just waited patiently for the response.

"First light?" I asked.

He grunted, this time in a tone I took as agreement.

"We'll stay on station then," I said, "move there tonight to save time."

"Okay," Dan agreed, shuffling back from the vantage point before standing out of sight of the far-off barricade and stretching his old back until it popped and cracked a few times.

"I'm getting too old for this shit," he grumbled, shooting me a sour look in the dying light as I made a grunt of agreement similar to his own. Nemesis stood up from where she lay down after I told her to stay, shaking herself off and shooting out her tongue at Ash's face to make him avoid her pestering, his eyes fixed on Dan's face.

"First light," he said, "see you afterwards." He reached out to bump my first, hesitating before offering the gesture to Lucien who smoothly returned it.

We doubled back, intending to approach the three-storey building from the direct rear to place the hulk of stone and brick directly in between us and our targets. We had our long guns on our backs and I led the way as I was the only one carrying suppressed weapons; an errant gunshot now would screw the plan up a little.

Lucien moved well as his light, strong body was almost as noiseless as mine. Moving stealthily was like that; it was control and strength and above all discipline to keep your body tense but flexible. He had those qualities, and another I held in far higher regard in that he watched someone perform a task and then replicated it. Dan was like that and I suppose I had become like it too.

Monkey see, monkey do. That's what Mitch called it.

Lucien adapted how he moved, keeping to the same patterns as my own as I weaved my way through the scattering of dead buildings towards our target. I knew that my own abilities were a mixture of Dan and Mitch in this sense, more Mitch in truth as I was replicating what he had taught me about fighting in urban areas. Dan had the edge on room clearances, just, but the skills of the British Army and the UK's armed policing manual lived on through me and, in turn, Lucien now. I made a mental note to give some explanations to him as to why I did the things I did, because replicating a skill without knowledge was often dangerous, and found myself actually looking forward to a quiet talk with him.

What the hell is happening to me? I thought. *Focus for god's sake!*

I switched back on as we reached the building we wanted, seeing that two of the ground floor windows had been smashed in or had succumbed to the weather over the years it had stood empty. Deciding on the best way to get to the roof ready for the attack at first light I scanned the only side open to us in the last of the evening light.

Lucien tapped my shoulder making me turn to him and follow the direction of his pointed finger. An external staircase, metal framework showing in silhouette against the lighter sky, stood jutting out of the left side of the building.

"Too risky yet," I whispered back to him, "exposed to the direction of the barricade until dark…" I paused, thinking, and turned back to him to whisper again. "Try and clear inside via the windows, if we can't get to the roof then, we go up there."

He nodded, readying himself to move again. I crept forwards, crossing the only exposed section of abandoned road to stack up against the nearest broken window and glanced back to Lucien who was angling away from me. Just as I was about to call out to stop him, my eyes shot towards his trajectory and took in the sliding glass doors I hadn't noticed. I moved down the building line, Nemesis silently following, and nodded at him before stepping inside and crunching my boots on the pebbles of broken safety glass inside. The floor was carpeted in a kind of rough tile, allowing me to scrape my boot along it to clear a path and avoid Nem picking up an injury. I considered going for the torch sticking out of the right side of the utility rail on my carbine, going so far as to reach out with my left thumb from the vertical foregrip which was placed just right to activate the light, but I stopped myself. Grimy windows overlooked the sloping, low ground leading towards the road and a torch beam could give away our position just as easily as a gunshot. Determined to get the building cleared with the last drops of daylight, I moved fast.

Clearing the corners, checking each room on the ground floor, I found nothing. No sign of recent activity, and certainly no trace of anyone having stayed there. I guessed that would change when winter hit, as I doubted those by the barricade would want to be sleeping outside when the temperature dropped, but for now they seemed to have ignored the building.

It was sectioned off into offices at one point in the past, as ranks of ergonomically curved desks and chairs with back support lay dormant and as useless as the computers they were there for. Moving up I cleared the next floor faster, then took the stairs to the third floor where I sent Nemesis to search each room by herself. I risked her emitting a single bark if there was anyone there, but as the footprints in the dust on the stairs belonged only to us I guessed it was safe.

And that was where our luck ran out.

There was no way up to the roof that we could find, and I turned to Lucien and shrugged, signalling that we would probably have to go back down and up the external staircase. He smiled, walking past me as he held my gaze in the dying light, and went to the large windows on the south-facing edge of the building.

He did something with the safety mechanism, opening a tall window before manipulating two plastic clips and pushing it open wider. Standing back, he gave me a sarcastic bow and invited me to step out onto the steel mesh of the fire escape.

"Wait for a bit," I said, "until it's properly dark."

He frowned and shrugged again, not in a way to indicate that he thought I was wrong but more than he hadn't thought of it, and slipped off his rifle and bag to sit against the wall. He looked up at me, patting the carpet beside him and flashing me a smile of white teeth in the gathering gloom. I slipped off my own rifle, resting it against the internal wall beside his own and shrugging out of the straps of my new bag which hadn't fully moulded to my shape yet. I frowned at that, the sting of losing my equipment still raw, and decided that it would be good to get my own kit back.

It would be better, I admonished myself as I sat, *to get Rafi back in one piece.*

Lucien produced a bag of dried fruit. Apricots and slices of apple which tasted much better than the shop-bought items I loved when I was a kid. We shared them in relative silence, chucking the odd piece to Nemesis who never failed to catch a tasty morsel sent her way, and I began to explain the urban combat manoeuvring I had displayed on our way in. He nodded along with my words, making the odd noise of surprise or understanding or agreement, and I realised I had never felt so relaxed with someone who was little more than a stranger to me.

"It is time," he said as he craned his neck to look out at the night sky, "is it time?"

"It is time," I said, rising and restoring my equipment to my back. I coaxed Nemesis out of the window, reassuring her all the while until I was forced to bring out the leather strap I used as a lead when I had no other choice. That was usually around sheep, as she seemed to be obsessed with annoying them; not that she was ever aggressive towards livestock, not like Ash was with cows, but she terrified them nonetheless.

She whined, unsure of walking on a surface that she couldn't see, but I managed to coax her up the two flights eventually until she could make out the pitch of the flat roof and jumped up. We moved forwards, heading for the slightly raised lip of the side facing our target for the next dawn, and rested down our equipment. I pulled out my bedding roll, which was a compact thing that could be partly inflated for comfort and warmth. Lucien did the same, placing his mat beside mine. I almost told him to move away, that we wouldn't be able to fire from the same position come daybreak, but I didn't. I didn't even know why I let him settle down beside me, his rifle lying down flat on the small bipod at the end of the gun's furniture, just as mine was rested against my bag. I pulled out an extra layer, a light-weight down jacket, and heard him do the same with a blanket which he wrapped around himself. I shuffled to the side of my mat, towards the centre to allow Nem to lay against me, and that had the effect of pushing me closer towards Lucien who, luckily for him, said nothing about it.

"Why do some people call you, Nikita?" he asked me after a

while in barely a whisper, breaking the silence of the night.

"A man called Rich started it," I told him, "he was a Royal Marine, and one of the bravest men I ever met. He had… *problems*, and he would never be able to relax. He called me Nikita because he joked about me being a child assassin. There's a book or something about it…" I trailed off, having no idea why I was telling him everything about me, especially things from when I was vulnerable. I didn't like people knowing that I was vulnerable, and not even that long ago in the grand scheme, but something about the man and the situation made me answer honestly.

"And where is he now, this Rich?" he asked, his pronunciation making the name sound as *reach*.

"He was left behind when we set off to find answers, back in England."

"And what has become of him?"

I sighed, remembering things my mind had blocked out to protect myself from the feelings that came with them.

"The others," I whispered, telling him the abbreviated version pieced together from the radio communication with Steve back there and from what Lexi and Paul had managed to recall, "the ones who stayed behind, they were attacked and taken away to a larger camp where they were kept as prisoners. People think that Rich discovered their plan, and they think he died because of it."

Silence hung over our rooftop as we both looked up at the bright stars, marvelling at how close to outer space you could feel when you were high up and where no unnatural light diluted the inky black.

"That is very bad," Lucien said, no hint of confidence or

cockiness in his words, "I am sorry for you."

"Thanks," I said, shifting my position and inadvertently brushing my hand against his. A jolt of electricity felt like it passed through me, and from his slight gasp I think he felt something too.

"Get some sleep," I whispered, my voice shaking and hoping that he didn't notice, "we'll need to be awake in a few hours."

I woke before the sun was up, but a smudgy-grey line cast an eerie glow over us from behind the mountains to our right. The blanket which had been on Lucien had somehow found its way over my shoulders during the brief slumber, and I gently pushed it off me to roll over onto my front.

"*Bonjour, chérie*," he whispered, stretching out with a wink and a smile as he uncoiled himself.

"Hi," I responded, feeling a little sheepish and vulnerable but unable to hide a smile for too long. "Did Nem, err... did Nem fart in her sleep?" I asked, hoping that any such accidental noises would be blamed on the dog and that would be the end of the matter.

"No," he chuckled, "she did not, but you were speaking..."

I leaned over, careful not to raise my head too much and give away our position in case any sharp-eyed bastard was looking directly at us and wiped the drool from where it had wet my chin.

"What was I saying?" I muttered.

"Something about the smell of burnings," he said almost dismissively, "but as nothing was on fire I decided that perhaps you were dreaming."

I ignored that. I knew exactly what I was dreaming about and if it wasn't being torn apart by dogs then it was replaying the burning of the barn after Joe's death. I rolled over to look at the direction the light was coming from before rolling back.

"Spread out," I told him, "I'll fire the first shot then you take everything to the left, I'll cover the right."

"Okay, *Nikita*," he said, and I just knew without looking at his face that he was smiling that devilish little smirk of his.

Focus, I reminded myself.

I saw some movement stirring in the disorganised camp below, ranging them at inside of a hundred and fifty metres. With our rifles, that distance offered no protection and I smiled grimly to think of the destruction we could rain down on them.

Don't get cocky, I told myself, *get the job done first.*

As the light crept towards the peaks and cast a beam down towards the barricade of cars I heard the muted sound of an engine come to a rest behind us.

"Show time," I whispered to myself, out of earshot of Lucien and ignored by Nemesis.

Strength lies in defence, I thought, not knowing where the saying came from or even why I thought of it then. In that moment I knew everything that these idiots had done wrong, and their downfall was in not garrisoning the building that we were about to use to pour death down on them.

I gave Dan another five minutes to get ready, to drop off all of his non-combatants, and I picked a target to start the day with death.

LEAD RAIN

Crack.

Crack, boom.

I fired first, having lined up on a man who was unzipping his trouser to irrigate the wrecked hulk of a car. He dropped in my sights at the same time as the report of my weapon echoed loudly out across the valley. I switched my aim, knowing that the man was dead the second I pulled the trigger, and found my next victim. Another man, younger but with a wispy straggle of facial hair around his open mouth, turned to look around him desperately. He tensed his muscles to start running, just as I squeezed the trigger and saw him fall in the same instant. Before I had found another target, I heard the duller report of Lucien's rifle booming out beside me. I didn't scan for his target, there was no point, instead I looked for another target to drop.

Boom.

Crack.

A woman, her hair a ragged mess as she ran around the corner of a tent with a rifle in her hands dropped to my next shot, flopping and tumbling as she fell to pitch forwards and drop the gun into the dirt.

Crack.

Another man threw himself down to grab the gun and come up pointing it in completely the wrong direction as the bullet tore through his chest in profile.

Boom.

No targets presented themselves in my area, and a twitch of the barrel to the left to pick up anyone in Lucien's sector. I saw a man in a crumpled heap, blood spurting vertically up into the air.

Boom.

Another man fell, his chest heaving and mouth open as he screamed silently. He hadn't been hit by Lucien's shot, instead he had thrown himself down in terror at the heavy bullets ripping the air around him.

Crack.

I took him down, a shot straight through the chest. Nobody else showed their faces, sensibly in my opinion, so I began putting rounds into the collection of tents and soft-skinned vehicles.

Crack. Crack. Crack. Crack. Crack. Crack. Crack. Crack.

Lucien realised what I was doing, adding the Boom. Boom. Boom, of his gun to the same ends.

It worked, as men and a few women began to pour out into the open as their foolish belief that being out of sight meant that they were out of reach of our guns. Dust appeared in the left of my peripheral vision as, my left eye still open and my right glued to the optic, I saw our van driving in hard.

"Keep an eye on them," I shouted to Lucien, stealth clearly no longer being a concern as we rained down death on them, "and check your fire."

Dan heard the first brutal reports of the heavy rifles ripping the peaceful early morning air.

"Let's fucking do this," he said, whipping himself up to perform with the words as much as they were intended for the others. There were four of them, Ash remaining with Neil and the others despite his grumbling. None of them had slept more than a couple of hours, with someone always awake and alert given their proximity to the enemy.

Dan, much like Leah, held no remorse for attacking these people without warning. Their leader had sealed their fate when he had turned down the sensible offer to release the prisoner and hand over the stolen items, and he had no illusion that these followers were just as piratical as the ones he had already met. To execute one of his own men just to prove a point, just to send a message that he was the biggest, baddest bastard around, sickened Dan to his core.

He threw the van into gear, tyres crunching on the gravelly surface as he floored the accelerator to launch them towards danger. He covered the half mile as fast as he could in the big, ungainly vehicle that was never designed for drag racing over uneven road surfaces. The tyres kicked up dust from the arid landscape as he pushed each gear to the limit of its power band before snatching the next until he arrested their forward momentum with heavy braking to slew them to a stop just outside the range of the killing shots from his daughter's position. He left the engine running, yanking on the handbrake as he slapped it out of gear and slid from the driver's door to round the engine block with weapon raised and body in the pose that was so familiar to everyone who knew him.

Knees slightly bent, body leaning forward into the gun tucked hard into his shoulder and torso fixed as though at one with the weapon, he moved forward on fast feet as his gun began to spit bursts of fire towards the melee ahead.

Bodies were down, strewn in awkward positions where they fell, and those few who ran did so in two directions; away from the danger and towards it.

That was always a test of a person's true nature, and no amount of simulation or conjecture could ever dictate what they would do given any situation. Often those who boasted of bravery would flee, and those who thought themselves cowardly would be the ones who stood and fought bravely.

Only a few of them tried to fight, and a rattling flurry of fire from those exiting the van cut them down in an instant.

"*Arrêtez!*" Dan bawled, repeating the order until all of his team stopped. They were left facing five people, all stunned after being torn from sleep by savage violence and surrounded by unexpected death. They had thought themselves superior, safe from attack, and the realisation that they were neither left them all devastated. Cable ties were produced and used as plasticuffs to bind the wrists of the remaining five, all men, before Dan swept the area one last time.

~

I watched them pour out of the van, guns up, then forced my concentration back to the barricade should any of them still be hiding and pose a threat to my people below. I saw Dan moving, his actions and posture identifying him instantly as he fast-paced forwards. I saw

Mitch sprinting for cover before raising his gun and tracking someone out of sight of our guns before firing off two bursts, and then it was over. I heard the shout to stop, to cease fire, and I flicked my safety on to find Dan in my scope again. He looked directly at my position and waved for us to come down as the prisoners taken, arms raised in surrender, had their hands bound behind their backs.

"Let's go," I said, standing and stuffing my roll mat into my bag before heading for the external staircase and snapping my fingers for Nemesis to follow. She had whined once during the firing but had stayed still at my side, waiting for a command.

In the daylight, the sun still not fully up but bright enough to light the landscape, the fire escape stairs were daunting. There was something about being able to see directly down three storeys through the steel mesh under your feet that unnerved me, even though I had never really been bothered by heights, and even though I forced myself onto the platform I could not get Nem to come.

I reassured her, escalating to giving her firm orders and then shouting at her but, try as I might to cajole her off the roof, she would not budge.

"Will she let me carry her?" Lucien asked from behind the distressed dog, making me think about it. I knew I could lift her, could get her through windows and over walls that she couldn't jump, but I doubted I could manage the staircase safely in case she freaked out and tried to wriggle free.

"Yes," I said, "but be really careful."

I reached out a hand, stroking her head and talking to her in a smooth voice to calm her, then held out the same hand for Lucien's rifle.

"Good girl," I crooned at her, giving him the nod to pick her and raising my voice when her head whipped towards him in protest. He lifted her, far easier than his slim frame would suggest he could but Dan always said that a person's strength wasn't obvious in their size.

I walked ahead, both long rifles on one shoulder and trying to keep eye contact with her as her lip curled in mild threat. The two flights were awkwardly managed, and as we reached the second-floor window we had climbed from only a few hours before Nemesis was struggling to break free from his grip. She almost threw herself out of his arms and he managed to direct her body to flow through the open window. I realised I had been holding my breath. I let it out in an exaggerated sigh of relief over such a trivial challenge and followed inside to take the stairs down to the ground.

By the time we had reached ground level, Nem had forgotten her ordeal and searched the area with her nose glued to the ground as though daylight made everything different. Jogging the short distance over the debris-strewn ground to rejoin the others, I smiled at Dan to communicate the whole, "Hey! I'm glad you didn't all die just then," thing, and we realised our mistake at once.

Shots rang out, coming from past the barricade as we dove for cover, and a pair of meaty thwacks indicated the strike of bullets into a prisoner who fell, crumpled really, wearing a look of shock and agony. He gasped once, then stayed silent.

We had ambushed the defenders, and then the defenders were ambushing us right back.

CLIFFHANGER

"No!" Jack exclaimed, rising up on his knees in protest as Peter held both hands over his mouth in mock horror. "You can't stop there!"

"Well," Leah said in a tone that sounded almost dastardly, "I can't very well just tell you the whole story in one go, can I?"

"Pleeeease?" Peter whined as Jack sat back and looked sullen.

"Tomorrow," Leah said firmly, "you have to go to sleep now and what comes next wouldn't help you do that easily."

The boys stood, Jack ruffling the fur on the back of Ares' head as he passed and both of them took it in turns to hug and kiss their aunt goodnight. Their cousin, Leah's daughter, was a tall, fierce young woman with a broad smile and a quick laugh. She waited patiently in the doorway, her hand held out for the boys to follow her and be tucked into bed. Before they left Jack turned back, his face completely serious as was his manner, and he fixed Leah with a stern look.

"Didn't you feel bad?" he asked. "Attacking the people like that?"

The woman in the chair leaned back, sucking in a breath through her nose and holding it as her eyebrows met in thought.

"Not really," she said, "not now anyway. Not after what we knew they had done."

191

"What did they do?" he asked.

"Tomorrow," she told him, "I'll tell you tomorrow."

Leah rose, taking her evening inspection at the pace of a sedate stroll so that she could enjoy the company of her old dog for a day longer. He had been through a lot with her, had comforted her when she lost Dan and Marie when human contact held too many pressures to talk about her feelings and force her to listen to their opinions. Ares never judged her, always knew when she was upset and the bond between them was, in her opinion, far stronger than she had seen before; even between Dan and Ash.

He grumbled as he sat stiffly, lifting an arthritic hind leg to swing it through the air as he lacked the flexibility to reach the itch behind his ear.

"Oh," Leah said, bending down to scratch it for him and make the grumble turn to one of satisfaction and affection, "poor old bugger."

Ares looked up at her, sneezing once and opening his mouth to pant lazily. She walked onwards, avoiding the steep stairs in favour of the longer way around on flatter ground to save his old legs. Instead of taking in the view from the ramparts as she usually did, she took him around at sea level towards the livestock pens, heading towards the shape of an old woman coming from the pens. Ares stopped to water a fencepost, staggering slightly as he couldn't lift his leg even half as high as he used to be able to. The sounds of chickens and pigs reached her just after the smell which, as unpleasant as it was, meant that they had food and were thriving. The shape became identifiable from how the old woman moved and Leah caught up with her easily.

"You're out late," she said, making the bent shape stop and turn stiffly.

"So is he," Sera answered, her voice a sibilant, toothless croak of the one who had spent years berating Dan at every opportunity. She pointed at Ares, his tongue lolling out as he padded towards them and wagged his tail slowly.

"He likes the evening air," Leah told her as she reached down for him to lick at her fingers, "less people around to stress him out."

"Hmm," Sera answered, giving no indication of whether she agreed or passed judgement, "you checking on the new pups?"

"I was going to poke my head in," Leah said, sounding as noncommittal as possible.

"Hmm," Sera intoned again as she turned away and patted Leah on the arm, "good night then."

"What do you think, boy?" Leah asked Ares, his partly vacant but happy face looking back up at her in the low light of the rare lightbulb fitted to one of the alternator setups. "I know, they're very young…"

She leaned over the gate into one of the stable stalls, seeing Ares' youngest daughter from his second litter returning her gaze tiredly as the six balls of brown and black fur bounced unsteadily over her exhausted body. They were three weeks old, still suckling and draining the poor girl and making her appear thin and drawn. She was being well fed, with fresh cuts of meat and fish with rice and other pulses being brought to her three times a day to keep her strong.

The lineage, started so long ago with a grey puppy found by random chance by Dan so many years before, lived on in the bundles of fuzzy fur on the blankets before her. She knew she would have to pick one of them in a few months, either to replace the old dog at her side or to not miss the opportunity to bond with her new partner at the right time when they were broken away from the bond with their mother. She was racked with guilt, with sadness for the imminent loss of her friend who had shared so many dark experiences and happy ones at her side.

"Life moves on, eh boy?" she said to him, seeing him tuck his tongue back up into his mouth and issue a huff from his nostrils. Switching off the light, she walked him slowly back to her room and slipped under the covers as her trusted companion settled down on the hearth rug. The other person in the bed stirred, rolling over and wrapping an arm around her waist as he tucked himself into the contours of her body. She kissed the hand once, readjusting it for comfort, and closed her eyes.

COUNTER ATTACK

We all reacted at once, dropping our bodies in the instant we heard the first shots ring out. That bullet-time principle struck me again; transforming time into slow-motion as irrelevant facts ran through my brain.

Small calibre, shotgun, semi-automatic, my brain tagged each of the three sounds to reach my ears in the same instant as my body still dropped and twisted to seek cover.

Mitch, further away from the barricade, stood tall and emptied his entire magazine towards the threat in the hope of suppressing whatever attack came our way long enough for our people to get into cover. The sound of unsuppressed firing stopped, only to return as a fresh thirty-round magazine replaced his expended one and the full-auto firing resumed.

I scrambled across the dusty road surface, low to the ground and breathing hard as the adrenaline flooded my system, glancing back to see a snapshot of our tiny force. Nemesis was beside me as I half lay in the tentative cover of a car's wheel. Dan was on one knee low down behind an engine block beside a flat tyre. Lucien, his wavy blonde hair falling over his eyes above his mouth which was wide open with shock and fear, was fumbling to pull his backup weapon from behind him without getting up and becoming an easy target. Mitch still stood, pouring murderous fire like a one-man relief force, until his weapon ran dry a second time in the space of a few seconds and then he too flung himself down into cover. Chloe knelt down, her body half obscured by the tent between us, but her body position was different. She didn't face the threat, nor did she seem to care that her cover stood no chance of stopping a bullet, and she was on both knees facing half away from the barricade. My eyes took it in, but my brain took a split-second longer to figure it out; she was tending to someone lying flat on their back with the toes of their boots pointing skywards.

Casualties afterwards, I told myself, knowing it was bullshit because if it was Dan or Mitch I would be running towards them already. *Deal with the threat first.*

Time seemed to return to normal speed, and with it the sound increasing like the world had been on pause for the briefest of moments. I glanced at Dan who had his eyes boring straight into me and saw him hold up four fingers before pointing at the other side of the barricade. Shouts reached my ears now; Chloe at the rear and other voices I didn't recognise in a language I didn't speak. I nodded, left my battle rifle where it was and brought the carbine round to my front. I got my feet underneath me, staying as low as humanly possible, and headed to my right away from the centre of the road as Dan mirrored my movement to the left side. Mitch still rattled off bursts of automatic fire, his intention not to kill specific targets but simply to keep their heads down for us to get into a position to end the conflict before they dug in. Some shots came back; the booming echo of a shotgun and the answering metallic peppering of shot against the metal skins of the vehicles. A second volley added to Mitch's, Lucien I presumed, and I took two steadying breaths before flicking aside the telescopic part of my weapon sight and swinging my body around the edge of a truck.

Target recognition and assessment, my brain lectured me in Dan's voice, *taking in the scene in an instant and weighing up all of the factors before taking a shot. It's what makes the difference between being a hero and being a murderer.*

He had told me the story, back when he was still healing from being skewered with his own knife by the Frenchman I had shot with a bow and arrow, of how he had weighed up all the factors back in the past and still made the wrong decision. That choice, that action, had ended his career and affected everything in his life to the point where it finally made sense why he enjoyed things so much after almost everyone died. Life just became more... simple.

As my right shoulder, head and weapon popped into view my brain slowed again, the adrenaline being used and channelled to hone my fight or flight instincts into a very sharp blade, and I fired.

Two bursts, one directly ahead and one slightly to the right, and both of them fell at once. My ears registered an echo of my suppressed shots, but in hindsight I realised it must have been Dan firing from the opposite end to drop the third and fourth attackers just as a fifth lost their nerve entirely and ran. Neither of us fired, as I had given the command to release Nemesis into the fray. I heard Dan yelling the order again to cease fire.

She accelerated away like a demon released from hell. Nemesis went to my command of, "Get him!" just as I had heard Dan use the same words to Ash so many times. I was up and following, gun raised in what Mitch told me was perfect symmetry to Dan rising from the opposite end as we tracked the dog and the man who, if he escaped, would destroy our plan.

Now Dan always said that Ash was fast *and* big, but I had to allow myself a moment of pride as Nemesis stretched out to time her leap and snag the man's arm and snatch him off his feet to land face-first on the tarmac and skid to a writhing, screaming stop as she lost her grip on the limb. She skidded and turned, pounced again and landed on his thrashing leg to sink her teeth in for added measure.

"Hold!" I yelled as I moved forwards, not wanting her to injure the man beyond his ability to answer questions. Dan caught up with me, his longer legs striding powerfully as we moved side by side.

"Nem! Back," I called, adding some gravel and dominance to my voice but literally lacking the balls to make it sound as deep and menacing as Dan did.

She released her quarry, leaving him to whimper and sob as he writhed on the ground in his own blood. He gripped his right fore-arm, blood seeping through his fingers despite clutching it so tightly that his fingers and knuckles shone white in the growing sunlight, and his mouth stayed open in a grimace of pain and shock so intense that it couldn't yet find sound. I glanced up, trying to figure out where he was hoping to reach before being brought down, and saw the only building in a wide expanse was one identical to the border post on the far side of the mountains in France.

Dan saw it at the same time, muttering for Nem to watch the bleeding man who wouldn't be able to run away, let alone be of a mind to try.

We went forwards with Dan on my right shoulder a few paces out and approached the small building head on, as being a glass box with views all around it offered no safe direction to attack from un-detected. Our guns moved everywhere our eyes did, able to bring fire to bear on anything we saw that offered a threat, and Dan laid his boot hard against the door to burst it inwards. Nobody was there, but the temperature and smell in the room told me that it was recently occupied, probably by the four who had run back to fire at us from the side of the barricade that we had assumed safe.

'Umption had been made an ass of in that respect, it seemed.

"Must have been using the barricade as an operating base," Dan said, "no wonder they didn't seem switched on; this was where they were standing guard, not there."

A cry of pain from outside pierced the air, lifting our heads. Guns up after exchanging a look, we went back outside to find the person making the noise, and what we found turned my stomach.

In some crude parody of crucifixion, a man and a woman were tied to the posts of the sign directing all vehicles to stop and prepare to be searched. The man, black skinned and long limbed but sagging down in a way that made me worry he had already succumbed to the torture, and the woman beside him who was far shorter and lighter. She was moving, weakly, and her lips moved under closed eyes with only intermittent noises coming from her.

Dan snapped, as he always did when such pointless suffering was inflicted on others, stepping forwards to draw his knife as he simultaneously dropped the gun to fall on its sling. He sawed at the bindings around the woman's chest as he moved behind her, grunting as he worked and made her weak body jerk.

"It's not rope," he growled, "it's electrical cord."

I cast one last sweep of the rising ground behind us leading into Andorra, then dropped my own gun to hang as I pulled the larger blade from the back of my vest. I forced the knife through the thick, rubbery bonds and levered it between the strands to try to stretch and snap them free, starting at the ankles and the hands then attacking the thick loops around his bare torso. Dan had freed the woman, laying her down in the knowledge that she still lived before stepping fast towards me as I struggled to free the larger man.

"They've been here a while," he snarled, disgusted at the treatment of people at the hands of supposedly fellow humans, "she's badly sunburned."

I finally managed to mangle the last strand of flex holding the weight of the man and stepped back as he slumped forwards into Dan's arms.

"Can you get her?" he asked, grunting as he manhandled the floppy weight of the unconscious man up into a fireman's lift, the strain evident on his face as he bent his legs and performed at least a ninety-kilogram squat with an uneven weight over his shoulders. I said nothing, instead going to the woman who was luckily far smaller than the man Dan carried. I was gentle about it, I couldn't be if I had to get it done, and I hauled her up by her arms as her head flopped back and a small whimper came from her mouth as I ducked fast and put my shoulder under her ribs to drive all my strength through my heels and stand with her weight added to that of my own body and equipment.

I walked in short, quick steps to cover the distance back to the barricade and shouted for help as soon as we got near. I left Nemesis watching the prisoner, satisfied that he wouldn't be making a move as the memory of her teeth was still a very painful prospect to him. Mitch heard us first and came running through the gap in the wrecked cars to assess which of us needed the most help. I was both ashamed and glad that he decided it was me, but my pulse throbbed in my temples and I was out of breath faster than any sprint had ever made me. My legs and shoulder burned even after he lifted her off me and carried her back like she was a child.

"Found them tied to a fucking signpost," Dan hissed from

under his burden, "dehydrated and sunburned. Probably been there a day."

Mitch said nothing, instead pressing ahead to where he had dropped his kit bag beside a small panel van peppered with bullet holes of differing sizes. He laid her down, turning to Dan who had arrived just behind him and helped set the man on the ground beside her.

"Top of my bag, I've got two bags of fluids ready to go," he said to me. I didn't answer, there was no need to, instead I just threw open the top flap of his old camouflage rucksack, his Bergen as he called it, and snatched up the IV bags.

"Him first," Dan said unnecessarily, as though I didn't know to treat the unconscious casualty before the one who still made noises.

I pulled his arm into a position where I could extend it and find a vein, squeezing his bicep and slapping at the flesh until I located one. Inserting the needle into his skin I extended the tube leading to the tough, flexible bag and called for some tape. A roll of metallic silver was handed to me and I tore some off to slap it over the bag which I stuck high up on the side of the van.

"Prisoner back there being watched by Nem," Dan said, prompting Mitch to call Lucien in from his position and instruct him to bring the man back.

I repeated the process with the woman, inserting the needle into a vein on the third attempt and taping it to the same level as the other bag. I stood back, looking at my work, when a thought from the brief firefight came back to me like a jolt of electricity.

"Jean?" I asked. "Was he hit?"

"Three in the vest," Mitch said, "he's alright but banged up.

Ribs broken probably."

I looked around to see Chloe kneeling by him, his back propped against another vehicle and his vest on the ground in a heap as he grimaced and screwed his eyes shut. I knew he would be in a world of pain. 'Bulletproof' vests gave the inexperienced wearer a sense of invincibility until they knew the sensation of actually being hit; like being punched by the smallest, hardest fist they had ever encountered and while the bullets hadn't penetrated they had dispersed all of their kinetic energy right into his torso. He was alive, but he was out of the fight.

Scuffs of boots on gravel and dusty road surface turned my head back to the other direction, and I dug back into Mitch's bag and the trauma kit he carried on top where it was most accessible to find a thick gauze pad and retrieve the roll of tape. Lucien had forced the man back under threat of his gun, but he also had the added bonus of Nem quite literally dogging his steps and snapping and snarling as he limped back in tears of pain and fear. I walked over to them, aware that a few sets of eyes were on me, and reached out to grab her collar and haul her forwards almost off her feet.

"Leave him," I growled, more authority in my voice than even I expected to hear and threw the man to the ground where he stumbled on his injured left leg and bleeding right forearm. I drew my knife, the smaller one from my shoulder, and slapped his hands away and he panicked. I cut the material away in a long line to expose the mess of torn flesh caused by my dog and slapped the gauze on it before wrapping the tape tightly over the dressing. I wasn't careful about it and didn't even wash the wound first, which would make it a miracle if it didn't get infected. Dog bites had a nasty habit of doing that.

I drew the knife again, cutting away the dirty blue denim jeans with a grunt of effort as he sat still and watched me with fearful eyes. I repeated the process on his leg, which wasn't injured so badly and was confined to the meat of his calf muscle. I stood, glaring down at him, and saw the hostility mirrored in his eyes despite his attempt to appear non-threatening.

"Someone go back and get the others? Dan asked, patting his pockets for the keys as his mind caught up and reminded him that he had left it running.

"I will go," Chloe said, knowing that neither Dan nor I would want to go, and the other options were her or Mitch as Jean was barely able to breathe, and Lucien had never learned how to drive. Dan nodded his thanks at her and stood resolute, his eyes switching between me checking out the freed prisoners and shooting daggers at our own captive. He said nothing, and the look on his face despite the obvious pain said that he had every intention of fighting back given the slightest opportunity. I had picked that up from his eyes in a heartbeat and I was sure that Dan would have seen it. He was probably thinking of retuning the guy just to put those ideas out of his head if I knew him at all. He satisfied himself with letting Nemesis terrorise him.

The sound of an engine pulled our eyes back to the road and the approaching van, where Neil now sat behind the wheel with Chloe riding shotgun. Alita and Mateo would be in the back, uncomfortable and probably already too hot as the sun gathered in intensity with each minute it rose higher over the mountains.

Neil stepped down after killing the engine, shotgun in hand and a worried expression on his face as he walked forwards via Jean to place a hand on his shoulder and offer a word of comfort. The others climbed out of the van, Ash bounding out to run low to Dan's side and sniff the air to try and figure out what his master had been up to without him. He froze, his eyes fixed on the bleeding prisoner, and a low growl rumbled from his throat.

Neil glanced at the man and the woman we had rescued, noting the bags of fluids snaking down from the panel van to their arms, then shot a look at the bloody prisoner who stared at him with un-disguised hatred. Neil had taken in the results, figuring out most of the facts and needing only to ask a few questions.

"Where were they?" he asked, pointing at the obviously inno-cent people receiving treatment.

"Tied to the border signpost," I told him.

"Been there a while by the look of it too," he said darkly. "What has fucknut said about it?" he asked, meaning the chew toy Nemesis had made friends with. That reminded me, and I called her back and sent her off with Ash to search, just to keep them busy and away from the man who would fetch a torn-out throat if he made the wrong move.

"Haven't asked him yet," Dan said, making us turn in panic as the sounds of scrabbling feet on tarmac sounded loudly. Before I had whipped my head around to face the threat, my hand automatically reaching for the grip of my weapon, my brain registered three meaty smacking sounds.

I turned in time to see the prisoner crumpling to the dirt, his knees made of jelly and his eyes rolled fully back into his head.

"Err," Lucien said, his hands up and balled into fists, "sorry?"

WELCOME TO ANDORRA.
AGAIN.

It turned out that the prisoner, despite having a badly chewed arm and a perforated leg, was a little tougher than he had made out to begin with. The arrival of Neil, coupled with the absence of the two dogs, had sparked him into action. Lucien explained haltingly, clearly nervous at having knocked the man unconscious in a heartbeat, saying how he had snatched out a hand for his assault rifle as soon as our backs were turned and that he had just reacted.

Neil laughed. Dan smirked. I tried to hide a look of admiration.

Mitch had seen the man make his move, had even got so far as to open his mouth and breathe in to issue a warning as he raised his rifle, but as his world moved in slow motion Lucien seemed to remain locomoting at regular speed. He didn't reach for a weapon, didn't step back or lash out to employ any of the distraction techniques learned through years of practice as Leah and Dan had, he simply adjusted his footing and let fly a blurred flurry of punches. The first was a right-handed jab which popped his nose; not a knockout blow but one that he pulled back as a shocker. The second was a left hook which connected low on the right side of his jaw and exposed the left temple perfectly for the right hook which was already swinging in an exquisitely timed arc to land on the left side of his face just above where the jawbone articulated. He was out on his feet, unconscious in mid-air, and he landed hard.

Lucien apologised again, profusely, as he knew that the man would not be able to answer questions with any coherence for many hours if he was any judge of it. He was concussed, that was without doubt, and his cognitive functions and memory would likely take time to reboot properly.

It didn't matter much to me, other than the flutter in my chest at seeing Lucien make good on the boast that he had been Olympic team material, and I asked Dan what was next.

"You tell me," he said, the smirk now gone from his face.

"Can't get a vehicle through there," I said as I pointed at the barricade, "and we have injured who need to rest. Secure here and I'll go in on foot."

"Not on your own," he said, "you and me."

"Fine," I said, "Mitch? You got this here?"

"Aye," he said, "on you go, missy."

From anyone else that would get a death stare, but I let it slide.

"It's a good few miles," I warned him, guestimating from the picture of the area map in my head, "sure your old legs can manage?"

"Fuck off," he quipped back without malice.

We started walking, stepping over the snoring man who was having his hands bound with the same tape, having been tipped on his side so that the blood from his bent nose didn't drown him.

"Keep Mateo off him," I said quietly to Lucien, flushing hot as he flashed me the smile and gave an understanding nod.

I had a thought as we approached the border post and called out to Dan on the other side of the road where he and Ash mirrored mine and Nemesis' path.

"I saw the others using a telephone at the other end in a toll booth," I told him, "worth a try?" He shrugged to try and indicate that making a phone call instead of walking miles uphill made no difference to him, which I knew was bullshit, so I went inside and picked up the phone.

It had a dial tone. I pressed a number and heard a beep, then a click as it started to ring in a weirdly dull tone.

"*Hola?*" a crackly voice said on the other end.

"Hello," I answered, "*Anglais?* Err, *Iglesias?*" I tried. Dan chuckled from the doorway, making me feel like an idiot as I realised I'd just asked for a singer by surname instead of a translation.

"I speak some English," the voice said on the other end, full of darkness and hostility, "what do you want?"

"We're not…" I said, realising that they thought I was one of the people keeping them prisoner inside their own country. "I was here a few days ago, with another man? And my dog…?"

"You are," the voice asked hesitantly, "you are not… *them?*"

"No," I said, "we are most definitely not *them*. Listen, we've just broken their barricade at your south road a—"

"You have what? Please," the voice said, "say slowly."

"We are at your southern road," I said slowly, probably sounding a little sarcastic as I did it, "and you probably want to send someone down here."

A pause on the other end. A staccato rattle of rapid language with rolling R's. A voice that reminded me of the woman in charge.

What was she called? Carla something?

"We come now. Please, no… no *traïcions*."

I could guess the meaning of that.

"They're coming," I told Dan, "they're nervous though."

"Wouldn't you be?"

"Probably. Guns down anyway," I told him. He shot me a look that questioned why I was giving him orders all of a sudden, which I ignored, and we waited.

"Well would you fucking look at that," Dan said incredulously less than twenty minutes later, his eyes shielded by his hand as he looked up at the two vehicles weaving their way down the road towards us.

"What?" I asked, seeing the vehicles at the same time as he did but failing to grasp the importance. It wasn't like vehicles still worked or anything.

"What?" he mocked, turning his appalled gaze on me. "Do you hear any engines?" he said slowly, heavy with sarcasm. I thought about that, straining my ears. I could make out a distant hiss of tyres on tarmac, but I couldn't hear the accompanying engine note to go with it.

"No," I said, "wait, are they…?"

"Teslas!" Dan exclaimed, unable to ever keep something inside and desperate to give over the punchline too soon. "Electric cars."

I shrugged. Using an electric vehicle made sense to me, as long as enough power could be generated from the wind turbines further down the coast from Sanctuary, which were already showing signs of needing maintenance. Not being a boy, I didn't see the attraction with their glee over vehicles and how they always talked about their figures and used acronyms I couldn't be bothered to learn as they were irrelevant to my life.

Something about the speed at which they approached set my spine tingling, and I called Nem to send her away to my left where I told her to get down and stay. Dan did the same with Ash, sending him off to the right where he lurked. No doubt the people in the lead car would have seen the dogs, but hopefully that would give them something to worry about if they intended us any hostility.

The lead car, a deep, shiny midnight blue, stopped twenty paces away as the second car, which was a plain red, pulled to one side of it. It was a very strange sensation to see cars moving and stopping without an engine note. It made me feel like I'd gone partially deaf.

The doors opened, and armed men got out to point little MP5s and shotguns like Neil's new Benelli at us.

"Knees!" one of them shouted in a tone of voice that said he had copied it directly from a movie. "On your knees, now!"

"Fuck right off, sunshine," Dan said lazily, "we've just helped you out, and this is how you repay us?"

I swallowed, it had dawned on me as they approached that the other group could have got inside and taken over, but everything about these people screamed fear of the outside and not the organised chaos I had seen from the ones who had attacked me.

"On your knees, I said!" the man with the small shoulders and the big mouth shouted, stepping forwards as he tried to sound and seem bigger than he was.

"And I said," Dan spoke quietly, "to fuck off." I knew why he had spoken softly, why he wanted the man to come closer and I had to prepare myself to roll with it. Dan would not simply submit to these people who he had never met, especially not to the fake hero who was inside easy pistol shot now.

"You will go to your knees," he said again, a hint of doubt creeping into his voice as he wavered slightly, "or I shoot her."

He turned the gun on me, keeping his eyes on Dan and not knowing how easily either of us could drop him before he got a shot off.

"Me?" I said. "What have *I* done?"

Movie-man switched his gaze between us, panic rising as he had clearly never thought of what to do if we weren't scared of his little sub-machine gun. He hesitated, eventually deciding to threaten the poor, defenceless female to force the big man to comply. He stepped towards me, totally failing to recognise the fact that I was pretty much dripping with guns, as his misogyny thought for him. He wrapped an arm around my neck, almost scared to touch me too much, and held the gun vaguely near my head as he turned me to face Dan.

"On your knees, now!" he shouted again, this time unable to keep the rising panic out of his words.

"*Mistaaaake*," Dan sang with a smile, "you'd be safer laying hands on me, pal. Let her go," he said, still speaking softly before pouring every ounce of threat and promised violence into the final word. "*Now!*"

He didn't, so I winked at Dan and reacted.

My left hand slammed downwards, hinged at the elbow, and slapped an open palm into his groin as my right hand pushed up and moved the barrel of his gun a few inches to make it totally safe if he pulled the trigger. My left hand shot up and gripped the barrel of the gun as my right hand pushed out and balled into a fist before I rammed my elbow upwards into his armpit. The gun clattered to the road surface, and I grabbed his wrist with my left hand before giving him another elbow to the lower part of his ribs. I stepped aside, spinning my body under his extended arm and pushed my weight through the joint and up into his shoulder to flip him onto his back.

In a blur, I whipped the Glock from my chest and dropped a knee onto his chest as the barrel pointed directly between his eyes, almost in an identical pose as the man I had killed when I had been ambushed the first time.

I glanced at Dan to see that he hadn't moved, instead he was just staring at the cars.

"Organ grinder?" he shouted. "Don't send monkeys to talk to us. Come out."

He loves that saying, my brain complained irrelevantly, *I wish he'd get some new material.*

I heard a car door open. It was an expensive sound; very solid and without a hint of metallic cheapness to it. It *clunked* instead of *clicking.*

"*Això és suficient per ara,*" a strong voice said, the R's rolling again before she translated it for ease. "That is enough for now." I winked at the terrified man under my knee and stood, holstering the sidearm and holding out a hand to help him up. He declined the offer, choosing instead to scramble backwards to his feet and shoot me a very wary look. I puckered my lips into a small kiss which I hoped the others didn't see.

"I am Carla Sofia Rovira," she said grandly, transporting me back a few days before I had been through the most recent shit in my

211

life, "and I am the... *or-gan grin-der,*" she finished with an accented attempt at humour.

"We've met," I said, seeing her face showed no new signs of recognition which told me that she knew who I was already.

"Yes," she said, "and since you left our country we have been attacked, shot at by snipers and had our people captured. How do you answer these charges?"

Charges? I thought, unable to believe what I was hearing.

"Err," I said, the sass in my voice coming from nowhere, "since I left your country I've been ambushed, had people try to kill me, had my friend kidnapped, lost my truck, weapons and bag, had to steal a car and walk half the way home only to come back to try and rescue you," I said, my voice reaching a pitch where, in Dan's words, I was close to losing my shit.

"And now," I went on, "after we've broken the barricade on your southern road, killed or captured the people you're so afraid of and rescued a couple others who were tied up, *now* you accuse *me* of being responsible?"

Silence hung for a moment.

"Fuck this," I snapped, "we'll be on our way, and screw you very much."

I turned to Dan, his look of amusement doing nothing to pierce the veil of anger which had descended on me before she spoke again.

"Wait, please..."

I looked at her, eyebrows up expecting an apology which I knew was coming.

"We had to be sure that you were not on the same side as To-mau and his people."

"Tomau?" Dan asked. "Tall? Bit of a fucking arsehole?"

Carla smiled. "You have met him then?"

"Yes," I said, too angry to let someone else speak in case I burst, "he executed his own man just to remove an advantage from us. He still has one of our people, and we'd *appreciate*," I growled through gritted teeth, "a little help instead of…" I waved a hand over the terrified man who was still too frightened to retrieve his weapon as he rubbed his wrist. "Instead of *that*."

Carla spoke rapidly, making the man scurry away from me. The six other men stayed still and silent, none of their weapons had been raised and they all seemed fairly neutral about the one with the big mouth getting humiliated by what they probably still saw as a child. I bent down and retrieved the MP5, the safety etchings beside the trigger guard seeming almost identical to the ones on my own weapon, and found it still locked in the 'safe' position. I held it up as I hit the magazine release catch and kept my eyes on the former owner as I caught it in mid-air. I racked the slide of the gun, expecting a glittering brass round to spin out into the air but nothing happened. I tossed the two parts back to him.

The moron didn't even have a round in the chamber, I thought to myself.

"Oi, dickhead," I called after him. He turned, and I tossed the gun into the air for him to catch which he did awkwardly and, I had to admit, did so in a way that was a little on the feminine side. "You might need that," I added as I sent the magazine through the air after it.

The atmosphere relaxed, and Carla stepped forward for me to introduce Dan. Her eyes met mine, an unspoken question in them as she sensed the strong bond between us. It was something we often got with differing degrees of judgement. I stemmed the flow of incorrect assumptions on her part by adding to the introduction that he was my dad. Her partly open mouth closed, and she hurriedly went on with the conversation.

We filled her in on what had happened since I left, and she did the same from their perspective. Our story ended with the breaking of the blockade, and on finding out that there were injured people she asked for a car to go down and bring them back.

"You'll need to leave a few men here at least," Dan said, "I'm sure they'll have a relief or something coming here after we showed up. Probably reinforcements if they have any sense.

Carla left five men there, keeping only herself and the two men driving the cars to ferry the injured and the captive back to her town.

I went in the first car as Dan waited back with the others, and Mitch came with Alita to bring the unconscious prisoner, who failed to enjoy the scenic drive over the mountain roads on account of being unconscious and being shut into the boot of the car like meat luggage.

Arriving back at the building which seemed to be their town hall only three days after leaving it, I stepped out of the oddly quiet car and looked up at the impossibly blue sky.

"Welcome to Andorra," someone told me.

"Again," I muttered to myself, hoping that this time I would leave in better shape than I had before.

LATE NIGHT

"Nooo!" Peter said, pleading and springing up on his knees as he always did being unable to sit still for more than a few minutes at a time. "Don't stop there."

"It's late," Leah said firmly, and looking over at her daughter, Adalene, who waited patiently for a natural break in the retelling of her mother's adventures.

"Come on, boys," she said insistently in her accented voice, "more tomorrow."

They left their aunt deep in thought, her mind racing back to the time after she had been so cocky, so full of herself to the point that she felt almost invulnerable just as Dan had done so many times before he got himself yet another blow to the head or shot or sliced up or found himself too close to an explosion only to sit there and complain as Kate berated him for needing stitches yet again.

She thought back to a time when she first learned caution, fear even, and it had humbled her. She explored those feelings, rising pensively to pour herself a refill of the fruity liquor they brewed in the town, and gently placed another log on the fire before she sat again.

She had people she loved, people she cared for and felt a sense of responsibility towards them, but she had never faced a sense of sudden and uncontrollable loss as she had back then, and that was why she didn't want to tell the boys the remainder of the tale. She wasn't ready to dive headlong down that rabbit hole that late in the night.

She sat in silence, her thoughts running over an event more than two decades old but still as fresh in her mind as the day before had been to her. Still as fresh as the day she had fled from Dan and Neil in fear, thinking that they were drug dealers or worse, back when she had really been a kid before being reborn into the company of the strange men who had shaped her life beyond measure. Before she knew it, her glass had been drained in small sips and she considered the pros and cons of another. She knew that if she opted for another it could easily become another after that followed by another; such was how she got when she melted back into the feelings of her past.

"Options," she muttered to herself, earning a slight raise of Ares' head as he opened one eye to be sure she wasn't asking him to wake up and lope into battle at her side once again. Just like he had in the Territory Conflicts before she had manoeuvred for, well *forced*, a peace agreement that secured a period of non-hostility in the area where all could benefit in safety. That peace still lasted, and if she was honest her actions over that year in her early thirties were among her finest achievements, after Adalene of course, but carrying and giving birth to her daughter when she was about the same age as she is now had taken a terrible toll on her mind and body and she vowed that she had done her part for the population of the human race.

"Options," she mumbled again, having made up her mind already and rose for a refill, deciding to bring the bottle over to where she sat to save the inevitable and risky journey back after her next glass.

She did this every so often, usually sparked by a story she retold of her past deeds and that of the others who the boys only knew by reputation, but it never bothered her husband as he preferred to go to sleep early and rise before the dawn to slip out and leave her to wake in peace. She called him husband, but there had never been a formal ceremony; just an announcement of their betrothal and commitment to one another. That was enough for the people of Sanctuary, but some still insisted on their old customs of a wedding. She had never been that way, had never dreamed as a girl of how her dress would look and what colour her bridesmaids would wear. Instead she had dreamed of her weapons and training as a teenager and had been sharpened over her formative years into an instrument of warfare to oversee the people under her protection with ruthless efficiency.

She never felt robbed of a childhood, far from it in fact, and never lamented of how things could have been. They just... *were*, and she was okay with that.

She stood, uncertainly, seeing that the fire had burned down to a point where another log would not revive it as she thought and drank. She couldn't leave her dog there, not in good conscience, so she gently coaxed the ancient animal up from his spot and ushered him towards her bedchambers where she removed as much of her clothing as she could in her state and fell into bed.

THE DANGER OF
UNDERESTIMATION

We were welcomed into the country as formally as I had been the first time, only without the air of happiness I'd felt before. Part of that, I knew despite the shame of it, was because I wasn't in charge this time and felt embarrassed about my inflated sense of self-worth. I was back under the leadership of Dan; once again the backup. Mitch never felt, or at least never seemed to be bothered by it, but he had been given orders to follow for most of his life. I had been trained as a leader, and Dan made no secret of that, so I think I felt the lessons that came with adversity and failure to heart more than others.

Either way, we were fed and embraced as friends for a meal and the niceties were observed. A glance at Dan made it clear that he felt as annoyed as I did to be exchanging inane pleasantries when there was a metaphorical wolf at the door and he hurried the conversation onto the more delicate matters until Carla invited us to speak in private.

"How are your people?" I asked, shamelessly manipulating her into feeling an emotional response and break down any resistance she may have had to our suggestions.

"They are better," she said with a frown of concern, "you have our thanks for all you have done for them, and for us all."

The bags of fluids I had got into them went a long way to promoting a revival, and their own medical people had taken over and even treated Jean with painkillers to ease the pain of his fractured ribs. Other than treating the symptoms, there was absolutely nothing that could be done for him. Either way he was out of the fight which at least two of us knew was coming soon. They had their own hospital, a small one granted but it was unmolested and kept in decent repair. Those with any form of medical knowledge had studied and trained to pass on their skills to the point that they had a decent working health system. Kate would have been overjoyed at it, especially as their hydroelectric power supply granted them working X-ray machines.

"You'll need to either block that road completely," Dan told her, "or else garrison it and keep it reinforced. Do the opposite of what they did to you."

Carla nodded, her politician's face showing that she was happy to receive advice on such matters from trusted military advisors but not going so far as to accept Dan's recommendations unquestioningly as she didn't know him.

"Much the same as the smaller mountain road is blocked," she said, "only that was a rockfall in our first year."

"How did they take your people prisoner?" I asked her, changing the subject and seeing her face darken.

"The two people you saved," she said carefully, "were not happy here. Not since Tomau and his people came back. They wanted to leave but I said that they could not."

Dan's eyebrows went up. He would never force anyone to

219

remain inside the walls of Sanctuary if they didn't want to and had even helped a group of people leave our old home years before by providing vehicles, weapons and equipment to see them on their way.

"But they went anyway?" I asked, knowing the answer.

"Yes, and those people obviously did not allow them to pass."

"Much the same as those people"—Dan pointed up the hill to where the tunnel entrance lay out of sight—"won't let you leave either. There's only one way to deal with them."

Her face settled into a mask so as not to betray her true thoughts on his opinion before she spoke.

"But we are not soldiers," she said, "we have weapons, yes, but we do not have the training or the knowledge to fight with them. What would you have us do?"

Even I saw this coming, and I was sure that Dan did too. She was trying to make us volunteer, to suggest that we be the ones to lift the siege on their behalf, to present the problem to the very people that could provide the solution.

"I'm aware that you are a…" Dan hesitated only briefly as he chose his words, but the pause was long enough to indicate a small hint of disapproval, "*peaceful* people, but that doesn't change the harsh reality of the world outside. You have a totally unique place here, and if you want to keep it then you have to fight for it."

"Tell me," she said, gaining control of her words before she spoke too fast or too harshly, "what you would have done in my position?" Dan looked to me, another test to see if I was on the right wavelength, so I answered her.

"Fortify the southern road," I said, "garrison it, just as you should the tunnel and the road over the top. Controlling who comes in and out is the only way to stay safe. When your borders are protected you can farm and scavenge everything you need from here," I said as I waved a hand over the stunning views, "and reform everything so that your people are fed and cared for. You say you're not fighters? Well neither was I, so I had to learn. You can too. There isn't an option any more just to choose to avoid conflict because conflict will find you. Look at the facts," I said, counting them off on my fingers, "you've got resources, some farmland, livestock, a position that can be defended, you've got an endless supply of power, and fresh water. People will want what you have and the only way to stop them is to be stronger than they are."

"Or at least *seem* stronger," Dan cut in. "It's like home security; if your house looks too difficult for a burglar to break in then they will go somewhere else that doesn't pose a risk to them. You can't stop people being people, *especially* not now, but you can out think them."

"But we are past that stage, are we not?" Carla asked.

"Yes," I said, "because the enemy is already here, right outside your gates, and they know everything about you already. There's only one option left."

"And what is this option?" Carla asked. Dan and I exchanged a look.

"The first time we were attacked," he said softly, "back in England where we had an undefended place with resources, we killed every last one of them. Then we went to where they had set up camp and searched for any more. We left nobody who would go off and gather support and come back to overpower us."

"The second time we were attacked," I said, "we did the same."

"And you would have us kill all these people? Without training as you have? Just march into their guns and die?

"Just ask me," Dan said, his tone dropping to one of intense resolve, "just *ask* me the question you want to ask."

Carla looked him straight in the eye, organ grinder to organ grinder, and spoke formally.

"Will you kill these people for us, please?"

"Yes," he answered, "but it will come at a price."

Her eyes widened, and her nostrils flared as her mouth opened ready to let fly a barrage of words before I cut her off.

"We aren't mercenaries," I told her, "we're not guns for hire, but we want an alliance."

She shut her mouth and seemed to deflate slightly, as though she took her finger off the trigger in her mind.

"What are the terms of this *alliance*?"

"Trade. Medicine. Use of your facilities when we need them," Dan said, "in return we offer protection, trade from our own town and the others also under our protection. We would want to come and go, just as you and your people would be welcome to do so in Sanctuary. We can share knowledge, exchange people with specialist skills to pass them on, we can send apprentices to you and you to us. We can be friends."

Carla seemed taken aback, as though she expected to have more than a pound of flesh extracted from her in exchange for us risking our lives.

"This…" she said uncertainly, "this is all you want?"

"I'll take one of your Teslas if there's one going," Dan said with a smirk, "but yes. This is all we want. It's in our interest to stop this bloke anyway; what if he takes over here and decides that he wants to come for Sanctuary next year? Or the year after that?"

"I understand," Carla said, a small smile of relief washing over her face, "so what will you do?"

"We go tonight," he answered without providing any further explanation, "and you need to sort out the defences ready for when it's done."

~

"They have taken the southern road," the messenger said, breathless and travel stained from his long journey around the mountains. The man he reported to kept his head down at the book on the desk, ignoring the arrival of the messenger up to the point that he began to feel distinctly uncomfortable.

"Did any of our people survive?" Tomau asked eventually.

"I," the man stammered and swallowed, "I saw one still lived, he was their prisoner."

"And they are now in my country?"

"Yes, they did not come back out of the blockade, but there are men with guns there."

"Just as there were men with guns there before," Tomau said softly, almost conversationally, "our men, only they failed to hold their position."

The messenger didn't know how to respond. He was starting to regret his choice to return to their leader to report the news, instead weighing up the benefits for simply pointing his motorcycle west and not stopping until he found somewhere safer to live out his life. Perhaps he could have found another group, one who wasn't led by a man intent on capturing an entire country.

"Go now," Tomau said gently, the softness of his voice implying violence if he didn't comply immediately. The man left, holding his nerve just long enough to not run. Tomau finished what he was reading, carefully placing a bookmark neatly against the inner spine of the book before closing it and placing it on the desk so that the edges aligned to that of the desk perfectly. This attention to detail, the fastidious observation of angles and neatness, was a new development for him and he found himself ready to fly into a rage if any of his possessions were disturbed. Now, if the barricade at the southern entrance to Andorra was counted as his possession, it had been disturbed in the worst possible way.

He opened a drawer, taking out a ledger which he kept in a neat hand, and wiped clean a small ruler before removing the cap from a pen. He placed the cap on the other end, aligning it perfectly with the writing running along the length, and scored a perfectly straight line through all of the names under the heading of the Spanish border, all except the messenger, adding a note to one side that one of them was assumed still alive and captive.

He counted the other names, coming up with a total of forty-one which was the true strength of his group despite inflated claims he made to anyone he met from the outside, and knew that he could arm most of them. He planned to advance his people before they could be attacked, and the second wave would be unarmed to take weapons from the fallen defenders.

He had wanted to hold out, to force them into submission and be welcomed home to take command after he had demonstrated his superiority and the weakness in the current leadership, the feeble democracy they all hid behind when times called for a more direct way, but his hand had now been forced and his timeline accelerated.

He had known that the man would be trouble, not when he had first seen him but after he had booby-trapped one of their vehicles and taken two more of his men. He had underestimated his enemy, and between him and the girl who he knew must be with them, he had lost six men at this end and sixteen at the south side. Almost fifteen per cent losses in people and weapons in a few days. He had to put a stop to it before that bleed became fatal.

"Caleb," he called out, "bring me the prisoner. I would speak with him."

"You, me, Mitch, Chloe, Neil," Dan said, "we go through the tunnel when it starts to get dark, Lucien"—the young man looked at him expectantly—"you set off earlier over the mountain road. Your job is to find their sniper and kill him first, then provide cover for us. Questions?"

"How many are there?" I asked.

"Their man didn't want to say," he replied, "but Mateo is quite... *persuasive.*"

"He threatened to cut his nob off then?" Neil asked innocently.

"Pretty much," Dan said, "however he did get the information that we should be facing almost fifty."

"How old is that intel?" I asked. Dan frowned but understood and answered.

"Two weeks, that's when he was rotated onto the barricade."

"Take off seven then," I said, "Nem killed one in the tunnel, I killed two outside and another three on the road. They killed their own man which makes seven, and I'd guess that those were among the bravest."

Dan pulled a 'that makes sense' face at me.

"So we're looking at around forty, of which we can assume most won't be trained given the balance of probabilities, and not all of them will be armed given that the group Leah encountered were sharing one shotgun."

That did make sense, but it sounded a little too much like an assumption to me.

Five of us. Five versus forty with a sniper giving us top cover, assuming Lucien could out shoot his opposition that was. I ran the numbers in my head.

"Eight to one," I said, feeling the unwelcome gaze of a few people who hadn't yet figured out the percentages in play.

"Piece of piss," Neil muttered glumly.

"I've already taken out seven on my own," I said, a little too cockily and sounding like I had no regard for human life, even if it was trying to kill me, "and we did for everyone at the barricade easily enough."

That truth sank in, most of them considering the concept of the force multiplication factors. We were well armed, well equipped and well trained, which stood for a lot when taking on greater numbers, assuming that those numbers were correct.

Assuming.

"We just need to kill eight each then," Dan said glibly, "get ready, we move in a few hours."

Rafi, eyes half swollen shut and speaking painfully through broken lips, answered Tomau's questions. He had no choice, not how he saw it, especially after they had beaten him for most of a day before even asking who he was and where he came from. He had told them about Sanctuary, of the impenetrable walls and plentiful bounty of the sea. Of the farm and The Orchards, of the trading post and of their supply of weapons. Weapons like the one that Tomau held now; its dappled tan camouflage paint fading from the countless times it had been handled. He had told them everything, just to make the beatings stop, and in return he had been given food and water before being locked in a room with just a bucket in one corner.

In the dark, in all the time he had been left alone, which by his disorientated count had been just over a week, he thought of all the people he had let down and especially of Leah who, along with her beautiful dog, would be dead because he couldn't save her.

He replayed the ambush, every brief second of it that he could recall, over and over in his head and found ways to change what had happened so that she got away, so that he wasn't knocked unconscious in the impact between vehicle and tunnel wall, so that he died in her place, *anything* that was different to how it had been.

"How will they attack me?" he asked Rafi in his menacingly quiet voice.

"They will come in force," he answered, "and overwhelm you

with their guns in the first light of day."

"And how many men does he command?"

"Many," Rafi said, "but I do not know how many he will bring."

Tomau made a noise, wondering if the man truly knew the nature of his enemy, and dismissed him with a wave which the guard took as his cue to remove the prisoner who shuffled painfully ahead of him, bouncing off the walls as he stumbled.

Rafi was dumped back in his darkened hole, the door shut behind him, and he took a breath. He straightened, rolling his neck to ease the stiffness in the muscles before flexing his arms. He was battered on the outside, that much was obvious, but he had found within himself a strength that could not be broken. Everything he had said, every scrap of information he had given up in a way that seemed so willing, was incorrect. Although based on fact, he had embellished and understated in varying degrees so that the men who would be facing judgement would do so without advantage.

DARKNESS

Dan, ever prepared, took two bundles out of his bag and handed me one. I unwrapped it, my eyes growing wider at the rare bit of technology that seemed like it had come from outer space in our normal world. The small binoculars attached to the headset, such a small item in the scheme of things, offered a tactical advantage that almost literally made the difference between night and day. The NVGs, powered by the precious batteries squirreled away over the years, made it awkward to walk sometimes but far less awkward than stumbling around in the dark would be.

Dan handing them to me meant that he and I would be taking the lead at the very tip of our small spear, just as soon as the sun set that was. The day was spent organising the men and women that they had assigned as guards, which I thought had been done completely wrong. They had chosen the unskilled, and in some cases the lame and the lazy, as standing guard wasn't seen as an important job. Volunteers had been reluctant, even before one of them had been killed without any warning, and even less so now that the air held a sense of imminent violence, like it was electrically charged.

I inspected weapons, offered tips and reassurance, ate with them and talked with them through Alita who had attached herself to me alongside Mitch. The smiling Scotsman had drawn a lot of gazes, from the vest he wore festooned with weapons and gadgetry to the big rifle and its underslung grenade launcher. We must have seemed like paramilitaries to them, or even something from a movie. They relaxed during the afternoon, talking more with us as they warmed up to our presence and seemed to feel comfortable enough to talk more.

We learned that, among everyone in Andorra, there were no warriors or soldiers or even anyone with any experience left. They only had a small police force and had no army to speak of. Being landlocked in the mountains they obviously had no navy either. Everyone left was either trapped there on holiday or else working in the tourism and service sectors.

I smiled when they said that, claiming a simultaneous innocence and apology that they weren't a war-like people, and told them a little about me.

"I was twelve years old when it happened," I told them, "I was a child, not a soldier. I learned how, learned from people who knew different things." I glanced around them, seeing them all glued to my words and hearing the cogs turning in their heads. "I learned things that the army taught," I gestured at Mitch.

"*British* Army," he corrected dourly, softening his admonishment with a wink. I bowed my head sarcastically. It mattered to him, just not to me because I was never part of it.

"Dan taught me things that the police learned too," I went on, "and Neil taught me other skills, as did Marie and another friend called Paul; someone else taught him about guns but he taught me how to fight without them. All of these things, these skills." I paused for Alita to catch up with my words after she placed a hand on my arm. "These skills were passed on from person to person, just as I pass them on to new people and they will change them and pass them on again. That's how we stay strong. That's how we survive."

They nodded in agreement, exchanging looks with one another and I dared to think that they were hopeful.

I left them with Mitch and Alita in the late afternoon, walking Nemesis at heel to the toll booth which was on high alert in comparison to the last time I had been there. I felt a sense of doom in a way, remembering the last time I had been there with no clue that I was going to have to fight for my life only a minute or so later.

I found Lucien there, beside the road to the right to afford him the best view into the tunnel as it bent to the left. Despite being exposed to the sun, he held his position as he lay down with his rifle, keeping watch on the dark scar in a bright landscape like it was some haunted doorway to the attic of an old house. Fear emanated from it, and just looking inside it made me feel colder. Three kilometres on the other side of that gaping entrance was our enemy, and with them the promise of conflict.

"You should rest," I told him, "we didn't sleep much last night."

He answered with a chuckle in rapid French, of which I only made out a few words.

"What was that?" I enquired sweetly, hiding the edge in my meaning.

"I said nothing," he answered as he stood, smiling and looking at me funny.

I thought I heard something involving the word 'wish' and my mind filled in the blanks.

"Anyway," I said, trying not to blush, "you should rest."

"I will be fine," he said, "how is it you say? Sleep when you die?"

"Sleep when you're dead," I corrected him pointlessly. "Fine, you'll need to set off soon and I want you to take Nem."

He looked at me, glancing down at the dog and back up to my face wearing an expression of uncomprehending confusion.

"How will I…?"

"I'll show you," I said, "the commands are simple; you tell her to heel, stay, get down."

"And she will do this for me?" he asked.

"She will if I tell her to," I said, "if you need her to take someone down you tell her to *get them*, and if you have a prisoner you've disarmed then tell her to *watch him*. It's that simple."

Lucien still glanced between me and the dog, trying to fathom whether it was that easy and whether I was serious.

"Try it," I told him, seeing him look at Nemesis and having his interest returned almost comically.

"'eel" he said, culturally unable to pronounce the *h*. Nemesis glanced up at me as though double-checking whether she should obey, and I told her to go on. She went, circled around his legs to sit down at his left side and looked up at him.

"Good," I said. Try a few more.

He walked forwards, looking down at her and making eye contact, and stopped before telling her to get down and stay as he walked away and turned back to see her lie on the ground where she had been left. She still glanced at me, still checked that she should be playing this new and confusingly simple game.

"'eel," he said again, smiling as she streaked towards him, ready for another command.

"Yeah," I said, "it'll work."

The locals took over the watch, allowing us to reconvene and be fed a meat and vegetable stew called *Ollada*, apparently, and was served with a heavy fresh bread that I had to force myself not to eat too much of in case I was slowed down in the night when I needed to be slick and switched on. I saw Dan push his own bowl away, leaving food which was something I had literally never seen him do. Mitch, sitting opposite me, stared at me until I met his gaze and responded to his smile by handing over the chunk of bread I had left. Unlike Dan, Mitch never missed an opportunity to eat or sleep, or even take the piss out of anyone he considered a friend.

The meal was eaten quietly, the knowledge of what we were about to do weighing heavy on the mood, and we all felt restless to get it done. Dan stood, thanking Carla quietly for the meal.

The last meal, I thought stupidly, allowing doubt and fear to creep into my head when I should have banished it in an instant.

And we left, heading for the darker black of the tunnel entrance as our small band of warriors moved with purpose. Lucien had already left an hour earlier, taking the looping route up and over the mountain to approach with the last of the light and hopefully find the perfect position to watch over us from. Dan would, if he had put himself in their position, be expecting an attack at first light. That was why we went in darkness to infiltrate beyond their lines well before daybreak.

"Stick to the left wall," he said in his low voice, "follow it all the way and if there's an obstruction we'll tell you."

"Gotcha," Neil said in a voice that wasn't his own, the stress of the situation still unable to prevent him from using an accent. His hand gripped the lead around Ash's neck, the dog watching his

233

master intently but a veteran of so many missions that he waited for his turn to be called up with all the professionalism of a seasoned soldier.

We set off, Dan and I with the bulbous binoculars strapped to our heads as we led the way into the dark. I glanced back once, seeing the line of Chloe, Mitch, Ash and Neil as they snaked their way inside and kept contact with the wall to guide their walk into the inky black ahead. In my goggles the dull sky outside the tunnel's entrance flashed brightly, forcing me to turn back to the ethereal green glow of the empty roadway ahead.

I always felt weird walking with night vision goggles on. Going through that tunnel made me wonder how the hell Steve ever landed a helicopter on a moving ship in the dark. I didn't know how he ever flew a bloody helicopter to be honest but that was him.

Moving through the ghostly glow of the dusty road I could hear my own breathing loud in the wide confines of the tunnel. It was both too big and echoing, yet claustrophobic at the same time. I concentrated on my footfalls, concentrated on pacing properly and scanning every darker patch of green ahead of me as though each shadow could hold one of them with his weapon trained ahead just waiting for us to step into their firing line to light us up and end the plan before it had started. I didn't want that, obviously, but something about the darkness unnerved me. I missed Nemesis at my side and thought that her body pressing into my left calf as I walked forwards would have given me the strength to keep my mind glued to the task.

I knew from my random decision to check the distance on my first trip driving through that it was about three kilometres, and at our walking pace moving tactically it would take us at least half an hour, probably more with the other three shuffling along in the dark without goggles. Knowing that didn't help me, because I hadn't checked my watch when we had set off.

I steeled myself, pushed my nerves aside, and pushed onwards.

"Stop," Dan said softly, just above a whisper and not loud enough to carry too far ahead. I stopped, turning awkwardly with the added weight sticking out the front of my skull to look at him. I took two steps to my left to be closer to him as my eyes faced forwards.

"The others need to stop," he said, "they're disorientated. You can see it in how they're walking."

I looked back, seeing what he meant as I focused on Neil at the front. His mouth was open, his eyes wide in the vain attempt to find more light and make them work again. His left hand traced the wall as his feet shuffled uncertainly as though he feared stumbling on something. Dan stepped closer, speaking so softly to them that I couldn't hear him. I dropped to one knee, keeping watch ahead as I felt the stiffness in my neck and back cramping. I tensed the muscles, rolling my neck and shoulders to try and ease it as I marvelled at how Dan had learned that skill of speaking in the black night and not be heard. An amateur would whisper, thinking that would prevent their words from travelling, but at night that sound would carry further than the soft words he employed. That was another trick of his that I tried to mimic.

We gave them a few minutes, the soft murmurings of Dan's voice barely audible as he reassured them. I knew how vital it was to move like this, silently and undisturbed, but that didn't make the task any easier. I couldn't imagine how hard it would be without the ability to see anything.

He gave the order to move again as the tunnel straightened for almost a mile and my legs began to burn with the effort of moving slowly. I thought I could make out a different shade of lighter dark ahead. I didn't know if my mind played tricks on me, whether I could begin to hope that the unexpectedly difficult ordeal was drawing to a close, and then I saw it.

I stopped. Slightly behind me and to my left I heard Dan stop too. I took two slow steps forwards, trying to be sure that the straight line I had seen at the very edges of my field of view was there or not. That was one of the odd side effects of using the goggles; I couldn't gauge any depth when I wore them, but it was there.

"Access door," I said quietly.

"Where?" Dan murmured.

"Ahead and right," I said, "thirty paces."

He stepped back and I felt the absence of his presence near me. I heard him speaking softly to the others, probably telling them to wait there for us, then the air beside me filled with the sense of him.

"Go," he said.

We went. I went to the right side as Dan went down the left. I stopped ten paces short, scanning the dark road ahead and clearly able to make out the semi-circle of the tunnel entrance in the electric-green gloom. Then I saw it and froze. Dan must have seen me go very still as I couldn't detect any sense of him moving on the far side of the roadway.

The guard sat in a chair near the entrance, tipped back so that it rested against the wall of the tunnel, and the faintest of snoring noises rattled towards me. The door was closer to me than the guard was, but there was no way we could get past them or inside without disturbing them. Going inside the door, into unknown territory in the pitch black, would leave an enemy behind us. That wasn't an option, obviously.

I turned my head slowly to Dan, careful not to move fast and disturb the air too much, but the guard stayed asleep. I pointed to the door and the guard in turn, seeing the ridiculous binoculared face of Dan turn to gauge the distance between us and the door, then the door and the guard. He looked back at me and I saw the twin circles of his goggles bob slowly up and down.

He took his right hand off his weapon, indicating with a bladed hand for me to take the door as he gripped the weapon again and stepped stealthily forwards. I reached the door, sinking very slowly to one knee so that the barrel of my gun pointed past the door towards the sleeping sentry. Dan came into view on my left, moving so slowly and silently, until he was within six feet of the chair. His carbine lowered, inch by inch, and when the barrel no longer pointed at the guard his right hand slipped away again and reached across his body to return bearing the Walther with its fat protrusion extending from the end of the gun.

Discovery was at the most heightened danger then, with either a shout or a flashlight able to spell our end, and I held my breath as he covered the final few feet and paused. He pushed the gun forwards, pressing the suppressor hard into the flesh beside his windpipe as his left hand clamped over his mouth. I wasn't close enough to hear, but I was certain that Dan would have shushed him. The man, woken in terror and darkness, rose from the chair very quietly and slowly, the front legs touching down on the road surface with the barest of sounds. He stood, and Dan's left hand ran swiftly over his body to remove anything he could use to escape or raise the alarm. He was turned and began slowly walking towards me as Dan held the back of his collar with his left hand and pressed the barrel of the

Walther into the right side of his throat. I knew why he did that; he was ready to shoot out his windpipe and weigh up the risk of the suppressed gunshot and the subsequent noise of the round hitting the concrete wall and flattening against the risk of a shout being heard. Dan reached me, slowly pushing him down to his knees so that his wide, terrified eyes shone brightly in my view. He seemed to look straight at me and I didn't know if the outside world offered some slither of light that he could see me in or whether he just sensed that someone was in front of him. I heard the *zzzip* and a small grunt as his hands were bound behind his back, then saw Dan reach around his neck in an exaggerated way to hook his right fist up behind the sentry's left ear. He issued an involuntary noise, a hint of a strangled yelp before he was unable to utter any other sound. His feet began to dance manically on the roadway and I lowered my gun automatically to secure his boots and keep the noise to a minimum. It took Dan maybe twenty seconds to put him out; strong forearms cutting off the supply of blood to his brain and rendering him a ragdoll who posed no threat for a while.

He was lowered gently to the ground and Dan rose, chest heaving from the effort of his burning muscles squeezing the man into unconsciousness, and he raised his gun again to turn back to the door.

I stacked up behind him, just as I had been taught, and placed my left hand on his left shoulder to indicate that I was ready. The drills we had practiced and perfected over the years had never been more important than they were then in the silent darkness as he opened the door. There was no lighter glow from inside, no sudden flash of light to white out our goggles, meaning that there were no lights on inside. There were only three rooms inside, one locked, one bearing ranks of electrical switch boxes, and one containing a grubby mattress and a shape in a sleeping bag. He lay on his back, mouth open and a chesty wheeze emanating from it, and his eyes shot open like headlamps hitting full beam when Dan simultaneously put a knee into his abdomen and pressed the tip of the suppressor hard under his nose.

Whoever he was, he got the message instantly. He didn't make a sound, didn't offer the slightest hint of resistance as he was bound and had a discarded T-shirt used to gag his mouth. I used another cable tie from my own vest, looping it through a second to secure them around a thick pipe and his neck to keep him sat up and still. Dan wordlessly went back outside and brought the other one in, still totally off the planet, and he was tied up beside him. I knelt down to put my face beside the conscious man, his face bumping off the goggles as I had forgotten he would be closer than I expected, and I asked a simple question after removing the gag and pushing the barrel of my weapon up under his chin.

"*Combien?*" I hissed. How many?

"*Ici?*" he answered in a quavering whisper. "*Deux.*"

Only two there. Perfect. I relayed this to Dan, and the others were brought inside. He went to fetch them one by one, leading them back with their hands on his shoulders until they were safely inside the windowless room. Only then did Dan warn them to shield their eyes before clicking on a tiny flashlight to bathe the small room in a dull, red glow. White light would have blinded us all, ruined any night vision the others would have developed, and the warning allowed me to finally remove the goggles and stretch my neck from the cramping effort of holding that small amount of extra weight up for so long.

My estimation of how long it would have taken us to walk

through the tunnel was ridiculously wrong, as Dan muttered to me that it had been a little over seventy minutes since we had set off, adding that we had three hours before sunrise.

Which meant it was two hours until game time.

We Meet Again, Mister Bond

I shot a glance up to the ridge above me, knowing that I wouldn't be able to see Lucien but hoping for some kind of connection with my guardian angel, meaning the devastating power of the 417 he held, and convinced myself that I wasn't thinking about him. We crept forwards towards the town, following the whispered directions of the conscious guard who was only too happy to tell us exactly where the people were housed in the town.

They had taken over the hotel which was at the furthest end of the tiny town, still in view of the tunnel entrance, but he helpfully informed us that a path ran from there to the tunnel which is how he went to his post each night and returned each morning. The other one had woken up, panicking at being so restrained, and insisted on making a desperate noise through his gag which resulted in Neil administering something he liked to call 'manual anaesthetic' via the medium of the butt of his shotgun to the head.

After that, the chatty one got even chattier.

He tried to explain that he had never hurt anyone, that all he did was stand guard at night and never involved himself with the politics of the others. He said that he barely knew their leader, some former policeman from Andorra which is why they had roamed back through Spain to take the country. He said that he wasn't a violent man, that he hadn't hurt anyone or taken part in any ambushes or attacks, and that he was only with them because they wouldn't let him leave.

I had believed some of what he said, not the parts about his hands being clean of all wrongdoing, obviously, and asked him where they would have taken Rafi.

"In the hotel," he had assured me, "on the first floor. There is a storage room beside the staircase where they keep him."

I had thanked him, leaving him to sit in silence for a moment, before looking at Neil and inviting him to step in with an open-handed gesture. He stood, readjusted his clothing, and applied a second dose of manual anaesthetic.

We followed the path, the dull glow of a lighter grey sky making the skyline behind us barely visible, and we followed the path towards the lights. They kept guards stationed there, just as lazy and unconcerned as the ones sleeping in the tunnel, and we stayed back in cover to watch them. I took off the goggles as they were more of a hindrance then and looked at Dan where I could just about see well enough to make out the dark and thoughtful expression on his face. He shuffled back from our makeshift observation post and reconvened in the dead ground.

"Chloe," Dan said, "swap your four-one-six for Neil's shotgun, then go back to the tunnel and collect their weapons. When you get the signal, you start firing their guns like there's a fight going on. Hold that position and shoot anyone coming to investigate who isn't us. Understand?"

"Yes," she whispered, "what is the signal?"

"An explosion."

Silence.

"Okay," she said finally, retreating to make her careful way back along the path to the tunnel.

"An explosion?" Mitch asked carefully.

"What's the range on your bomb-lobber?" he asked.

"Three fifty to four hundred," the Scotsman answered blankly.

"Good," Dan said, offering nothing more for a few tense seconds before adding, "they'll be expecting us to attack at dawn, right?" The question was rhetorical. "So we hit them before sunrise. You fire a 40mm towards the direction of the tunnel and Chloe starts rattling off like there's a firefight happening there. They'll come out of the hotel and we drop them."

"Easy as that?" I asked, filling the silence that fell after the plan was declared.

"On my signal," Neil intoned in a Hollywood voice, "unleash hell."

"Yeah," Dan said, ignoring Neil's inappropriate levity, "we take the rest as it comes. Get ready, spread out. Mitch and Neil take centre and we'll take left," he said meaning he and I would be the ones to cut down anyone making it out of the door and heading towards the tunnel, "and confine fire to ground floor only, remember we have a friendly on the first floor."

We settled in, gun barrels pointed towards the small hotel in the cluster of the twenty buildings in the small town. It was the biggest building there, and as the grey of the sky grew lighter it showed its bulk more clearly. Dan checked his watch repeatedly, his nervous tension evident and picked up by Ash who fidgeted and nudged him until a reassuring hand went to his large head.

Still a puppy, I thought, *no matter how big and bad he is.*

The fact that I could make out the shape of Ash beside him reminded me that it was almost time to start; to wage a tiny, small-scale war between a handful of hairless monkeys on a ball of rock and water spinning around the biggest natural power plant going. In the grand scheme of things our imminent conflict was irrelevant, but to us, right then, it was all.

Dan knew it too, as he could make out enough detail below to start proceedings.

"Mitch," he hissed, "now."

Mitch wriggled back down into the dead ground and rolled on his back to point the rifle up and away towards the direction of the tunnel. He gauged it from memory, aiming further to the right to be sure he didn't accidentally pepper Chloe with shrapnel, and pulled the trigger of the launcher. The metallic and percussive *ffoomph* of the small bomb launching up and away in an arc had barely faded when the sharp pop of the resulting explosion echoed loudly out over the small valley. Silence followed, and I saw the two men outside the entrance to the hotel stare at each other in sudden, uncomprehending fear. They had obviously been told to expect an attack later in the day, not when the sky was still dark, but the sounds that followed spurred them into action as they ran inside and shouted loudly.

Boom, rat-at-at-at-at, boom-boom.

The sounds of Chloe's mock gunfight drifted down to our position, clear and precise and very convincing. She fired intermittently, clearly pausing as she set down one weapon and picked up another as though two people exchanged fire in panic from cover.

"Get ready," Dan said unnecessarily, as they began to run out of the main doors to the hotel in ones and twos. Mitch sensibly left the first few, allowing us to pick them off with measured bursts from our suppressed carbines before the majority realised they were under more direct attack than they feared.

They ran blindly into our kill zone, only faltering when bullets kicked up sparks from the road and the crumpled bodies of the others before the accurate fire cut them down. The flow faltered, as though only a handful were dressed enough to join the fight. I counted nine down and called over to Mitch who still hadn't fired a shot in anger yet.

"Stir the nest," I said, meaning for him to start stitching the windows of the hotel, but instead he rose to one knee and reached for the trigger mechanism under his barrel again.

Ffoomph-BANG, the launch and answering detonation sounding as though no time separated them at all. Mitch slid open the breech of the fat tube and pushed in another of the 40mm bombs from his vest, snapping back the open section and pumping a second one into the windows on the left side of the ground floor this time.

It worked. People ran from the main entrance where they had clearly been cowering and waiting for orders, and the staccato rattle of the unsuppressed rifles of Mitch and Neil rang out loudly in the grey end of night. Bodies fell, some answering the barrage with shots of their own indicated by the differing light shows of muzzle flashes from inside. Glass shattered everywhere until the return fire simply stopped.

"We've done it," Neil answered, then ducked and swore savagely when bullets began to impact on the rocky ground ahead of him. He tucked up like a hedgehog and threw himself down the slope to avoid death, which for some unknown reason I found hilarious in the moment. It stopped being funny when the intensity of the returning fire grew so strong that Mitch was forced to duck back also. He looked at me, the whiteness of his eyes just visible in the growing light, and the head they were set in shook. I poked my head above the crest to see muzzle flashes and silhouettes on the roof as they poured fire down at the position in front of the main doors.

Trapped, my brain said, *no way out of the dead ground. They have the height advantage.*

I popped up, pointing the barrel of my gun at the moving shadows on the roof, and let fly the whole magazine in three long bursts. Dan did the same, sixty rounds flying towards half-seen targets in the hope of killing or suppressing them, but the fire turned on our position and forced us to duck back down.

"Fucking bollocks!" Dan roared, the fingers of his right hand dabbing at a cut on his cheek where a slither of stone had been thrown up by the onslaught.

We were pinned down, still with probably half of their force in play, and it was all going to shit.

There was this brief moment of fear, fear of failure more than death, as each of us tried to figure out a way to break the deadlock. As I took a breath, fresh magazine seated in my carbine and heart beating out of my chest, I rolled a metre to my right and prepared to rise again and pour fire back at them. Just then a sensation of warmth, barely detectable in the chaos, touched the back of my head and made me turn to see the sun crest the mountains.

Then, the sweet sound of a high-velocity bullet passing through the air ripped my senses back to the present. It was followed by more, each of them coming down at a steady, rhythmic rate like some wrathful and vengeful god smiting the unworthy.

Lucien had crept up the winding road during the evening, his eyes alert for any sign ahead of the enemy, but the dog walking uncertainly beside him made no sound to warn of another human being in sight or smell. Nemesis had spent the first hour issuing small whines as she looked back down the road, clearly not fully understanding why her master had left her. That abated when the town below dropped from sight, as his careful movements forced her to recognise that the prospect of enemy was a realistic one. She stalked beside him in silence, claws clacking only occasionally on the smooth tarmac, which had baked dry during the hot day, until he reached the summit of the road. He moved off the easy path, electing instead to angle across the rocky ground to where the two roads would converge and make his careful descent under the cover of darkness to a spot he had picked out at dusk, and he sat and shared his snack with the dog.

Taking his time so as not to disturb the night air, he crept forwards with the dog and settled himself in beside a sparse bush to overlook the town below. And he waited.

A sudden popping explosion tore him from a daydream he had lapsed into as Nemesis raised her head and growled deep in her throat. Gunfire echoed back, sounding like a battle was taking place below him but he saw no sign of movement or muzzle flashes to support what his ears were telling his brain. Before he understood that, more gunfire rang out with another pair of muted explosions, and the angle of his spot hid the source from his sight.

"*Faut-il partir? Faut-il rester?*" he asked himself, receiving a nudge from Nem and decided that they should go instead of staying where they were. Moving, he knew, was risky because the sun was starting to rise in the far-off landscape over his left shoulder, and detection as a sniper was fatal.

He went, leaving his bag and roll mat where they were in favour of speed over comfort. He ran, skipping low over rocks and clumps of stiff grass until he half saw the flashes of gunfire ahead and below him. He dropped to the nearest patch of flat ground, settling himself as he squirmed towards the battle, and put an eye to his scope. Ten or more shapes poured from the hatch, where they stopped near to the ledge of the roof and aimed their weapons ahead of them. Firing sounded heavy and constant, faltering only once before resuming with greater intensity than before, and just as the sun broke cover to illuminate them, he fired.

Boom.

Two of them fell to one bullet, so he switched his aim and squeezed the trigger again to drop another two and spill a third over the unprotected edge to fall to the ground below. He fired again and again, not taking such careful aim but just pouring the heavy bullets into the people who threatened his own, who threatened his friend and the young woman he suddenly decided that he very much wanted to see whole once more.

˜

"Pretty boy!" Dan exclaimed gleefully, readying himself to rise and fire again. We did so as one, popping up like reanimated corpses to unleash a coughing rattle of hell and death at the bastards who had trapped us in the dead ground below them. And just as rapidly as it had begun, the firing stopped. Nobody could have been alive or showing themselves on the roof as the cracks and booms of the distant rifle ceased, and as I scanned the shattered glass of the entrance to the hotel I saw the most bizarre of things.

A table cloth, at least I guessed it was one, hung limply from the barrel of a gun as the man carrying it stepped into the light with his hands held wide.

"Mitch, Neil," Dan said, "hold position."

He rose to his feet and I followed, as did Ash. We stepped awkwardly down the slope and raised our guns, stopping in the only low cover between us and the man appearing to surrender.

"Everyone out," Dan called, "slowly."

The man turned back over his shoulder and spoke. I hadn't clearly seen his face when I had him in the scope of my bigger rifle the first time, but the way he carried himself was the same. This was their leader. Six others came out, the last of them with a long barrel protruding over his shoulder and a pistol held against the head of the person he pushed in front of him. He I recognised instantly, despite the bruised and swollen face.

"Rafi," I said to Dan, just in case he hadn't realised. In answer to his reaction at seeing our man so mistreated, Ash issued a low snarl as though he was our elected spokesperson.

"I must congratulate you," the man with the makeshift white flag said in a tone of voice that made my trigger finger twitch, "I expected you to come, but you have done well."

"Shut your mouth," Dan snapped at him, "drop your weapons and let him go."

"I cannot do this," he answered stiffly, "until you allow me to go."

"Let him go and then ask," Dan responded hotly, "you don't have a choice here."

"This is where you are wrong," he said, a smile creeping over his face as he dropped the white cloth from the end of the gun and exposed what he held.

It was my M4, the sight of the faded dappled tan camouflage sending me into a rage. I held my nerve, and if Rafi wasn't there I would have filled the bastard with holes, but I couldn't with his life so endangered.

He solved that problem for us, pitching forwards as though overcome with sudden pain as he gasped and whimpered. The gun fell away from his head just long enough to provide a clear shot, and I took it.

I wasn't the only one, as Dan's own gun spat a single bullet at the same time. The remaining men raised their weapons uncertainly but didn't fire. Tomau looked shocked, defeated almost as the panic of losing hit him. Rafi stood, dusted himself off and walked stiffly to stand in front of Tomau.

"Rafi, move!" I yelled. He ignored me.

"The others should go free," he said, half turning towards me but keeping his eyes on the man, "but this one cannot."

The five surviving members of his gang of mercenaries backed away, distancing themselves from him as though they understood that their survival depended on disassociation from their leader.

His eyes narrowed, and he began to raise the weapon to Rafi who snatched at the barrel and pushed it down. The two men tussled, pushing and pulling as the others scattered away from the danger of a stray bullet hitting them as Tomau's finger squeezed the trigger involuntarily to stitch a handful of rounds into the shattered front of the building. Tomau broke free, losing his hold on the gun as he did but whipping his hand to his hip and bringing it back with a pistol gripped firmly. Gunshots rang out and he seemed to dance and pirouette before dropping to the ground almost gracefully. He was done. Dead. And his siege of his country was ended.

Repair, Rebuild, Move On

The surviving five, together with the two groggy prisoners from the tunnel, were given food and water for a day and forced into a vehicle found in the town. They were very clear on what would happen if they were seen again, and their instructions to head back to Spain and not head this way again were taken with a solemn silence. The man emerging as their leader, or at least their appointed speaker, tried to apologise for the actions of the man they had fallen in with. Dan didn't want to hear it, and he stopped trying to explain. Neil had driven back through the tunnel to return with a strong contingent of others to collect weapons and resources from the town they had been denied access to.

After being searched for anything of use as a weapon, the survivors were sent away and not seen or heard from again.

Carla had asked Dan why he had let them leave, and he turned on her with an anger that she didn't truly deserve as the last of the adrenaline left him.

"Because I've had enough of killing," he snapped at her. "I'm a protector, not an executioner."

She backed away, wary of his hostility, but busied herself with taking control of the people and reform them in the image of the future she had been shown by our words.

I sat with Rafi, using my small trauma kit from my vest to clean and dress the worst of his wounds which had already scabbed over. A cut on his head should have been stitched, but the time for that had passed and he would be left with a long scar for the rest of his life. One of the smooth electric cars came back, unnerving me as it made its almost silent and alien progress towards me, and they took him back to the hospital for treatment and rest.

As I watched him being driven away a bark behind me made me turn I bent and slapped my hands onto my thighs to make Nemesis bound forwards towards me as she slunk low to the ground and wagged her tail rapidly. I fussed her, looking up from the direction she came from and saw Lucien approaching with his rifle cradled in his arms like a baby. He reached up and swept the hair off his face, smiling as he stepped close. He opened his mouth to speak, but I silenced him.

I silenced him by wrapping my arm around his neck and pulling him down to me, our equipment clanging together as I kissed him.

"*C'etait inattendu mais pas inappreciable,*" he murmured, saying something about the kiss being unexpected.

"Shut up," I told him softly, "thank you, my guardian angel,"

He smiled at me, melting my heart and pressing his nose into mine.

"*Ahem,*" came a voice from behind us. "Work first, canoodle later," Dan said sternly.

"*Canoodle?*" I said. "How old are you again?"

"Piss off," he said, walking away to hide his smile.

Rafi stayed in Andorra, after a week to recuperate with Mateo at his side. Chloe remained also, to assist him in passing on the knowledge and skills to the appointed defenders and show them how to clean and maintain the weapons taken from Tomau's group.

They closed the southern road securely, blocking it with rocks and vehicles to seal it and allow them to concentrate on their tunnel as though it was the main gate inside their huge, natural walls.

We returned home, our uncomfortable van having made the long journey back around to be loaded with our people. Another van was gifted to us, loaded with produce and dried tobacco much to the delight of Dan. And we went home. Life moved on just as it always did. There were guard shifts to stand, people to train, weapons to clean and fish to catch. There were supply runs to escort, people to keep focused and in line, records to keep and lessons to be learned.

Reaching my own bed after a week on the go I threw down both bags, one ransacked and battered and the other full and new, then stripped my equipment off and fell onto the bed as my dog huffed through her nose as she relaxed beside me.

It struck me that I had visited another country, twice in a week, and I considered the concept of taking a holiday. If nothing had changed, if my life had turned out just as it was expected to, then I would probably be looking at some kind of foreign holiday with my girlfriends the following summer. Drinking and dancing and staying in grotty hotel rooms in some costa-del-cheap resort and coming home exhausted and broke after a week of partying.

I scoffed at my own thoughts, startling Nem into looking up at me before laying her head back down in annoyance.

Who wants that? I thought. *Not when I've got all of this.*

I fell asleep, having only summoned the energy to take my boots off and unfasten my combats, deep in thought and thinking of cleaning my old carbine to remove all trace of the unworthy hands that had held it for a short time.

I didn't know that the renewed period of peace would last less than three years, that I would be forced back into conflict before I grew restless again, but that was a story I didn't yet know.

EPILOGUE

"But what happened to them?" Jack asked, his face wrinkling up at the seemingly unfinished tale. "The ones you let go?"

"I don't know," Leah said, leaning forward in her chair, "but they never came here, or to any of our other settlements as far as I know."

"So they just disappeared?" Peter enquired.

"They just... stopped being our problem," she told him, "you see, some people are dangerous. Take me for example. *I'm* dangerous to anyone who would try to threaten us, but am I a good person?"

"Of course you are," Jack said, almost annoyed. He hated the grey areas in life. "But their leader wasn't, was he?"

"No Jacky-boy," she said, "I'm not saying he was. But people like him are only a problem when they have others around them to do their dirty work. He needed followers, and without enough people to follow him I doubt he would ever have amounted to much again. If he'd lived, that was."

"But we're still friends with Andorra?" he asked.

"Yes," she replied matter-of-factly, "very much so. It's just that the journey takes a few days now that we don't use cars any more, and they come to us at the start of every summer with carts of things to trade. They take salted fish and meat back to see them through the winter. They don't bring much tobacco any more, I think it was just your grandfather who kept that trade going, but we are still friends."

"And if someone attacked them again?" Peter asked. "Would you go back there?"

"I would," she said, her expression so genuine that they believed her utterly, "but I'd have to let the younger men and women do any fighting because I'm so old now…"

She waited for their protests about her age to pass, smiling and feeling reassured that they didn't agree with her.

"But now it's time for bed," she said, holding up her hands to ward off the barrage of moans and protests as they always did when she told them a story.

"Tell us another one," Peter pleaded, "tell us about Steve and the people back in the old country."

"Another time," Leah told him. "I've still got lots to teach you and right now you need your sleep, so you can grow up big and strong and take over from me and be responsible for everyone here. Just like your grandfather was, and just like I am."

They rose, stroking Ares and making the dog grumble in response for the last time, before Adalene stood up from the chair she had been listening from to tuck them into bed. Her belly was only just starting to swell now, the child inside her growing strong which explained why she was so sick each morning, and Leah leaned back to smile as she remembered all that she had seen and done in her life, vowing to leave her legacy in the children that came after her.

Children are life, she told herself, *and they are our future. Children are all.*

She didn't take the usual evening walk around the town, instead she put two extra logs on the fire to give Ares some warmth to sleep beside as he was too tired to follow her to the bedroom. She slipped off her clothes before pulling back the covers and fitting her own body into the contours of the man already half asleep.

"You are freezing," he complained sleepily, making her press her icy feet into his warm legs and prompt a gasp of shock.

"Stop complaining," she told Lucien as she kissed her man's shoulder. Her man. Captain of the town's defenders and leader of their civilian militia. Father to their daughter. Uncle to the boys he took on so willingly as his own after the passing of their parents, vowing to teach them everything he had learned.

"Sleep," she said softly, kissing him again, "or I shall tell you a story to send you off to slumber too."

Ares didn't wake the following morning, having drifted off into a peaceful and well-earned slumber in the night. Leah knew he had gone the second she woke, and a single tear of sadness and regret fell for all the times she would think of him in the years to come.

She carried him, wrapped tightly in a blanket as though he still felt the cold, up the mountain path for as long as she could manage, only then allowing Lucien to bear her burden as she took the two shovels from him. They set him down, the proud, old warrior being shown the reverence he had earned and deserved, and dug the hole in silence near to his four-legged ancestors where she imagined him and Ash, who he had never met, with Nemesis beside them, sitting peacefully on the cliff overlooking the town they had all defended without question or cowardice for their entire lives as they sniffed the evening air, ever watchful for a threat to their people.

They had no words to say, not out loud anyway, but each stayed silent in their thoughts for a while. They returned to the town, barely a word said between them as they descended in peaceful companionship.

And life moved on, filling their minds with new tales of adventure, learning and teaching new skills for the next generation to keep alive and pass down to their own descendants as the years passed.

Sanctuary was no longer a place, no longer stood as just a physical entity or inanimate walls. It was no longer a town that offered them safety in the turmoil of the remains of humanity, but instead it was a people. A concept. A way of life. A model of how to exist with others.

And it was Leah who told the stories which kept that spirit alive for generations to come. They were the chronicles of her extraordinary life. And she had many more to tell.

ABOUT THE AUTHOR

Devon C Ford is from the UK and lives in the Midlands. His career in public services started in his teens and has provided a wealth of experiences, both good and some very bad, which form the basis of the books ideas that cause regular insomnia.

Facebook: @decvoncfordofficial

Twitter: @DevonFordAuthor

Website: www.devoncford.com

The *After it Happened* series

Set in the UK in the immediate aftermath of a mysterious illness which swept the country and left millions dead, the series follows the trials facing a reluctant hero, Dan, and the group that forms around him.

www.vulpine-press.com/after-it-happened

CPSIA information can be obtained
at www.ICGtesting.com
Printed in the USA
BVHW081058111219
566310BV00003B/367/P

9 781912 701247